WINTER WALTZ

As Georgie turned from the table, she found Whitfield looming over her. The light in his eyes sent warmth racing through her. "Thank you," she said impulsively.

His broad smile flashed. "I haven't even asked you to dance yet."

"That's not what I meant, and you know it. You've been wonderful about dancing with the dowagers."

"I'm glad to see my efforts haven't been wasted. But I've come to claim my reward."

Her gaze flickered up to meet his, then lowered at once. "Pray, do not be absurd. I'm a chaperon."

"Your time of chaperonage is almost at an end, so why shouldn't you enjoy this one dance?"

"You are quite absurd," she informed him. "And I am quite serious. I do not dance tonight."

A wicked gleam lit his eye. "Then you will create the most shocking scene if you persist in refusing, because I intend to drag you onto the floor and dance with you."

Without realizing she had moved, Georgie found she was clasping his hand and dancing in the steps she had practiced so many times with Louisa, only it wasn't at all the same, nothing like she had ever dreamed. It was exhilarating, wonderful, her heart pounding, her breath coming rapidly. His gloved hand held one of hers tightly as they moved through the open steps, then she daringly rested her other hand on his shoulder as they spun together for those few glorious turns. Then they separated once more and she could barely breathe with the sheer delight of it all. . . .

from THE FAIRY TALE WEDDING by Janice Bennett

WATCH FOR THESE REGENCY ROMANCES

BREACH OF HONOR   (0-8217-5111-5, $4.50)
by Phylis Warady

DeLACEY'S ANGEL   (0-8217-4978-1, $3.99)
by Monique Ellis

A DECEPTIVE BEQUEST   (0-8217-5380-0, $4.50)
by Olivia Sumner

A RAKE'S FOLLY   (0-8217-5007-0, $3.99)
by Claudette Williams

AN INDEPENDENT LADY   (0-8217-3347-8, $3.95)
by Lois Stewart

A Winter Wedding

Janice Bennett
Carola Dunn
Monique Ellis

Zebra Books
Kensington Publishing Corp.
http://www.zebrabooks.com

ZEBRA BOOKS are published by

Kensington Publishing Corp.
850 Third Avenue
New York, NY 10022

First Printing: January, 1998
10 9 8 7 6 5 4 3 2 1

Printed in the United States of America

Contents

The Fairy Tale Wedding

Janice Bennett

One

If the snow kept her housebound for one more day, Miss Georgiana Simms reflected ruefully, she would go stark staring mad. She loved the winter itself, with its icy nip, its intricate patterns of frost on the windowpanes, and the crackling fires filling every hearth. Unfortunately, the magical silence outside produced by the heaviness of the drifting flakes served only to intensify the noise inside the London town house on Half Moon Street. If something didn't happen to allow Georgie to escape the company of her spoiled charge, she might just go so far as to forget herself and murder the girl.

Miss Louisa Granleigh, at seventeen, knew her own mind, and it had been rapidly brought home to Georgie that Louisa's betrothed, Charles, Lord Carlisle, knew his as well. For more than an hour now, the two had gone over the same sore topic, neither showing the least sign of either yielding so much as an inch or tiring of the subject.

Georgie had tired of it long ago. She gripped her mending with whitening knuckles and steadfastly ignored the argument that raged on the other side of the drawing room. On the afternoon after Boxing Day, with the sky darkened by the storm, she needed every last remnant of daylight to set her precise stitches.

No, she could no longer see clearly. With a sigh she laid

aside the torn lace. There went her only excuse to ignore the couple she nominally chaperoned.

Miss Louisa Granleigh perched on the edge of a sofa, fine-boned hands clenched in her lap, her large blue eyes sparkling. A cloud of blond curls haloed her piquant face. The girl was so lovely, it was no wonder she'd received the accolade of being named last Season's Incomparable.

Her fiancé stood before the hearth with one arm laid negligently on the mantelpiece. His gaze rested on his future bride's blushed and lovely countenance, a besotted expression on his own. Argue they might, but this was one fish that Louisa had firmly hooked.

"Georgie!" Louisa turned to her cousin *cum* companion. *"Will* you make him understand? I want there to be snow. Beautiful white piles of it, not that filthy sludge we get once we're into February. I want it fresh and beautiful. I want the setting to be as perfect as all the other details. Why can't he see that? I won't—I cannot!—be cheated on my wedding day."

"My dearest Louisa—" Lord Carlisle began.

"You're not listening to me!" the girl protested with a complete disregard for the fact it was the other way around.

Georgie forced her expression into a conciliatory smile. "We frequently have fresh snowfalls—"

"Frequently!" Louisa uttered the word with scorn. "I don't want to count on frequently. I will not be disappointed. I cannot be." Her lower lip trembled, a tear slipped over the lower lid of one eye, and her voice took on a forlorn note. "It—it is my wedding."

Carlisle sprang forward at once, his handkerchief in his hand. He caught the determined little chin in his palm, turned the beguiling face upward to his, and dabbed away the moisture. "Hush, my love. My cousin will get here in time, never you fear. You just go ahead and plan all the details except the date."

"But what if he doesn't come?" Louisa wailed. "How

can Lord Whitfield be so disobliging as to remain on his estate when we need him *here?*"

Carlisle possessed himself of her hands and settled at her side on the sofa. "There's a great deal for him to do. I well remember the interminable hours I had to spend with my man of affairs when my own father died. Whitfield's earldom has far more extensive properties than my barony."

"Well, I think it is most unkind of him, when you wrote begging him to come to London. It's been an age!"

"A bare month," Carlisle corrected Louisa. He lowered his voice to a whisper, his mouth pressing close to his beloved's ear.

Georgie discreetly turned her attention to the window. The storm had slowed, and now delicate flakes drifted past, swirling in the wind. Louisa, Georgie feared, had become a trifle spoiled by her success. The girl had taken the *ton* by storm with her initial appearance, and had her pick of any number of eligible gentlemen. From the very first she'd set her cap at society's most handsome and fashionable matrimonial prize, Lord Carlisle. For more than a month he'd appeared impervious to her charms, thereby guaranteeing that she would wage an all-out offensive against his defenses. Then he'd looked her way, and the betting ran high in her favor at the clubs. With the coming of June, and the removal of most of polite society from the metropolis, it appeared as if she'd lost. The absence of the summer worked its magic though, for within a fortnight of the beginning of the Little Season, Louisa had brought Lord Carlisle up to scratch.

It ill befitted her, Georgie knew, to criticize her charge. As a penniless companion, the poor relation elevated from a nightmarish governess position to introduce Louisa to society after the death of the spoiled beauty's mother, Georgie supposed she should be glad just to have a roof over her head. Though at times, such as now, she actually longed to be back with those six screaming children rather than endure one seventeen-year-old's tantrums and unreasonable demands.

Outside, the solitary figure of a gentleman turned the corner and strode up the street at a perilous pace. The slipperiness of the paving stones didn't seem to bother him in the least; he moved with surprising grace and ease. He was a large man, Georgie noted, who swung a walking stick in a manner that bespoke boundless energy. A dusting of snow covered the broad shoulders of his greatcoat and his tall, curly beaver. He slowed as he neared the house, then drew to a halt in front of it.

They weren't expecting anyone as far as Georgie knew. Curious, she peered down at him, but the brim of his hat obscured his features. The town might be dreadfully thin of company, but anyone—or anything—would prove a welcome break from listening to those two argue. With a sense of heightened anticipation she watched him mount the front steps and heard the distant, insistent ringing of the bell. She waited, alert, and after a couple of minutes she was rewarded by the muffled footfalls on the carpeted steps. Relieved at the proffered interruption, she turned toward the opening door.

The slight, graying figure of Dauber, the ever-correct butler, stood on the threshold. He cleared his gravelly throat and announced in his haughtiest tones, "His lordship, the Earl of Whitfield," then stood aside.

Carlisle's errant cousin stepped forward to fill the doorway. Georgie, subjecting him to a rapid survey, found herself favorably impressed. While presenting all the appearance of a man of fashion, he favored none of the dandyish extravagancies sported by his young relative. His coat of blue superfine bore the unmistakable stamp of a tailor of the first stare, yet did not seem to fit so tightly as to require the services of his valet to ease his broad shoulders into the garment. His starched shirt points reached only to a moderate height, and the creases in his neckcloth bespoke an elegant simplicity. His pale yellow inexpressibles remained unmarred from the storm outside, and his top boots had been wiped clean of any smears before he presented himself upstairs.

Her gaze moved upward to a face more striking than handsome. Humor-filled hazel eyes dominated the rugged features, and dark hair waved back from the high forehead. A practical man, she decided, and liked him for it.

"Vare!" Carlisle sprang to his feet, relief flooding his expressive countenance. He hurried across to clasp the new arrival's hand and grip his shoulder. "You've come. I was beginning to think you'd never break free."

"As was I." Whitfield's deep voice held a smiling note. "How do you go on?"

"I'm the happiest man on earth, of course." Carlisle turned his laughing face to Louisa. "It's my cousin Vare! I told you he wouldn't fail us." He dragged the earl forward. "This is Miss Granleigh," he announced, pride heavy in his voice. "Louisa, this is my cousin Verrick, Lord Whitfield."

Whitfield bowed over the hand Louisa extended, murmuring a polite acknowledgment, then turned to Georgie.

"Oh, this is just Miss Simms. Louisa's companion," Carlisle said in the dismissive tone to which Georgie had long ago grown accustomed.

Whitfield's eyebrows rose, and his eyes glinted with sudden humor. "Indeed? How delightful for her." His assessing gaze rested on Georgie's face as he took her hand, then he bowed over it with the same deference he had bestowed on Louisa. "Charmed," he declared in a tone that implied he actually meant it.

But that would be the height of absurdity. Logically, Georgie knew that. But when faced with the smile that lurked in his eyes and the firmness and warmth of his handclasp, logic ran a poor second to wistful thinking. She found herself returning his smile in a manner quite unbecoming a lady in her situation. Vexed with herself, she lowered her gaze and schooled her countenance into a less revealing expression. With cool civility she said, "It was good of you to come directly to see us."

"Yes, it was, wasn't it?" he drawled.

Startled, she looked up to see a quizzical gleam in his eye.

"Much better. I infinitely prefer to see a person's face when I talk with them."

For a moment she stared at him, speechless, then she burst out laughing. "You are quite absurd," she informed him with considerable force.

"You are being kind. Usually I'm told I'm abominable." He shook his head. "A sad reflection on my character, I fear."

"Yet Lord Carlisle has told us you've been at the Congress in Vienna. It's enough to make one wonder how you went on there," she said before she could stop herself.

His eyes gleamed. "I've been a sad trial to Lord Castlereigh, I fear. He was quite glad to grant me leave at the beginning of November to come home and settle my affairs."

She had a strong suspicion the case might be quite the reverse, that he was, in fact, a very valued member of his lordship's staff; but she knew far less than she wished of the great events taking place in Europe. The newspapers reported so little. Louisa's father could have told her more, but whenever he embarked upon a discussion of current events, he inevitably became entangled in a morass of philosophy, necessitating his immediate departure to seek out like-minded cronies with whom he could properly thrash out the vexing questions. As for Lord Carlisle, that fashionable young gentleman approached the problems of piquet with more energy than he did the division of the Continent.

To hear the latest news of these stirring talks, especially from someone who had actually been present, would be a treat of no mean order. "Were you present when—" she began.

"Really, Cousin Georgiana," declared Louisa in the overly loud voice of one trying to reclaim the attention. "How can you monopolize Lord Whitfield, when you know we have my wedding to plan? Now that he is here, we may finally proceed."

A slight crease formed in the earl's brow, but it faded almost at once. The sparkle returned to his eyes as his gaze rested a moment longer on Georgie, then he turned to rejoin the couple, taking up Carlisle's abandoned position by the hearth. "I am entirely at your disposal. Where do we begin?"

Carlisle, now that his cousin had arrived, bore the carefree appearance of one who faced a cloudless horizon. He grinned. "Oh, we have nothing to do now but show up on the day."

"Yes." Louisa cast her bridegroom a speculative glance from beneath her full lashes, then smiled archly at Whitfield. "I am so grateful, my lord," she added, "that you could spare the time to come to town. It seems Carlisle must refuse to wed unless you will stand with him as his groomsman."

Whitfield inclined his head. "So he has told me."

"So now," the girl pursued, "perhaps we *can* name the day upon which he has only to show up."

"Why the haste for the wedding, Chaz?" Whitfield cocked an eyebrow at his cousin. "I would have thought you'd plan it for the coming Season."

"Everyone marries in the spring or summer," Louisa protested. "Or even the fall. *I* shall have a winter wedding. Just think of it." The girl's eyes focused on a point outside the window. "All of London will wear white for me. And I shall be like a fairy princess, all in silver, like a snow crystal."

A spasm crossed Whitfield's features, which he brought

under control almost at once. He glanced at his cousin, but Carlisle remained oblivious to all but Louisa, gazing at her with that besotted expression that seldom seemed to leave his face these days. "Very nice," the earl commented dryly.

"Nice?" Louisa refocused on him. "It will be like a fairy tale! I'll be the envy of every lady in the *ton.*"

"Except they won't be there to see you," Whitfield pointed out.

Louisa tilted up her chin and looked down her dainty nose at him. "The Polite World will flock back to London for my wedding. I—Carlisle and I—are more important than some beastly hunting season. You will see."

"Indeed." The corners of the earl's mouth twitched, but his voice made the single word ambiguous, so it could be taken either as an agreement or a question.

The mantel clock chimed the quarter hour; Carlisle glanced at it and frowned. "The time! Louisa, I must dash. An appointment I cannot break. Vare, I'm sorry to abandon you so soon after your arrival."

"I have managed quite well on my own for a very long time now, bantling. Off with you, then. As your second, I shall remain and learn a little more about your wedding plans."

Carlisle clasped his cousin's shoulder. "My thanks. I know I can leave it in your hands. Have you arrangements for dinner yet? Will you join me at White's? Until later, then." He bowed over his bride's hands, pressing fervent kisses into her palms, then hurried out the door.

Louisa cast a dubious glance at the earl, as if uncertain whether she faced a supporter or a foe.

Whitfield ignored her and turned to Georgie instead. "Who has been placed in charge of organizing the wedding?"

"I have," she admitted.

He nodded, as if she had confirmed his guess. "How much has been settled?"

Louisa flounced to her feet, obviously miffed at not being the center of attention. "It is plain that nothing new can be settled now that Carlisle has had to leave. Cousin Georgie, you may deputize for me. Be my second, as his lordship has called it. Will you hold me excused, my lord?" She offered Whitfield an artificially sweet smile.

"But you cannot leave!" Georgie protested. Not, at least, on what seemed such a dreadfully inauspicious beginning to Louisa's acquaintance with her betrothed's favorite relative. It boded ill for the future.

Louisa laughed. "My dear cousin, surely you cannot feel there is any impropriety in my leaving you two alone? The prospect is absurd!" And on that note, she exited.

"That's not what I meant!" Georgie declared as the door slammed behind the girl. With an exasperated sigh she turned back to Whitfield. "I'm sorry, my lord."

"Don't worry," he said cheerfully. "I'm far too much the gentleman to compromise you on such short acquaintance."

She couldn't help but laugh. "Whoever called you outrageous was quite right," she declared, struggling for a touch of severity. "As Louisa pointed out, it is quite absurd." With regret, she acknowledged this fact, that so important a man never could have any interest in her.

The humor faded from his eyes as he studied her. After a long while, he said, "We have a wedding to discuss." He then added with disconcerting straightforwardness, "She's confusing it with a fairy tale. You appear to be a young woman of sense. Are you keeping this affair under control?"

Her mouth twitched at his accurate reading of the situation. Fighting back her smile, she arranged her features into an expression of reproach. "You haven't an ounce of romance in your soul," she informed him.

His ready grin returned. "Good God, I should hope not. For that matter," he added reflectively, "I would have sworn that my cousin hadn't either. I doubt this fairy tale nonsense is his idea."

She lowered her gaze to study her hands. "Louisa knows her own mind," she said with infinite diplomacy.

A short bark of laughter escaped him. "Which is to say she's stubborn and won't be budged."

At that, she looked up, meeting his quizzing gaze with a challenging one of her own. "You seem to have taken her in dislike."

"Let us say, rather, that I'm not blinded by beauty."

"As is your cousin?" she inquired with false sweetness.

"I've offended you." He made it a statement of fact, devoid of any apology. "But I can't help wonder if they will really suit."

She raised her eyebrows and regarded him with her haughtiest expression. "What reason—or right—have you to doubt it?"

"None," he admitted. "Except that I know my cousin very well."

"And Louisa not at all," she shot back.

He inclined his head. "As you say, I know Miss Granleigh not at all. Does Carlisle?"

Here, at least, she was on safe ground. "They have known each other since the beginning of last Season. It is quite absurd to be suggesting that he fell in love with her face and offered for her without due reflection."

"I am only amazed he waited so long."

Her eyebrows rose once again. "Do you doubt me, my lord?"

"Not in the least. It's just that I had not thought Carlisle to be such a slowtop."

To her annoyance, she felt her cheeks flush under the steady regard of his bright hazel eyes. "I believe he did not make her the object of his gallantry until the end of the Season."

"So he had other fish to fry, did he?" His remarkable

eyes glinted with amusement. "And only after that did he become aware of Miss Granleigh, and then almost at once he was separated from her by the summer months."

Her mouth tightened. "You mean to imply that he fell in love—oh, in absentia, I suppose?"

"He did offer for her at the beginning of the Little Season, did he not?"

"This is absurd! Many gentlemen make up their minds far more quickly."

"And many of them to their regret," he shot back.

Georgie regarded him with a kindling eye. "Do you know, my lord, I believe it would be best if we bring this interview to an end. It would be a shocking thing should we come to cuffs."

An answering gleam sprang to life in the depths of his own eyes. "Shocking, indeed." He rose on those words and, taking her hand, bowed low over it. "Miss Simms, it has been a delight to make your acquaintance. I shall see myself out."

With that, he turned on his heel and exited the apartment, leaving Georgie fuming.

Two

Verrick, seventh Earl of Whitfield, studied his reflection in the cheval glass, then set another crease in his neckcloth. Behind him, his man, Gottleigh, paid scant heed; he focused his attention on the coat of blue Bath cloth for which his master would call within a few minutes. His unerring eye had detected a fleck of fuzz on one sleeve, and although the earl might not view this in a serious light, Gottleigh recognized it for the solecism it was. Even if the earl were not a dandy, his valet still had both of their reputations to consider.

Lord Carlisle, straddling a chair, his arms laid across its back with his chin resting on them, watched the earl's progress with amused interest. "Lord, Vare, since when did you care a fig for the niceties?" he demanded as his cousin set a final crease and examined the results.

"I thought you wanted me to make a good impression on Miss Granleigh," Whitfield countered.

Carlisle eyed him critically. "Well, if that's what you want, I can teach you to tie something with a bit more dash."

"No." Whitfield gratified his waiting valet by allowing the man to assist him into his coat. "This suits me well enough. I'm too large to go aping the dandy set."

At that, Carlisle laughed. "Nothing, my dear Vare, would ever make anyone accuse you of being a dandy. You've been spending too much time with diplomats and officers."

"True. I've become as dull as ditchwater, haven't I?"

Carlisle, still chuckling, shook his head. "Not you. I can see you now, cutting some jest, and not one of the prosy old bores realizing you're funning. How have you managed to endure it?"

"By cutting some jest." With a nod and word of thanks, he dismissed Gottleigh. As the door closed behind his man, Whitfield turned once more to the mirror, this time under the pretext of rearranging his hair. Catching his cousin's eye in the glass, he asked, "How will Miss Granleigh like your estate, do you think?"

Carlisle blinked. "What's not to like about it? Oh, I admit it's not in the grand style, not like Whitfield Court, but it's spacious enough. No drafts blowing down the halls either, and you can find your way from your chamber to the dining room without having to ask directions every few corridors."

Whitfield let these aspersions on his own ancestral home pass without comment. "Miss Granleigh appears to be more accustomed to living in town than the country. Won't she miss it?"

"Lord, why should she? How can anyone not love the country? It's only because of her father and all his societies, they don't remove."

"I see." Whitfield selected an enameled snuffbox and slipped it into his pocket. "She hunts, I presume?"

Carlisle stared back blankly. "I have no idea. The subject has never come up."

"But of course it wouldn't bother you if she doesn't," Whitfield added smoothly.

"Well, no, I don't suppose it would." Carlisle laughed, but it sounded a touch forced. "Besides, she has only to grace a ballroom for anyone to be bewitched by her."

"You certainly have been," Whitfield said dryly.

"She's the most glorious creature, isn't she?" His eyes brightened with eagerness. "Such beauty and such grace. The first time I saw her—*really* saw her, I mean—she was waltzing with Faversham. I don't think I noticed anyone else after that."

"No," remarked Whitfield. "I don't think you did." It also seemed apparent to Whitfield that his cousin had failed to notice anything else about Miss Granleigh once he'd been floored by her beauty. He certainly appeared oblivious to her tastes, preferences, and even temperament. It didn't seem probable that infatuation with a face, when unaccompanied by any understanding of the lady's character, could lead to any degree of matrimonial happiness. He brooded on this for a few moments, until Carlisle's enraptured voice recalled his attention.

"Anyone!" his cousin declared. "She could have had her pick of anyone! Yet she accepted me." His smile became a trifle smug. "Carried her off, right out from under the noses of the lot of them."

For a moment Whitfield toyed with the idea of asking the identities of these other suitors, then forbore. Instead, he inquired with the most casual of tones, "What about this nonsense of a winter wedding?"

Carlisle shrugged genially. "Makes no odds to me. We could be married at midnight on All Hallows' Eve for all I care, if Louisa took a fancy to it."

Whitfield selected a signet ring from his dressing table and slid it over his knuckle. "What about her determination? She seems amazingly set upon having everything just as she wishes."

"Typical of a female. They take such odd fancies. And since the wedding is of far more importance to her than to me, why shouldn't she have her way over it?"

Whitfield shook his head in a funning way. "It's obvious you'll soon be living under the sign of the cat's foot, my dear cousin."

Carlisle laughed, but a flicker of sudden apprehension lit his eyes.

For the moment, that satisfied Whitfield. He'd planted

the first seed of reason. But only an extremely obtuse gentleman could believe it would be sufficient to prevent Carlisle from making what Whitfield firmly believed to be the gravest of mistakes. Whitfield knew himself to be far from obtuse. Subtle tactics would not do the trick, he decided. He would have to see to it that reality confronted Carlisle in a manner the young man could not ignore.

And that, Whitfield acknowledged to himself, might not prove easy.

"He's pompous," Louisa declared. The girl glared into the fire, refusing to look at Georgie, who sat on the edge of the wing chair across from her. "He's ill-natured and overbearing, and I cannot understand how my dear Carlisle can be so blind to his cousin's obvious faults."

"Perhaps Carlisle knows him better than do you," Georgie suggested.

Louisa turned at that, her large, lovely eyes open wide. "But that is just what I mean, Cousin Georgie. How can he be so deceived? To hear Carlisle speak, one would think Lord Whitfield to be a gentleman possessed of every amiable quality. A veritable paragon! Yet when he looked at me, he made me feel like the most insignificant mushroom instead of a—a diamond of the first water. And you need not laugh, Georgie, for you know Faversham called me that. And so did several other gentlemen! Why, I was the Season's reigning Incomparable. So how dare Lord Whitfield look at me as if I were a mere nobody and wholly unfit to be the bride of Carlisle?"

"How, indeed?" Georgie fought back her smile. "But perhaps he fears that his cousin has been dazzled by your beauty, and has not properly considered whether or not you should suit."

A puzzled expression flickered across Louisa's brow. "Oh. Well, Lord Whitfield is quite old, of course. Why, he must be five-and-thirty if he's a day! I suppose he is past the age of romantic fancies, poor man. But my dear Carlisle is not, and so we do suit very well."

"Do you?" Georgie asked with a touch of diffidence. "Lord Carlisle is certainly an amiable young man, and—"

"I never thought I would say it," Louisa interrupted, "but I begin to fear he may be just a little too amiable. Oh, I don't mind, of course, when it concerns me. But his cousin is quite another matter. You cannot deny Lord Whitfield appears to be of a controlling temperament. In fact," she went on, warming to this theme, "I suspect that is behind his animosity. He cannot bear the thought that he will be losing Carlisle to me." Her brooding gaze fixed once more on the blazing hearth. "Do you know, Cousin Georgie, I would not be at all surprised if he were to try to prevent my wedding to Carlisle—if he could. But if he tries, he will find he has met his match in me."

"Will he?" Georgie murmured. She well knew Louisa's strength when it came to a battle of wills, but she recognized the earl as an unknown quantity whom it would be foolish to dismiss lightly.

Louisa appeared not to have heard the interruption. She clasped her hands, her expression thoughtful. "I do very much fear Lord Whitfield to be my enemy," she said at last, "and that cannot be desirable. I fear I shall have to wean Carlisle from his cousin's influence. Once we are wed, it should not be too hard. I know whose voice my bridegroom will listen to, and it won't be—"

She broke off as the door into the sitting room opened and Dauber ushered in Carlisle and Whitfield. She rose gracefully, moving forward to greet her fiancé with a sweet smile, and his cousin with a flickering glance of uncertainty.

"You see, we have come to settle the wedding plans this morning," Carlisle told her gaily. "I told you all would be settled in a trice once my cousin arrived."

Whitfield bowed over Louisa's hand, then looked toward

Georgie. They had parted, Georgie recalled, upon the worst of terms. Yet there he stood, smiling across the room at her as if they had never exchanged anything but the merest pleasantries. Distrust stirred in her heart, only to encounter an unexpected resistance.

His eyes, she decided as she watched him approach, were the problem. The corners crinkled, holding such amused understanding for the awkwardness of this meeting. They quite disarmed her. Except it was more than that. Why must it be that when a man passed thirty, he became more masculine, more attractive, with a rakish air that could assail the defenses of even the most hardened spinster? Yet a woman who passed the dire age of merely twenty lost her first blush of youth and was called an antidote, beyond her last prayers. It was entirely unfair.

He stopped before her and took her hand, the solemnity of his expression belied by the sparkle in his eyes. "I have come to apologize," he said softly so only she would hear.

She raised her eyebrows. "Have you changed your mind?"

"Since the engagement has been announced, it is not my place to interfere," he said.

"We are in agreement about that much, at least. Though I am well aware you did not answer my question."

He inclined his head. "If Miss Granleigh has no wish to cry off, then there is naught for me to do but accept their marriage. And so I have come to offer whatever aid is needed."

"Very handsome of you." Or very devious. But she kept that last reflection to herself. She didn't trust him, she realized, and that fact both dismayed and stimulated her. She must, of course, regret his displeasure in his cousin's impending marriage; yet her long-buried fighting spirit rose with reprehensible alacrity at the promised battle. He'd make a formidable opponent, especially if he intended to play some sort of undergame. This seeming affability of his would not fool her in the least. She would enjoy crossing swords with him.

Three

From the depths of one of the wing chairs drawn up near the hearth, Georgie faced the Earl of Whitfield across the low table that separated them. A tray rested upon it, bearing two decanters, one filled with wine and the other with negus. The fire crackled in the hearth, emanating a comforting warmth throughout the room. It ought to be a cozy scene. Perhaps, if she trusted him more, it might be.

Louisa, seated on the sofa beside Carlisle, leaned forward. "The date is of the first importance. We must order cards upon the instant."

"I believe you wished for snow," Whitfield reminded her.

"Oh, yes!" Louisa's eyes glowed, but she directed a suspicious look at him.

"Snow," he repeated. "And you, Carlisle, wanted a wedding in the spring, I believe?"

"Well—" Carlisle cast an uneasy glance at Louisa. "It is more traditional."

Georgie regarded Whitfield with a fulminating eye. "I might have known you would try to reopen the one issue we had settled."

The smile the earl turned on her held amusement, and something she couldn't quite fathom. It stopped her, causing her to study him more closely.

"Not in the least," he said smoothly. "But the first rule of any negotiation is to clearly state the initial demands of each side. That now has been done. My principal has agreed to grant your principal her way on this issue in exchange for future concessions."

In spite of herself, her lips twitched. "Is this how it is done in Vienna?"

"Of a certainty."

This time there could be no mistaking the warmth that lurked in his eyes. It startled her, and to her dismay she discovered within herself an answering spark. Apparently he intended to while away the time before the wedding with an idle flirtation. It behooved her to depress his pretensions, to not let herself be beguiled, but she realized with a sinking heart he had already succeeded in that regard. She would be hard pressed not to succumb to the temptation to indulge him in this pastime that for her might not be as innocuous as she would wish.

"But when, exactly, is it to be?" Louisa broke in.

Carlisle, his gaze resting on Louisa's profile, said, "Let's have it soon. If it must be in winter, let's not delay."

"But that's impossible!" Louisa shook her determined head. "There's so much planning! And we'll have to order cards, and—"

"You don't really think anyone will come in the middle of winter, do you?" Carlisle broke in.

"Of course they'll come. Why, no one will want to miss—"

"Whether they come or not isn't the issue," Whitfield declared, interrupting the argument. "What matters is that cards must be sent. Miss Simms, is that on your list?"

"I need only to know the date," Georgie assured him, "and how many to order."

"Carlisle, name a date," Whitfield declared.

"A date? I mean, I hadn't thought about it that much. Perhaps—"

"Fine." Whitfield cut him off without any compunction. "Miss Granleigh? How about you?"

"We must have a little time. Toward the end of the month, I suppose, but not so late as to—"

Whitfield shook his head. "Exact dates only. Miss Simms?"

She looked up from the calendar she had created earlier. "The twenty-ninth of January," she declared. "That will give us plenty of time to notify everyone and finalize our plans."

Whitfield nodded approval. "Do we have any objections?" He looked from his cousin to Louisa. "Very well. The twenty-ninth of January it shall be. Congratulations."

"Just allow me to speak to the rector." Georgie tapped her quill point on the paper. "Yes, I can do that first thing, and have the invitations ordered before noon."

"There will even be time for the banns to be read." The glint in Whitfield's eye belied the solemnity of his tone.

Georgie fixed him with as cool a glance as she could manage. "As you say. All the proprieties are thus observed. Lord Carlisle? Are you in agreement?"

Carlisle, thus finding himself the focus of three pairs of eyes, flushed. "Yes. That is—It's of no real matter to me. Whatever Louisa wants will be fine."

Louisa clasped his hand and murmured, "Dear Carlisle." The next moment she dropped it and sprang to her feet. "We must not sit about here. We must settle it with the rector, and then the stationer. I shall run and fetch my bonnet this instant. Carlisle, if you will—"

"No! I mean, I'd love to come with you, of course, but I can't. Vare and I are promised this morning."

"Are we?" the earl murmured, and encountered a speaking look from his younger cousin. "Of course. How forgetful of me."

"Craven," Georgie murmured.

That captivating smile danced in Whitfield's eyes. "Yes, it is, isn't it? But you will manage much better without us, you may be sure." He rose. "Miss Simms, your most obedient servant."

"But there are still other matters to be settled!" she protested.

His eyebrows shot upward. "When every moment matters in the rush to place this order?"

A vexed exclamation escaped her. "I suppose you are right, and nothing else can be so much as discussed until that is taken care of. I'm sorry, then, that you have come for so little purpose this morning."

"On the contrary." He took her hand. "I have had a most enjoyable time."

The warmth of his clasp startled her. She broke the contact quickly, disturbed to discover that she very much would have liked to maintain it. She made the mistake of looking up into his smiling face, and encountered an expression that caused her breath to catch in her throat. For the first time in her six-and-twenty years, her normally ordered mind melted into a quivering morass. She moved away, placing a prudent distance between them.

If he noticed her disordered state, he gave no sign. He took his leave of her, collected his cousin, who stood gazing down into Louisa's lovely face, and dragged him ruthlessly out the door.

Georgie closed her eyes. She urgently needed a time for quiet reflection, to consider what had just passed between them. Her first reaction, to feel as giddy as a green girl, to indulge in daydreams, she knew to be dangerous. That he intended to flirt with her she could no longer doubt. That she would find it enjoyable and flattering she also did not doubt. To what extent he intended to carry it, though, she had no way of knowing, and that was where the trouble lay. A lighthearted flirtation might cause her some pangs when it ended, but that would be infinitely preferable to the alternative. A serious flirtation could lead only to his making her an offer, and in her experience, the sort of offer noblemen tendered toward penniless companions had nothing to do with marriage.

Louisa spun to face Georgie, interrupting her thoughts. "We have done it! We actually have a wedding date. I thought Lord Whitfield my enemy, but indeed, I must have been wrong. Come, I don't want to waste a moment. We must order the invitations this very morning."

"Of course." Georgie banished the image of Whitfield's tall, broad-shouldered figure from the forefront of her mind. With an effort she shook off her troubled reflections and returned her attention to Louisa. "Do you know what it is you wish to order? And how many?"

Louisa laughed. "Hundreds! I want to invite all of Polite Society!"

"As long as you are aware they will not all attend," Georgie reminded her.

"I won't let you depress me this day no matter what you say. We will invite them, and they will come. The church must be filled." Louisa clasped her hands, delighted by the envisioned throng.

Georgie regarded her with misgivings. "Must it?"

Louisa threw her a scornful look. "Of course it must. I want this to be a glorious event, one that will be the talk of next Season. I want it to make all the other young ladies jealous."

"Most commendable," Georgie murmured. "But how does Carlisle feel about turning his wedding into a social event? I know it is not uncommon to hold an extensive gathering for the wedding breakfast, but the ceremony itself is usually quite small."

"Not ours," Louisa declared. "Carlisle will be quite gratified when he sees the influence we have with the Polite World."

"Will he?" Georgie, by no means convinced, fell silent. It didn't seem at all the sort of commotion a gentleman would like to cause, but she knew herself unequal to the task of convincing her stubborn charge of anything of the kind. For Carlisle's sake, she could trust only in the hedonistic nature of the members of the *ton* to prevent them from bestirring themselves from their country idylls at this inclement time of the year.

Whitfield hunched his greatcoated shoulders against the chill wind that whipped the falling white flakes into a frenzy along Half Moon Street. "That was craven, and most unworthy of you," he informed his cousin.

"I didn't hear you correcting me," Carlisle countered. "If you'd prefer, you can go back there now and escort them to the stationer."

"That might prove the wisest course. Have you consulted together about the style and number of the invitations?"

"Lord, I've no interest in that," Carlisle assured him. "Let 'em pick what they will."

Whitfield regarded his young relative with a thoughtful frown. "And is that your attitude toward every aspect of this wedding?"

"Oh, as to that, I daresay there won't be any problems. How much planning does a wedding take, after all?"

"The guests, to begin with," Whitfield reminded him. "How many people do you intend to invite?"

Carlisle considered a minute. "I suppose all the aunts and cousins will be offended if they're not asked to the breakfast, even if they have no intention of coming to town for it. I doubt if so much as a quarter of the family will turn out."

"Do you think Miss Granleigh intends to invite only family?"

Carlisle scowled. "She'll want to invite the entire *ton,* of course. I'll leave it to Miss Simms to curb that ambition. Though I don't suppose it matters who gets an invitation. They won't come. Not in the middle of winter. It'll be a snug little affair, never you fear." He brightened. "Now, there's a good reason for getting married in January, isn't it? No chance we'll be overwhelmed by a crowd of people. Dashed uncomfortable, that's what that would be."

Four

The visit to the stationer forced Georgie's own problems to the back of her mind. The choice of invitation offered seemed infinite, and she had her hands full dissuading her charge from embracing the more opulent of these. Here she was aided surprisingly by Louisa's own innate good taste, which compelled her to listen, albeit with reluctance, to reason.

No such considerations intervened over the *number* of invitations to be ordered. Louisa wanted quantity, and two years of chaperonage had taught Georgie when her charge could not be influenced. In comparison with other issues it seemed a paltry matter, so she gave in with good grace. Her only qualms stemmed from the reflection that it would be she who would be expected to address all three hundred of these cards.

They were well under way compiling the prospective guest list when Whitfield and Carlisle called upon them late that afternoon. Georgie looked up as the gentlemen entered the room, met the gaze of the earl's smiling eyes, and discovered how inconsequential breathing really could be. She flushed, and called herself severely to task for such foolishness. He might be attractive, he might even stir her longings; but she was considerably more than six, and knew the difference between daydreams and reality.

Whitfield strode forward several paces, then stopped. "You look vexed. Have we come at a bad time?"

She rose, masking her fluttering nerves beneath a polite social veneer. "Indeed, not. You provide a most welcome break."

"You could not have picked a better time," Louisa added. "You may help us, Carlisle. I must have the names of anyone you particularly wish to invite to our wedding."

"Lord, we've talked of nothing else this age *but* the wedding," Carlisle protested. A sudden gleam lit his eye. "Come. We shall now do something different." He held out his hand to Louisa.

"Come where? Really, Carlisle, we've so little time, and there's so much to be done. I do wish you'd concentrate on the matter at hand."

"I would if the matter were more to my taste. But I'll tell you something that is. Do you play piquet?"

"Piquet?" Louisa stared at him as if he had just uttered the most irrelevant question imaginable. "No, of course not. Why ever should I? Really, Carlisle—"

The gleam in his eye hardened. "You should because I'm very partial to a game."

"You may play whenever you wish, and it needn't concern me in the least," she informed him. "Unless, of course, I have need of your escort. What does concern me is the invitations."

"And what concerns me is being able to pass an agreeable evening at home, playing piquet with my wife if I so choose," Carlisle informed her.

"Playing . . ." Louisa's voice trailed off.

"Playing piquet," he affirmed. "I believe I shall teach you."

"Of course you shall—if you really feel you must," she said without enthusiasm. "But right now—"

"Yes." Determination replaced his usually easygoing expression. "Right now. You can spare the time. Send for a pack."

"But—" Louisa began.

"An excellent notion," Whitfield intervened. "I will provide Miss Simms with the names and directions of Carlisle's relatives, and he will have only to approve them."

Georgie regarded the earl with a measure of trepidation but kept her tongue between her teeth. She unearthed a pack of cards from a table drawer, and Carlisle dragged the still-protesting Louisa to a table on the far side of the room, where they would not, he expressed the devout hope, be interrupted with all the talk of the wedding. With that, he set about the task of instilling in his bride-to-be some understanding of the rudiments of piquet.

Whitfield met Georgie's frown with a disconcerting twinkle in the depths of his eyes. "We are now free to further the wedding plans without hindrance," he informed her.

"It is their wedding," she protested. "Does it not occur to you that they should take part in its planning?"

"Emphatically not!"

Georgie glanced at the couple. "Louisa would not agree with you."

"True. One can tell already that cards bore her."

"Only because she is so eager to settle the details about the wedding. It is only natural that any other pastime must seem of little interest to her at the moment. What on earth could have possessed Carlisle to insist on teaching her now? And you, to have encouraged him?"

Whitfield drew his snuffbox from his pocket, took an infinitesimal pinch, then closed the lid with a snap. "I think he is showing excellent sense. Would you rather they did not discover each other's tastes and preferences until after the wedding, when it is too late to call off an unfortunate mistake?"

"Why are you so certain it is a mistake?" Georgie countered.

"They won't know that unless they know each other better, will they? And don't fear," he added as Carlisle's light laugh followed a vexed exclamation from Louisa. "He has only to compliment her to keep her from falling into a fit of the sullens."

"She doesn't!" Georgie said quickly. "It is only that her mind is quite naturally focused on the wedding, and—"

"And she has no interest—or apparently, aptitude—for cards," he finished smoothly.

"You are determined not to like her."

"I am determined my cousin shall not make a mistake. If Miss Granleigh is indeed the right bride for him, I will support them in every way."

"But you don't think she is."

For a long while he frowned in the direction of the younger couple. "She can think of nothing but this fairy tale of hers," he said at last. "I still maintain that if they are unable to work out their differences on something as basic as their wedding—or, for that matter, how to pass an afternoon in amity together—their chances for marital happiness are very slim indeed. What will they do when some greater issue looms?"

"For Louisa, at this moment, there is no greater issue," Georgie confessed.

"Very true." The earl held her gaze. "Miss Granleigh appears to be a young lady of determined ideas and a single focus."

"I believe I mentioned that she knows her own mind."

A sudden smile flickered in the depths of his hazel eyes. "Every moment that passes, she makes that abundantly clear. Unfortunately, she will find that Carlisle also has his share of determination."

"He has been all that is most amiable," she assured him, then added, giving herself the lie, "at least they seem to enjoy their arguments."

"They've been giving you a difficult time of it, have they?" he hazarded to ask. "Perhaps you have already discovered that although Carlisle says the details are of no importance to him, the opposite is actually the case."

"Of course not. That is—" She broke off and regarded him with a touch of unease. "They do tend to disagree a great deal."

"Let's have the word without bark on it, if you please. Each knows exactly what he or she wants, and neither is willing to budge so much as an inch."

"They have compromised now," she pointed out.

"Only with my intervention. I—or you, for that matter—will not always be present."

She considered the truth of his statement, dismayed. "Surely they cannot be so far apart in their ideas as all that."

"Oh, we'll bring them around to agreement—at least about the wedding. Never you fear. But it will take negotiations every bit as tricky as those currently under way in Vienna."

"Where you would much rather be."

He shook his head. "Where I would rather be is at Whitfield Court. But that's of no matter at the moment. Once we get this business settled, I may go where I will."

"Then it behooves us to make all speed. Where do we begin?"

"I already mentioned the first rule of any negotiation is to state the initial demands of each side. That way we know how far away we are from agreement. The second rule is to determine on which points each party is the least willing to yield ground."

Georgie sighed. "Louisa wants a very large wedding with as many of the *ton* present as she can drag from the country. And on that point she is immovable."

Whitfield nodded. "Carlisle wants a very small wedding. And he wanted it sometime in the late spring. On the latter point he's already yielded, and I believe he'll be willing to do so on the former as well."

Her eyebrows arched quizzically. "Are you sure you should be admitting that to me?"

"I feel certain," he said, eyes gleaming, "you will not try to take ruthless advantage of my honesty. Now, what is the next issue?"

"Oh, the wedding breakfast, I suppose. Louisa—"

"We shall have it here, of course," Louisa called to them, showing on which conversation she had focused her attention. She threw down her cards without further ado and made her way to the fire.

Carlisle, apparently resigned to this turn of events, followed. "There's still plenty of time," he muttered.

Louisa ignored him. "We must hire a caterer, of course," she continued, animated by this return to her favorite subject.

"Gunter's for the bridecake. The breakfast too, I suppose," Georgie murmured, jotting down notes. "Berry Brothers and Rudd for the wine—"

"Christopher and Company," Whitfield corrected her. "That is, I presume Miss Granleigh would prefer French wines?"

"The very thing!" Louisa turned her delighted smile on him. "How very clever of you. If only they did breakfasts as well. I fear Gunter's may not be up to the occasion. The breakfast must be special, like everything else."

A sinking sensation assailed Georgie's stomach, and she laid down her pen. "What do you have in mind?"

"A fairy tale feast, of course. Dainties and delicacies, with spun sugar and—"

"No, I say!" Carlisle protested. "Everyone will be wanting a real meal, I shouldn't wonder. Something substantial."

Louisa stared at him, wide-eyed. "You don't like my idea? But you know that nothing ordinary will do for me."

"No, of course not," he corrected her hastily. "But I have the most famous idea. It's the hunting season, isn't it? Shooting, and all. My friends will have to leave their sporting to come to town. So I think we ought to make it up to them. What we want is a real banquet with fresh game.

Send to the estate for whatever the gamekeepers think is prime."

"Game?" Louisa spat out the word with loathing. "And I suppose you want me to wear a riding habit instead of a wedding gown? And perhaps ride a hunter up the center aisle of the church? Are you mad? This is my wedding!"

"I must say, that would be something like." A gleam lit his eye. "You know, Louisa, we'd certainly be the talk of the *ton.* That's what you want, isn't it?"

"No! I will not make such a figure of fun. How can you even suggest such a—a dreadful thing! You would make a spectacle of our wedding!"

Whitfield cast Georgie an amused glance. "At least we had them in agreement for a full minute."

Georgie glared at him, then turned her attention to the outraged beauty. "Louisa, he is only funning. Lord Carlisle, please, you know Louisa envisions herself a fairy princess for the affair."

"She could be a fairy princess on horseback," he suggested.

"We were discussing the wedding breakfast, not the ceremony," Whitfield reminded them. "One thing at a time, or we'll never have this settled before the chosen date."

"He is quite right," Georgie stuck in before Louisa could protest. "Louisa, a feast of spun sugar would not be at all the thing. And, Lord Carlisle, a hunting banquet would hardly be suitable. No, Louisa, I agree that the ordinary will not do for you. I suggest you leave the matter in my hands, and I will speak to Gunter's. I make no doubt we shall hit upon something that will carry off the mood to perfection."

"There ought to be fresh game," muttered Carlisle.

"To be sure, there will be," Georgie promised rashly. "And spun sugar and all the fairy cakes you could desire," she added to Louisa. "But we must have something substantial enough to satisfy everyone. There, is the matter settled?"

"It had better be," Whitfield declared. "Carlisle, unless I am much mistaken, we are promised to old Enderby this night. Miss Simms, we shall call on you first thing in the morning—No, you will have the caterer to see. We shall call upon you shortly after noon to continue." He picked up his hat and started for the door.

Carlisle lingered, his arguments with Louisa forgotten in that moment of temporary parting.

Georgie, ever discreet, followed Whitfield. "Thank you," she said, as they stepped out into the hall.

"Oh, I believe this latest victory goes to you. A compromise of no mean order. I hope they all may be so easily settled."

She looked down, embarrassed by so simple a word of praise. "I had best finalize it before they can change their minds or think of some new objections."

"Another of the principal rules is to never renegotiate once you've reached an agreement. It's fatal."

"How well I know it. You can have no idea how many times we've gone over the same ground."

He frowned, and his intense gaze rested on her. "It seems to me that when a man and woman contemplate a union, there should be an underlying desire to compromise, or even to allow the other to have his or her way."

She shook her head. "Not all people are the same. Theirs is a livelier sort of relationship."

Humor once more flashed in the depths of his eyes. "That's one way to phrase it, I suppose."

"And how would you phrase it, my lord?" she asked guardedly.

"They're engaged in a sparring match," he responded promptly. "Carlisle's so besotted, I doubt he realizes it yet, but he's more than ready to meet any challenge she throws at him."

She frowned. "Cross and jostle work, do you mean?"

"But I should never be so ungentlemanly as to use boxing cant in the presence of a lady," he protested.

At that, she smiled. "My father had no such qualms, I assure you, my lord. Do you truly think that each is trying to pop in a hit over the other's guard?"

His smile deepened. "Perhaps that would be putting it too strongly. Though I do confess, I feel more like a second for a duel than a groomsman for a wedding."

"Well, we have arranged the time for the meeting, at all events. Let us hope it is to be breakfast for more than one. That leaves us only with the problem of choosing the weapons. Shall I assume that Louisa is the challenged party?"

He shook his head. "I fear that it will be we who find ourselves severely challenged before we see them safely wed."

Five

Georgie stood on the snow-covered cobblestones in front of Madame Thérèse's elite establishment off Piccadilly. After days cooped up within doors by the storm, she found it an inexpressible luxury just to stand in the open air and breathe. But it was still London. Not even closing her eyes could enable her to imagine herself in the country. Still, she tried.

Footsteps approached, but she paid them no heed until Whitfield's amused voice asked, "Is it not rather cold out to be playing statues?"

She looked up to see him standing before her, tall, ruggedly attractive, so very much a commanding presence. For a moment she allowed herself the pleasure of simply studying his features, then she prudently looked down. "I am waiting for Louisa. She is having another fitting for her trousseau."

"And you found it too stifling to remain inside." He made it a statement rather than a question. "Do you know, I have the distinct feeling you would prefer not to be in London."

"It's well enough in the spring or fall, when it's neither too hot nor too cold. But right now it's too confining. Winters should be spent in the country, where one may go for an agreeable tramp without worrying about appearances."

"My sentiments exactly." His gaze rested on her. "Is that what you are accustomed to do?"

"I was very lucky in my last post," she assured him, temporarily ignoring the existence of six whining, ill-favored children. "The family spent much of the year in Sussex, where I was able to ramble about the countryside whenever I had a spare moment."

"Do you hunt?"

"Not in recent years. When I was young—no, don't smile at me like that. When I was a child, I would take out one of my father's retired horses, and the master would let me follow the pack. But since then I have not had the opportunity." With an effort, she banished the reminiscent longing. "What has brought you out here this morning?"

"Like you, I am enjoying the fine weather. We called in Half Moon Street, and your good butler informed us you were to be found here."

"For quite some time yet to come, I should imagine," she said with only a touch of dryness in her tone. "But you said 'we.' Is Lord Carlisle no longer with you?"

"He should be again shortly. He noticed a snuffbox in a shop window, you see."

"I do see." She eyed him speculatively. "Perhaps they have more in common than you seem to suspect."

"I do not consider a shared tendency to purchase items upon impulse to be a quality destined to assure matrimonial success." Amusement colored his words, but his eyes held an unaccustomed serious look. "Any more than do you, so stop trying to gammon me. You have doubts about their compatibility too. Don't you?"

Resolutely, she shook her head. "They both care about their positions in the *ton*. That will form a solid bond between them. It must."

"Would it be sufficient for you?"

She could feel his gaze resting on her, but she didn't dare look up to meet it. "I am not Louisa. For that matter, you are not Lord Carlisle."

"What would be important to you?"

A longing swept over her to tell him, to see if they shared

any common ground, but prudence prevailed. Again she shook her head. "That's of no moment."

"Isn't it?" he asked, but before he could pursue the topic, Carlisle strode up to them.

"See, Vare," he called gaily, and waved his newest acquisition. "Just the thing, don't you think?"

"Bang up to the mark," his cousin drawled.

"Elegant," Georgie assured him.

"I rather think so." Carlisle, beaming, admired the little enameled box. "Just what I need." He looked around with the air of one for whom all is right in the world. "Beautiful morning, isn't it? Not a cloud in the sky for a change. Maybe we should all take a drive in the park, enjoy it while we can."

"Oh, I should like that of all things," Georgie said, then broke off, vexed with herself. It was not the place of a companion to accept such an offer.

Whitfield regarded his cousin with approval. "I was about to suggest the same thing. With the top up on the curricles, and a hot brick for their feet, the ladies might be quite comfortable."

"There is no need for me to go," Georgie declared quickly. "There can be no need for Louisa to be chaperoned in her fiancé's company for such an expedition. Then you need take only the one curricle."

"But I wish to go," Whitfield pointed out. "You would not ask me to ride bodkin with that pair, would you? Since I shall need my own curricle, I would be grateful if you would bear me company."

"Where?" Louisa demanded from behind them.

Georgie turned, relieved at this interruption.

"For a drive in the park," Carlisle said gaily. "Enjoy the good weather before the snow returns."

"Go for a drive?" Louisa repeated. "You must be mad! I should take a chill. No, really, Carlisle, it's no good looking disappointed. You must see it's quite ineligible. Besides, you must order your coat for the wedding."

"No need," he announced cheerfully. "I've got several perfectly good ones. One just delivered from my tailor that's all the crack. Just the thing."

"It won't do at all," Louisa said firmly. "But it is far too cold to stand here discussing it. Cousin Georgie, when is the carriage due to return for us?"

"At one."

Whitfield drew his watch from its pocket. "Not for another half hour," he said. "But we are barely five blocks from your home. We may walk the distance in only a few minutes. If you will accept our escort?"

"Walk?" Incredulous, Louisa stared at him. "In the snow? Carlisle, be a dear and find us a hackney."

"But it's bracing weather," he protested. "Just the thing to get the cobwebs out of your head."

Louisa fixed him with a compelling eye. "A hackney, please." Her voice might be gentle, but there could be no mistaking the determination behind her words. "I shall wait inside." With that, she turned on her heel and returned indoors.

"A hackney." Carlisle, somewhat deflated, set off in search of one.

"Now, why," Whitfield mused, "did I have the impression that Miss Granleigh loved the snow?"

Georgie's lip quivered. "Her enthusiasm for it at her wedding does not extend to actually walking through it."

"I gathered. But what is this about Carlisle's coat not being suitable? She hasn't seen it, has she?"

Georgie's humor faded. "I don't know. She hasn't said a word about it to me. I suppose we shall have to wait to find out until we return to the house."

A hackney drew up, and Carlisle jumped down. Louisa emerged from the shop, followed by two assistants bearing bandboxes. Carlisle handed Louisa up, then passed in her packages. Whitfield declined the ride, and Carlisle agreed, saying it was too fine a day not to walk. Georgie, in complete agreement with Carlisle, reluctantly climbed up after her charge.

As the carriage moved forward, Georgie settled against the squabs and regarded Louisa with wariness. "What is this about Lord Carlisle's coat?"

"Oh, not now, Cousin Georgie." Louisa leaned her head back. "Wait until I am inside and warm. I know my dear Carlisle will be delighted with my plans, but I am really too cold to explain anything at the moment."

She fell silent for the remaining few minutes of the drive. When the hackney drew up before the house, two footmen hurried out to take charge of the bandboxes. Louisa vanished after them, in the direction of her apartment.

Georgie retired to her own room to remove her bonnet and straighten her hair. To her dismay, she found herself taking far too much care over this. She tried to tell herself it was only because she was female and naturally liked to look her best, but she knew she was trying to hoax herself. It was because Lord Whitfield would be there.

She was a fool to permit him to haunt her daydreams. And she was a fool for taking such pleasure in his exchanging pleasantries with her. Why must he single her out for such attentions? He did not behave like an ardent flirt, so any hope that she might have that his attentions were merely a means of passing an otherwise boring interlude seemed ungrounded. That he meant to seriously engage her heart she couldn't be sure about. That that was well on its way to being accomplished she greatly feared. Perturbed, she made her way down the stairs to find her charge there before her, and Carlisle and Whitfield just being shown into the drawing room.

Carlisle, appearing somewhat uneasy, followed his cousin to the hearth but did not remain for long. He strode restlessly back and forth, until Dauber, who had entered with

a tray of refreshments, had withdrawn. "What is this about
my coat?" he demanded as soon as the door closed behind
the servitor.

"I've had the most wonderful notion, my dear Carlisle."
Louisa leaned forward, eyes shining. "We shall both of us
be all in silver against the white backdrop of snow."

Carlisle stared at her for perhaps a full five seconds before exclaiming, "Good God! No, really, Louisa. I may be
a dandy, but I follow poor old Brummell's lead. I'm no
Tulip or Exquisite. You go ahead and wear your silver. Very
becoming it'll look on you too. You'll see how well it'll fit
with my blue coat."

Louisa froze. "Silver," she said with distinct clarity.

The tone sent a shiver through Georgie.

"No, really, you can't be serious," protested Carlisle. "I'll
not cut such a figure of fun before the *ton."*

"There won't be many there to see it," Whitfield stuck
in, only to receive a glowering look from his cousin.

"You won't look a figure of fun," Louisa protested. "You
will look like a fairy prince! It will be the most romantic
thing ever, and it will quite take everyone's breath away."

"No, it won't, because I won't do it!"

Louisa straightened, her piercing gaze transfixing her
bridegroom. "Do you mean you won't do such a simple
little thing just to please me? I never thought you could be
so selfish."

"Selfish! Of course I'm not. But it dashed well isn't some
little thing you're asking me to do."

A dangerous note crept into Louisa's voice. "You won't
even make such a very little sacrifice, just to please me?"

"No!"

Louisa rose to her feet, her face pale with wrath. She
began to tug at the engagement ring Carlisle had placed on
her hand such a short time before.

"Wait!" Georgie sprang forward. "You are both of you
overreacting. Louisa, do sit down. And, Lord Carlisle, will

not you as well? Now, Louisa, you must see that for a gentleman to so fly in the face of fashion would not be at all the thing. And, Lord Carlisle, you must admit Louisa has a point in her desire that your coat should set off her gown. So why do you not compromise?"

"Yes." Whitfield watched her with an odd expression. "By all means, let us have them compromise. How would you suggest they do this?"

For a moment Georgie stared at him, at a loss. "I don't know. Perhaps he could wear a silver waistcoat. There would be nothing odd in that, surely."

"But his waistcoat would barely be seen," Louisa protested. "It must be his coat!"

Whitfield's gaze rested on Georgie's face. "Your principal wishes my principal to make a considerable sacrifice."

"Not a sacrifice, but a compromise!" Georgie corrected him.

"A compromise," he agreed. "What is she willing to give up in return?"

Grasping at this proffered straw, Georgie spun on the indignant Louisa. "He's right. On what other aspects are you still in disagreement?"

"Nothing, of course. How should we be?" Louisa declared.

"Oh, yes, we are," Carlisle put in. "What about the wedding trip?"

"Now, Carlisle, you know we plan to tour Europe. Just like the Grand Tour of your father's and grandfather's days. We've spoken of it often."

"No, we haven't. *You've* spoken of it. I don't want to go gallivanting all over Europe for months. We'd miss the whole of the Season. I won't do it."

Louisa frowned. "I don't know what has come over you, Carlisle. You know perfectly well that you wished to go."

"You wished it."

"Then there's your compromise," Georgie put in quickly.

"Louisa, you wish for two things that Lord Carlisle does not. You may have your way in one, and Lord Carlisle will have his in the other."

"But—" Louisa stared at her, dismayed.

"I'm not wearing a silver coat!" Carlisle stuck in.

"No, that would be too much to ask of anyone," Georgie assured him. "But I've been thinking. Would it be so terrible to have a coat of pale blue cloth shot through with silver thread? Just enough to blend with Louisa's gown?"

Carlisle's brow furrowed.

"An interesting suggestion," said Whitfield. "Carlisle, if you agree to that, where will you decide to take your wedding trip? Is there no location on the Continent that would appeal to you?"

"Not Paris," Carlisle said slowly. "But Italy, now. That might be something I would like." He brightened. "What do you say, Louisa? Shall we go to Italy?"

"Will you wear silver? Oh, all right," she added at a nudge from Georgie, "pale blue shot through with silver?"

He grimaced, but nodded.

"And thus another crisis is averted," Whitfield murmured to Georgie some twenty minutes later as he took his leave of her. "Your bargaining abilities leave me quite in awe. We could have used your assistance in Vienna."

At that she smiled, but shook her head. "They are at least learning to compromise."

"Are they?" Whitfield glanced to where their two principals stood before the fire. Louisa was saying something softly, and Carlisle stared down into her face. For once, though, his expression appeared absent. "What do you want to wager that Louisa does not suggest that they stop by Paris, or Vienna, or even Munich, since it wouldn't be so very many days out of their way, and it would be a shame to have come so far without ever seeing them?"

"It sounds exactly the sort of thing Louisa would say," Georgie admitted.

"That's much better," he said softly. "I much prefer it when there are no pretenses between us."

The warmth of his tone flustered her. She forced a soft laugh. "You would have me betray my principal," she accused. "Surely seconds are not supposed to do that."

"You serve her best when you are honest with me."

He took her hand and, to her consternation, kissed it. She tried to withdraw it from his clasp, but he resisted, his thumb caressing her palm in a manner that made her pulse speed and her breath quicken. She looked up quickly into his eyes, then realized her mistake, for the force of his gaze held her, making it impossible to look away. Slowly, deliberately, still with his gaze locked with hers, he turned her hand over and pressed a kiss into the exposed palm.

Gently, he smoothed back a wisp of her hair, his fingers brushing across her cheek. "I find there is much more happiness in agreement, do not you?"

She tried to pull away, and this time he released her. "You are pleased to flirt with me," she said, her voice tight from the emotion that raged within her.

"It would please me to do much more," he said softly.

His deep tones rolled over her, buffeting her gently, yet leaving her raw with longing. She closed her eyes, turning away. He had all but stated his intentions out loud. When they were through with this wedding, when Louisa and Carlisle were safely and respectably leg-shackled, he intended to offer her a very different sort of alliance. That it would be as pleasurable and wonderful as it would be ruinous for her, she had not the least doubt.

She could not let it happen. Yet if he ever spoke the words, would she have the resolution of character to turn him down? She could hope so, but she had grave doubts. It would be best to keep him at a distance, discourage him, prevent him from voicing the words she both longed and dreaded to hear.

Behind her, he said, "I must return to my estates tomorrow."

She spun back to search his face. "Will you be gone long?"

His smile caressed her. "Not a moment longer than I have to, I promise. But I doubt I can be back in less than a fortnight."

"Well"—she tried a laugh, striving for a lighter note—"I doubt they can cause me too much grief in that time. I shall manage quite well, I promise you."

"That's my fear," he said, and with that, he was gone.

Six

The days passed quickly for Georgie. Carlisle continued to call—though not as often. Each time he arrived, she looked up quickly, hoping beyond any reasonable hope to see Whitfield's tall, vibrant figure follow him into the room. She hid her disappointment, and lectured herself firmly that it was only for the best, that to see him was far too dangerous. Yet not seeing him was becoming every day more painful.

She had no lack of things to do. The invitations arrived from the stationer, and she spent several days inscribing them and setting them aside for Carlisle to frank for her. When the last of these had been dispatched, she next turned her attention to Gunter's. Fortunately at this time of year there was no trouble in obtaining what she requested, though she could not give the caterer any precise idea as to how many people would be present.

Within a very few days, the first acceptances came back, from those friends of Louisa's father who lived in London throughout the year. As these were all members of the various academic and philosophical societies at which that gentleman spent the better part of his time, it could not be considered a social coup. Refusals from the *ton* also began to appear, but Georgie was surprised and Louisa triumphant at the surprising number of acceptances from the members of the fashionable world. Yet there was only one person from whom she wished to hear, even though she already knew he would be present at the wedding. She missed Whitfield more than was wise.

She now turned her attention to the ball, which had been planned as an inducement for their guests to make the tiresome journey to London. The days continued to pass without any word from Whitfield, but she found herself able to keep on organizing, attending to details. Louisa and Carlisle took to bickering, but she assured them both this was merely due to nerves. Carlisle declared that he wished Whitfield would return, a sentiment with which Georgie found herself in complete agreement.

As the second week drew to a close, Dauber brought a letter to her while she was in the drawing room, compiling a list of those who had accepted. The butler's manner was so secretive, his smile so fatherly as he handed the folded sheet to her, it instantly roused her curiosity. For a moment she didn't recognize the handwriting, then she deciphered Whitfield's frank. Suddenly she felt as nervous as she had on the day she arrived to take up her first post as a governess. She managed to thank Dauber, then broke the wafer with trembling fingers.

He wrote only a few words, apologizing for his prolonged absence. He hoped, he added, it would not be many more days until he could once again aid her in her wedding chores. Not by so much as a single word did he betray any feelings for her, any indication that he regarded her in any other light than a business associate, yet she folded it with tender care and secreted it away, as warmed as if it had been the most passionate of love notes.

What a fool she was, she reflected. He had undoubtedly changed his mind, found game more to his liking. When he returned, the warmth she had come to relish would be missing from his manner. It would be for the best. She repeated that to herself several times, but found little solace in it.

By the time he finally arrived toward the middle of the

following week, the last-minute details were driving her frantic. She looked up, startled, when the butler announced him, and a disconcerting mix of relief and joy flooded through her as she met the gaze of the earl's penetrating hazel eyes.

He strode forward into the room, took her hand, and kissed it. "Forgive me for taking so long," he said simply. "There were many details I had to attend to. Tell me how you go on."

"Very well," she managed to say. The passage of a little more than three weeks had not given her as great a perspective as she had hoped. He was still the most attractive man she had ever encountered. And her heart, she discovered with sinking dismay, had not in the least recovered during his absence. She realized he studied her closely, and warm color flooded her cheeks.

"You have been working too hard," he said abruptly. "Tell me how I may help."

"There is really very little," she assured him. "You could hardly take Louisa for her fittings."

"Are you still plagued with that? Send her on her own," he said.

"No, you forget. I am her companion."

His mouth tightened. "How about this ball? Let me see what you have left to do. You have a list, I presume?" He held out his hand.

She shook her head, smiling. "I begin to suspect, my lord," she informed him as she drew the sheet from the desk, "that you are of a very managing disposition."

"Of a certainty." He studied the list for a few moments, then looked up at her with new respect. "I had no idea there were so many things to be taken care of."

"How should you? It is not something that would ordinarily come in your way."

"Well, the musicians will. That much I can handle." He perused the list once more. "Silver fabric and ribands?"

"Louisa wishes to transform the ballroom into a—a fairyland," she admitted.

"Good God. And you can do this, I presume?"

"Oh, yes. I have already checked with the linen draper. We won't need much, of course. Gauze will go a long way to creating the effect she wants. I shall begin the decorating work tomorrow."

"Yes, I have been away far too long. The wedding is in only five days. Have they plagued you very much?"

"Oh, no. They have not argued—oh, above a dozen times," she said lightly. "We have worked out compromises."

"I would wish you well out of this," he declared.

"Yes, and so I shall be all too soon." She didn't express the dread this thought brought with it. Once her charge was safely wed, Louisa would have no further need for a chaperon. Georgie would have to find another position. The prospect of returning to a governess's post held little appeal. While dealing with Louisa had been difficult at times, she had enjoyed considerable leisure, even experienced some of the elegancies of life once again. All that would shortly be over. She thrust it to the back of her mind.

"And you are worried about your next position."

She didn't look up, afraid he would read the confirmation in her eyes. "Right now I am more worried about the things I still must do."

"Is there anywhere you need to go?"

"Layton and Shears," she admitted. "I must finalize the order for the fabric."

"I will take you."

"Nonsense. That cannot be of interest to you." Resolutely, she ignored his smile, which played havoc with her senses.

"As your fellow second, it is my duty to help with the burdens laid upon you. Come. My groom is walking my horses."

She hesitated, but knew she didn't stand a chance. "Let me just put on my bonnet," she said, and fled the room.

When she returned, warmly wrapped in her pelisse and with her bonnet securely tied beneath her chin, it was to find the curricle at the door, and Dauber himself placing a hot brick for her feet. Whitfield handed her up, then swung into his seat at her side and produced a rug which he spread over her knees. Once he had assured himself of her comfort, he gave his horses the office.

She sat silently for some time, until it dawned on her that they were not headed in the proper direction. "We should be going to Henrietta Street," she told him.

"Actually, we are going to the park."

"The—no, please, my lord. I have far too much to do."

"You are going to take a short rest, and will then be able to work much more efficiently. No, short of causing a vulgar scene, which you will not wish to do, there is nothing for it but to make the best of it and enjoy yourself. We shall make a circuit or two of the park, and you may pretend you are deep in the country."

She shook her head. "I was right. Quite managing."

He looked down at her, his expression unfathomable. "Do you truly mind so very much?"

"Well, I am also very much accustomed to having my way, you see, and—"

"Vixen," he murmured with appreciation. "You know very well I meant the expedition to the park."

She was silent for a moment. Then she admitted, "I ought to mind," with too much honesty.

"No, you most emphatically ought not."

The curricle was very well sprung, and she found herself surprisingly comfortable with the brick and rug to lend her warmth. Even had she been denied those two items, his mere presence warmed her. They swung through the gates and proceeded along the tanbark, empty at this time except for a couple of grooms exercising horses. She could almost envision herself in the country.

"Even the air smells fresher," she said. "Almost like a garden."

"Do you enjoy setting out flower beds?" he asked. His attention appeared to be taken up with his horses.

"I've never had the chance. Someday, perhaps, I shall have a small garden."

"My mother started one at the court," he said. "It has been sadly neglected of late years. Does Miss Granleigh share this interest?"

Georgie hesitated over her answer. "I do not believe she has had any opportunity. She has lived all her life in a town house, you must know."

They completed their first circuit and began on a second. Georgie found herself relaxing, enjoying herself. If only she weren't so vividly aware of the powerful man who sat so close at her side. To divert her mind, she asked about the Congress, and he spoke readily enough of the negotiations, touching upon the personalities involved in a humorous manner. This so delighted her that for a little while she actually forgot the pressure of the tasks still before her.

Passing the gates to the park recalled her mind to them, though, and with a pang of guilt, she realized she had lost all track of time. She protested, adding, "I really must visit the linen draper, my lord. And there are other errands awaiting my attention."

Somewhat to her regret, he turned the horses, and in a very short time they pulled up in Henrietta Street before the establishment of Layton and Shears. Not only did the earl insist upon accompanying her inside, but his presence garnered for her far more attention than she had previously enjoyed. Several clerks hurried to present before her various bolts of fabric; the proprietor himself tried to press refreshments upon them; and within a surprisingly short time, she had purchased sufficient fabric and ribands of white and silver to create a respectable fairy kingdom, even if one not quite up to Louisa's standards.

"For I cannot bring myself to rig the footmen out with silk wings," she confided to the earl as they set off for home.

"I should think not," he responded, considerably revolted. "It is to be hoped it is your hand that will prevail."

"Well," she said, considering, "since Louisa merely makes sweeping decisions and leaves the actual accomplishment to me, it seems likely."

He pulled up his pair before the house, but as he prepared to escort her inside, she stopped him, saying, "No, please. I must meet with a seamstress within the hour, and I have a great deal to do to prepare."

He took her hand, retaining it in his warm clasp. "Remember, you have no need to worry about the musicians. I will see to their hiring."

With a mixture of regret and relief she watched him drive off. She would have been wiser not to have gone to the park with him, but it had been so tempting. Surely she at least could be wise enough not to lose all sense of judgment over the man.

Fortunately, she had no time to think about him anymore. Several more details awaited her attention before the seamstress came, and the fabric for the ballroom would arrive by midafternoon. It would be best if she started decorating at once, which would leave her more time for any last-minute disasters. She had no leisure to indulge in daydreaming.

And once this wedding was over, she would have the problems of finding a new position, then all the bustle of taking up her residence and duties in a new household. One thing she could say in favor of the life of a governess: It left little time or energy for personal reflections or regrets.

Seven

Georgie stood near the door of the ballroom as a country dance began. This was the first quiet moment she had experienced, and she welcomed it, taking the opportunity to look around and admire her handiwork. The room was really quite lovely, bearing out the hint of snow without being mawkishly fairy tale-like. The musicians were superb—she must thank Whitfield for finding them if she got a chance to speak with him.

In fact, the whole evening promised to be a success. Although by no stretch of the imagination could the room be called filled, there were sufficient guests present so as not to be an embarrassment. Carlisle, who had arrived with his cousin in time for dinner beforehand, now danced with Louisa. Lord Whitfield she spotted gracing the floor with Mrs. Pettering, the wife of one of Mr. Granleigh's friends from the Royal Institution. The poor woman's husband had deserted her almost the instant they arrived, vanishing to the sanctuary of the library, where he and Mr. Granleigh would undoubtedly indulge in philosophical discussion, oblivious to all else. The gentlemen's intention to remain thus secluded they had made very clear, directing Georgie to send any of their other friends to that room as soon as the poor fellows arrived. That this left their wives unsupported, not one of them seemed to care. Their attitude appeared to be that having escorted their ladies to the ball, their obligations ceased. This also left the numbers sadly unequal, but there was nothing Georgie could do about that now.

The dance ended, and Georgie busied herself securing partners for as many of the ladies as she possibly could. They had an odd assortment of guests, mostly town dwellers, some whose estates lay not too far removed from London as to make a winter ball an inducement. Carlisle, she noted, did his duty by one of his aunts, while Whitfield attended to another of the scholars' abandoned wives. That was really very well done of him, and one more thing for which she would have to thank him later.

Louisa, she noted, had gathered a sizable court about herself. Georgie bore down on them, and within minutes had presented the hapless young gentlemen to various ladies. She watched with satisfaction as they all took the floor.

By the next dance Georgie fully expected the earl to reward himself by partnering one of the several rather pretty girls present. But again he surprised her, this time raiding the ranks of the dowagers and drawing the laughingly protesting Lady St. Albans onto the floor.

"Very well, if you must have your way," that lady declared, shaking her head. "You never were one to give in."

"Confess, ma'am," Georgie heard Whitfield say, "there is nothing you would rather do, is there?"

"You know perfectly well I have always loved to dance."

"Then let us not be concerned with public opinion."

Several soft exclamations sounded behind Georgie, the "public" whose opinion Whitfield and Lady St. Albans chose to ignore. Georgie glanced at these dowagers and chaperons, and in relief detected no real disapproval. Several, in fact, bore decidedly wistful and envious expressions. Georgie made a mental note of their identities and determined to point them out to Whitfield at her earliest opportunity.

She headed for the refreshment table to check that all

the trays had been safely placed, only to encounter Louisa coming toward her.

"It's the dullest party," that young lady declared in tones far too loud for Georgie's comfort. "There is almost no one of any consequence present, and Carlisle seems determined to dance with every nobody here."

"And very grateful I am to him," Georgie declared. "The first duty of a hostess is to assure herself that all her guests are enjoying themselves. You will find, at the first ball you and Carlisle give together, how lucky you are to have a husband who will do his duty like this. When it is obvious to all he would much rather be with you," she added.

At this, Louisa's expression softened. "It is most tiresome," she declared, and moved off.

Georgie checked the table, sent one of the footmen for more champagne, then began to arrange more partners as soon as the dance ended. The strains, though, were not the country dance she expected, but a waltz. Looking quickly toward the musicians, she discovered Louisa just moving away from them. Well, she supposed she couldn't blame her. Of all things, to waltz with one's betrothed, only a little more than a day from one's wedding, was of all things the most romantic. Firmly she banished a budding longing of her own, and steered a young gentleman toward one of Carlisle's maiden aunts, who had been watching the proceedings with avid, eager eyes.

As she turned from them, she found Whitfield looming over her. The light in his eyes sent warmth racing through her. "Thank you," she said impulsively.

His broad smile flashed. "I haven't even asked you to dance yet."

"That's not what I meant, and you know it. You've been wonderful about dancing with the dowagers."

"I'm glad to see my efforts haven't been wasted. But I've come to claim my reward."

Her gaze flickered up to meet his, then lowered at once.

"Pray, do not be absurd. I don't dance tonight," she said, not pretending to misunderstand him. "I'm a chaperon."

"Your time of chaperonage is almost at an end," he reminded her, "so why shouldn't you enjoy this one dance?"

She glared at him, all the more vexed because she longed to dance with him. "You know perfectly well I cannot."

"I have been dancing with every dowager, maiden aunt, and chaperon present, for no other reason than to assure that you would not have an excuse to refuse me. In fact, it would look very singular if you did refuse me."

"You are quite absurd," she informed him. "And I am quite serious. I do not dance tonight."

A wicked gleam lit his eye. "Then you will create the most shocking scene if you persist in refusing, because I intend to drag you onto the floor and dance with you."

"You cannot!" she exclaimed, flustered, for from the determined expression on his face she could see that that was precisely what he was likely to do.

"Oh, can't I?" he murmured, and took her hand.

She backed away quickly, but he pursued, still clasping her hand. Several people stared at them, she realized in dismay. "Please," she begged, but he shook his head. The only possible course was for her to give in with good grace. Reluctantly, she allowed him to lead her onto the floor. "You are placing me quite beyond the pale, and it is most unhandsome of you," she informed him.

"It is," he agreed, "and I beg your pardon, but it's an opportunity that I don't want to let slide by, for who knows when it can be repeated?"

His words sank in, his smile melted her heart, and suddenly she no longer cared about what people might say. He was right. It would never be repeated. Once Louisa married, Georgie would return to obscurity and poverty. Never again would she attend a ball, never again would she wear a gown worthy of the occasion, and never again would she face Lord Whitfield while the strains of a waltz played in her ear.

Without realizing she had moved, she found she was clasping his hand and dancing the steps she had practiced so many times with Louisa, only it wasn't at all the same, nothing like she had ever dreamed. It was exhilarating, wonderful, her heart pounding, her breath coming rapidly. His gloved hand held one of hers tightly as they moved through the open steps, then she daringly rested her other hand on his shoulder as they spun together for those few glorious turns. Then they separated once more, and she could barely breathe with the sheer delight of it all.

The rest of the dancers became little more than a blur to her, a hint of swirling color against the glittering of the candles in the chandeliers. All other sensations and thoughts held no importance to her; she lived for this one moment, memorizing the sensations, knowing this would be the only memory she would ever have. She intended to make the experience as complete and exact and as wonderful as she could. For this one moment she allowed herself all the joy and excitement of knowing herself deeply in love.

When the music stopped, she could only wonder how any dance could be so short. Yet for a few moments, time had extended until it seemed to stand still. In a daze, she allowed Whitfield to place her hand on his arm and lead her from the floor.

His eyes smiled down at her, caressing her. "Was that really so terrible?"

"Of course it was," she declared, rallying, trying to bury her emotions beneath a cool exterior. "I went along with it only to prevent a scandal."

He stopped, turning her to face him. Raising her chin with one hand, he compelled her to look into his face. "Is that true?" he demanded.

Hot color flushed her cheeks, and she pulled away. "I must get back to my duties. I never should have abandoned them."

"Georgie."

He spoke her name softly, yet it seemed to fill her ears, her entire being. She longed to turn back to him, to meet that teasing challenge she knew would be in his face; but she knew if ever she did, her life would never be the same.

Resolutely she walked away, refusing to give in to her longings. No amount of wishful dreaming could ever span the vast social gap that lay between them. True, he had fortune enough not to require any in his prospective bride, but his was an old family; they had been prominent long before there had been an earldom of Whitfield. And they were proud, their members marrying always for social advancement. That the head of such a family might for so much as a moment contemplate anything but the most casual of liaisons with a pauper governess from an insignificant family was ludicrous. She had been foolish to indulge in that dance.

Louisa strode up to her, seized her by the arm, and propelled her into an isolated corner. Georgie, startled, and still in the thrall of her unhappy thoughts, made no protest until they were virtually alone. "Whatever is the matter?" she managed to ask.

Louisa looked daggers at her. "That was the most absurd display. Oh, Cousin Georgie, how could you make such a figure of fun of yourself? To be so blatantly setting your cap at someone like Whitfield!"

Georgie straightened, facing her young accuser. "I do wish you would not be so dramatic, Louisa. It is not in the least becoming."

"Becoming! Oh, no, cousin, that's doing it too brown. When it is you who have been behaving so foolishly. You must know his attentions to a companion could never be serious. You have been—"

"I have been doing my duty here this night, and that is all. Now, pray, talk no more such rubbish, for you know perfectly well there is not an ounce of truth in it."

Louisa glowered at her. "It's being talked about all over

the ballroom. Never did I think to be put to the blush for my companion."

"That is quite enough nonsense," Georgie snapped, and turned away, trying desperately to hide her mortification. Resolutely, she stared straight in front of her, not daring to meet the eyes of any of the guests. They laughed at her, there could be no doubt of that. Or was it worse? Did they speculate upon Whitfield's less than honorable intentions—and her own willingness to accede to them?

She dashed a tear from her eye, and wished she dared grab a moment alone to deal with the other tears that threatened. She had known how shocking her behavior had been, yet she had gone ahead, succumbing to impulse. It had been her fault, she must have led Whitfield to believe she had been casting out lures to him, making him think she could be so lost to all propriety. Surely Whitfield would not have insisted upon the dance had she not erroneously led him to believe she might be willing, despite her protests. So what if he had threatened a scene if she refused him? Had she but held firm, behaved like a lady rather than a wanton, lovesick fool, he would have relented. He was too much the gentleman to have persisted.

She had used his joking threat only as an excuse to behave in a manner both shocking and unforgivable. She could blame only herself, bitterly, for being such a fool—and also for entertaining such feelings for him, for wanting to continue to feel such things, for allowing herself, for those few moments, to dream of love.

She turned, unable to stop herself, and met Whitfield's gaze, where he stood some distance away. The burning glow in his eyes wrenched her heart. At that moment she actually considered abandoning the respectable but unfulfilling life of a companion for the unknown but undoubted joys of becoming his mistress.

Eight

Georgie's distress continued to haunt her long into the night, until sheer exhaustion at last brought on the oblivion of sleep. She awoke late to a lingering headache and the nagging sensation that all was wrong with her world. A few minutes' consideration confirmed this latter, and it was in a mood of determined and totally false enthusiasm that she descended the stairs to face the trials of this last day before Louisa's wedding.

Time-consuming and elusive details haunted her throughout the morning and well into the afternoon. She had to contact Gunter's with the revised numbers for the wedding breakfast. The seamstress arrived late for the last-minute fittings for Louisa's silver gown. The wine merchant had insufficient quantities of the vintage she had requested, which necessitated a second visit to the caterer with the altered wine list.

Upon her return, she hurried directly to Louisa's room, where not one but three seamstresses attended the imperious beauty. Two sat by the window, stitching, while the third, Madame Thérèse herself, examined the hang of the gown with an experienced eye.

Louisa turned eagerly from the cheval glass to the door as Georgie came to a halt just over the threshold. "What do you think?" the girl demanded.

"It's stunning." Georgie shook her head. "It could not be more beautiful." And in this assessment, she told the simple truth. They had decided at last on a plain underdress of white silk shot through with silver thread. A robe of silvered gauze partially covered this, its tiny puff sleeves and low décolletage boasting tiny knots of silvered silk rosebuds and ribands. More of the knots caught up the skirt. A length of silvered sarcenet, still being hemmed by the diligent needlewomen, would drape across her fair hair.

Louisa turned back to the mirror and preened. "Against the white snow, and with Carlisle dressed to match me, I think I will create quite a sensation."

"Indeed you will. Except there won't be any snow in the church."

"As long as it is decorated to look as if there were. And outside there will be. Oh, I hope there will be sun in the morning. It would create such a dazzling effect."

The church decorations. She hadn't yet assured that the fabric and flowers had arrived at the church. Mentally she added this to her list of chores that kept mounting. She would probably have to arrange them herself as well; that wasn't the sort of thing of which one could ask the rector to take charge. She had better see to it right away.

She was just requesting that the carriage be brought round for her, when Lord Whitfield arrived on their door-step. Georgie stared at him in dismay, fully aware of the awkwardness of the meeting after the events of the night before. Only when he greeted her as if nothing untoward had occurred did she realize that he had remained unaware of the unpleasant aftermath, of the gossip that must be circulating about them. Yet that did little to restore her composure. She stared at him, tangle-tongued and flustered under the effect of his mere presence. Her cheeks burned, and her heart beat faster with an awareness that was entirely unfair.

"Have I come at a bad time?" he inquired when she made no response to his greeting.

"No. I'm sorry. That is—" Her cheeks flamed more hotly. "I was just on my way out, to the church."

His smile was warm, supportive. "Then allow me to drive you."

"No, I couldn't. I'm sure you have other, more important things to do this day."

"Not in the least." His eyes gleamed. "The part of the groomsman, I assure you, is simplicity itself. All the work has fallen on you. It seems only fair I should assist in whatever way I can."

She knew she should repulse him, make it clear she neither needed nor wanted his assistance, but this she could not bring herself to do. Saying that she would be only a moment, she hurried upstairs to fetch her bonnet and pelisse. As she donned the former, she caught herself studying her reflection with too much care. She did not want to make herself attractive, she assured herself, blatantly lying. She wanted to impress Whitfield with her neatness, her aloofness, her propriety. With that intention she knotted her hair back in a grim and forbidding chignon, tied her bonnet prosaically under her chin, and rejoined him in the hall.

The earl assisted her into his curricle, then swung up beside her. When he had settled her with rug and warm brick to his satisfaction, he started his pair. His groom stood back, then swung up behind as the carriage moved past him.

"I see you are far too busy today," he said in a purely conversational voice.

"Well, it will all be over with tomorrow." Firmly, she shut the door on the inevitable fears and speculations about her future that thought brought to mind.

He cast her a sideways glance. "And how does Louisa go on today?"

"Oh, she's in high gig. Her gown is perfectly beautiful. She truly will be a sensation in it. It's a pity so few people will see it, though I daresay she will wear it for a ball later on."

"There are times it seems that dress and the fairy tale effect are all she cares about." He kept the words light, as if he merely teased her.

She wasn't fooled. "You wrong her. Of course she cares about her wedding, but it is marrying Carlisle that matters to her."

"Don't be vexed." He fell silent as he maneuvered his pair around a wagon that stood blocking the better part of the street. He didn't speak again until they pulled up in front of St. George's in Hanover Square. He helped her down, then retained his hold on her hand, smiling into her eyes. "Don't worry. I have arranged everything for the best."

"And what am I supposed to make of that?" she demanded, albeit somewhat breathlessly. Looking into his eyes almost proved too much for her, and she had to struggle against the longing to sway against him, to feel his strong, comforting arms about her.

"Just what I have said. All will be for the best." He led her up the steps to the church.

The circumstance almost proved too much for her, driving all else from her mind. If only this were her own wedding, to Whitfield—

But that was truly an unattainable dream. She knew all too well that only two possibilities lay before her once Louisa and Carlisle had wed. Either Whitfield would vanish from her life, or he would force her to choose between him and her virtue. If he did, it would be the most difficult choice she'd ever have to make.

The carriage that brought the wedding party to Hanover Square that chill morning set them down before the church barely a minute before the designated hour. A fresh falling of snow during the night had blanketed everything in white; Louisa had gotten her perfect backdrop. And now the sun shone bright, sparkling off the ice crystals. Nothing, as far as the girl was concerned, could be more ideal.

Shivering, Georgie stepped down and hurried up the steps of the church, leaving Mr. Granleigh to assist his daughter. As soon as Georgie was inside, she removed her pelisse, revealing her own dress of the purest white gauze. White ribands threaded through her brown hair, making her appear one more snow-covered element in Louisa's fairy tale. Then Louisa hurried in, and Georgie busied herself readying the bride. In another minute her charge stood before her, the very vision of a fairy tale princess all in silver and white. Georgie adjusted the fine sarcenet that covered the girl's pale hair, then stood back in admiration.

Mr. Granleigh, a slight man with a nervous manner, peered nearsightedly into the sanctuary, then frowned at Georgie. "There seem to be an unusual number of people present for a wedding."

"Yes, sir. It's what Louisa wanted."

"Oh, it is, is it? Well, I don't know anything about the Polite World. Left all that to her mother, rest her soul. Well, if it's us for whom they're all waiting, I suppose we'd better get on with it. Coming, my dear?" He offered his arm to his daughter.

Louisa shook her head. "Let them wait a little longer. I want to savor this moment."

Georgie fidgeted, nervous, wanting only to get this over with. Her night had been tortured by Louisa's bedtime scene; the girl had threatened not to go through with the wedding if everything were not perfect. She had imagined and dreamed about every detail, she'd exclaimed; if anything should go wrong or be different, it would ruin everything.

But all had gone well. They had made it. Nothing could go wrong now.

At last Louisa nodded, and Georgie started forward through the doorway. As Mr. Granleigh had noted, a gratifying crowd filled the pews. Then her gaze focused on the three men who stood before the altar, and an awareness swept over her, so great she could barely breathe. Whitfield stood facing her, as if he waited for her to come to him, to take his hand in the sight of God—

The pain of that thought overwhelmed her, yet still she gazed at him, unable to look anywhere else. Each step seemed to take an eternity. All of her handiwork in white, the draping of cloth, flowers, and ribands, passed by her in a blur. It might have been real snow, considering the chill and emptiness that settled in her heart. Then she was next to him, then moving aside to take her place.

A startled murmur from the gathering penetrated the fog that filled her mind. She'd expected gasps of awe, but this sounded nothing like the reception Louisa had prophesied for her appearance. Filled with sudden foreboding, Georgie looked over her shoulder.

The bride had abandoned her father near the door, and advanced up the aisle on her own. This was not the delicate fairy princess of the plans, but a raging termagant. The bride blushed, but with anger rather than a pretty show of nerves. She strode in a most unladylike manner to the front of the church, then confronted her bridegroom, arms akimbo.

"How dare you!" she breathed. "Oh, how dare you overset everything like this! I worked so hard to make it all so perfect, and you only had to do one little thing for me. Only one! And look how you have betrayed me!" Her voice rose with each word, until even those in the rear pews must have had a fair idea of the bride's emotional state.

Carlisle straightened, and one hand ran along the lapel of his coat. Of his deep blue coat. Not pale blue, not shot through with silver, but *blue.* Georgie stared at it in bewildered dismay.

"You promised me!" Louisa cried.

Carlisle's mouth set in a firm line. "I looked a dashed fool in the thing you'd have had me wear. That's not the sort of thing any female could ask of a gentleman."

"But I wanted us to look like a fairy tale!"

"That's all you care about. Not me, just your dashed fairy tale! Now, listen, Louisa. I'm not one to live under the cat's paw."

"How dare you!" Louisa exploded. "How—how selfish you are. Well, I can only say I'm grateful my eyes were opened in time. I'll not stand for this. The wedding," she informed him at a rather high pitch, "is off!" With that she turned on her heel and marched right back down the aisle, her bewildered father scurrying after her.

Georgie started in pursuit, but Whitfield stopped her, catching her hand. "No," he said softly. "Let her go."

"But—" She looked at him, confused, as everything fell apart about her.

Carlisle, staring after his erstwhile bride, shook his head. "You were right, Vare," he said in a strangled voice. "Lord, what a narrow escape. How could any man of sense find happiness with a spoiled chit who cares more for the appearance of a coat than for the man who wears it?"

"She'll be sorry in a little while," Georgie assured him. "It was only nerves, you know."

"I know nothing of the sort," he retorted. "She has the makings of a real shrew."

The scandalized chatter of voices filled the church. Georgie, desperate, turned to Whitfield. "What do we do now?"

An intriguingly slow smile lit his eyes. "I suppose we should go on with the wedding, albeit with a different bride and groom."

"A—" Georgie shook her head. "This is no time for funning, my lord. How ever do we smooth over this scandal?"

"Just as I suggested. I admit it's not what I had in mind.

I'd intended a much quieter affair, once we'd gotten our charges off our hands, but it would be a shame to let all our planning and efforts go to waste."

"But who—"

"And here are all these people, lured to London with the promise of nuptial festivities," he went on smoothly, ignoring her interruption. "It wouldn't be right to disappoint them. Carlisle, will you do me the honor of standing as my groomsman?"

His cousin grinned. "Of course."

"Thank you." From his pocket Whitfield produced a folded piece of paper which he handed to the distraught rector. "A special license," he explained to Georgie. "The rector had already promised to meet us back here later this afternoon."

She shook her head. "But you cannot marry me! Your family—I'm a nobody. And the scandal—"

"That's exactly what I hope to avoid," he informed her. Firmly he took her hand in his. "Quit arguing with me, my love. Our own, and very unexpected, wedding will cause such a sensation that it will overshadow Louisa's behavior. You will marry me, won't you?" he added, his eyes dancing with inner laughter.

"How can I? My lord, it would be such an unequal match, it would be thought such a—a freakish start on your part. It would cause the most vulgar talk, and—"

"Now, what's all this? I hadn't thought you missish, my girl."

"Missish, no. But prudent. My lord—"

"Do you want to save Miss Granleigh from this scandal?"

"Yes, of course, but—"

"Can you suggest a better way than to provide society with a more romantic *on-dit?*"

She regarded him soberly. "So you wish me to marry you to avert a scandal?"

"I wish you to marry me for reasons that decorum prohibits me to describe in front of other people. Do me the honor of wedding me, and I will explain them to you in the greatest of possible detail as soon as we are alone. Surely you must have known how I felt?"

"I—I had thought you intended—something—" She broke off, unable to voice the suspicions that had haunted her.

"Good God, did you take me for the sort of loose fish who would trifle with a lady of your quality? No wonder you hesitate to wed me!"

"No! That is—Oh, surely you must understand how unsuitable I am for you."

"The only thing I understand is how much I love you. Now, will you marry me, or will you create another scandal by following Miss Granleigh down that aisle?"

Torn between laughter and tears, she blinked up into his humor-filled yet determined face. "It seems I have no choice," she said.

"None whatsoever," he responded promptly.

With a look that left her weak with desire, and set her heart singing, he drew her to his side, and together they faced the rector.

A Match for the Season

Carola Dunn

One

"Well now, poppet, it seems you have done the thing!"

"Done what, Papa?" Looking up from the note she was reading, Cecily gazed fondly across the breakfast table at the earl.

A beam on his square, ruddy country-squire's face, he waved his letter. "Your mama will be *aux anges.*"

A flutter in her middle effectively destroyed her appetite for the hot roll she had just spread with damson jam. At present only one occurrence could render her mother ecstatic, and Cecily was not at all sure she was ready for it. "Lord Avon has requested an interview with you?" she asked apprehensively.

"Near enough, This is an invitation from Pembroke to spend Christmas at Felversham."

"But the Duke of Pembroke is a particular friend of yours, is he not? He dined here twice last spring, when he came up to Parliament, and I recall you and Mama were guests at Felversham once, when I was still in the schoolroom."

"More than once. However, Pembroke makes a point of including you in the invitation at his son's request!" said her father in triumph.

"Oh." Since her arrival in town for the Little Season, Lord Avon had certainly been most assiduous in his attentions—hence Mama's raised hopes. He stood up with her twice at every ball, and generally took her in to supper. He drove her in Hyde Park, escorted her to Hookham's Library and the opera, bought her ices at Gunter's.

Just the other day he had told her about his father's splendid winter house-parties. After a quiet family Christmas, the Duke of Pembroke always invited a crowd of guests, young and old, to celebrate the New Year and Twelfth Night at Felversham. Though the duchess's crippling arthritis prevented the Pembrokes' spending the Season in London, she enjoyed entertaining friends and relatives. The fortnight was always filled with music, dancing, and such outdoor activities as the weather allowed, culminating on Twelfth Night with a masquerade party for guests, servants, and tenants.

It sounded like a great deal of fun, but Cecily could not help wishing her suitor had inquired whether she would like to visit rather than simply asking his parents to invite her. And an invitation for Christmas, which he had described as a family occasion, was alarmingly significant.

Her less than beatific response dismayed her papa. "You have not taken Avon in dislike, Cecy, have you?" he asked anxiously.

"Oh, no, Papa. He is charming and handsome and conversable and . . . and amusing. . . ."

"And wealthy and heir to a duke and son of an old friend. Nor have I heard anything to his detriment beyond the little peccadilloes excusable in a spirited young fellow. I need not tell you, my dear, that I should be as pleased as your mother to give your hand to the Marquis of Avon."

"Yes, Papa. May I go and tell Mama about the invitation?"

"Certainly, and give her this enclosed letter from the duchess, but finish your breakfast first. We don't want any lovesick wasting-away," he teased.

"Yes, Papa." Cecily obediently ate the roll and drank a cup of tea before making her way upstairs. She went first to her own lilac-and-ivory chamber, where she sat down before the dressing table and stared at herself in the looking-glass.

Lovesick wasting-away? She did not love Lord Avon.

She liked him as well as any gentleman she had met during her first Season last spring, and better than most. Besides, he was by far the most eligible bachelor presently on the Town, a splendid match for any young lady. To the vast majority of the Beau Monde, that was more than sufficient basis for marriage.

Did he love her? She inventoried her assets: hair thick and glossy, curling easily into ringlets, though neither blond nor dark but merely a middling brown; eyes of a dark blue that had the more poetically inclined of her admirers in raptures; straight little nose; clear complexion with rose-tinted cheeks; mouth a trifle wider than was strictly fashionable, but only a trifle; chin—did gentlemen care about a lady's chin? One never read sonnets to a chin!

Standing up, she cast aside her cashmere shawl and studied her figure. Her height was somewhat above average, but Lord Avon was tall, so that would not disturb him. Slim in the right places and rounded in the right places, the whole was enhanced by her morning gown of primrose jaconet, designed by Madame Ernestine, the most exclusive modiste in town.

Quite pretty, she thought, though the title of Incomparable was due less to her looks than to her being the only child of the Earl of Flint, with a fortune of fifty thousand pounds.

Altogether a suitable bride for a duke's heir looking to set up his nursery. She was a goosecap to wish for love. Mama and Papa went on quite contentedly with no more than habit and a mild fondness for each other. An agreeable husband was the best their daughter dared hope for.

With a sigh she picked up her shawl and went to tell her mother the good news.

Lady Flint, propped against a mound of pillows, glanced

up from her post and smiled as Cecily entered her chamber. At forty, she scarcely needed the flattering light cast by ruffled pink bed curtains on her round face and lacy nightcap.

"What a fetching headdress, Mama," said Cecily. "Is that the cap we bought yesterday?"

"Yes, my love, the one you chose for me. There is nothing like the real Valenciennes." She pushed aside a pile of papers. "So many hostesses desirous of our company, one might suppose it to be the height of the spring Season instead of the end of November! Come and sit down and let us decide which invitations to accept."

"I have brought another." While her mother perused the duchess's letter, Cecily perched on the bed and leafed unseeingly through the heap of cards beside her.

"Christmas at Felversham!" crowed Lady Flint. "My dearest child, you have brought it off. Not that I supposed for a moment you would not," she added stoutly. "There's not a girl in the *ton* can hold a candle to mine. A winter wedding, I think. I do not approve of long engagements, and you will enjoy next Season as a married lady."

Cecily smiled. "Now, Mama, who is forever telling me not to count my chickens before they hatch?"

"Nonsense, child. It is very proper for Avon to wish to make you known to his parents before he formally offers for your hand, but the duchess writes that he informs her you are . . . ahem! Well, I don't wish you to grow quite puffed up!"

"Pray tell, Mama! What did he say?" Cecily asked hopefully. Perhaps he did love her after all.

"Let it suffice that he has persuaded both her and the duke you are in every way fitted to be his wife. What is more, she especially looks forward to the connection because of your father's long friendship with her husband. So you see it is perfectly plain. You shall be the next Duchess of Pembroke!"

In the face of such delighted enthusiasm, Cecily did her best to put aside her doubts. She knew very well all her friends would be green with envy. The world would consider her the most fortunate of creatures; who was she to dissent?

"How are the aches and pains today, ma'am?" Iain Macfarlane took his aunt's knotted hands in his with the familiar twist of helpless pity. What was the use of being a physician if he could not cure the woman who had been a second mother to him? He bent to kiss her cheek, scented with the faintly astringent sweetness of cologne water.

"I do believe the ginger and willow-bark tea has helped, Iain," the duchess said cheerfully. Reclining on the blue-brocaded chaise longue by the window in her cozy private sitting room, she smiled up at him.

A near cripple before she was fifty, the Duchess of Pembroke bore her affliction with patience and tried without complaint every new remedy Iain prescribed. Reluctant to disappoint him, she had at first avoided telling him when one of his ideas failed to alleviate her symptoms. He had persuaded her to be frank, so now he could be sure the latest medicine really was useful.

"However," she continued with a mischievous twinkle, "the improvement may be due to Jasper's news. You have heard he means at last to do his duty?"

"He mentioned in a brief note that he had resigned himself to parson's mousetrap."

She laughed. "He told me that if you were in the line of succession, nothing should make him toss the handkerchief, but the thought of his cousin Rodney as duke is more than he can stomach."

"He and Rodney were ever at odds." Iain frowned, vaguely troubled. Cutting out a disliked relative seemed a poor reason for marriage and hardly fair to the young lady in question. On the other hand, in worldly terms no one could deny Jas was a splendid catch for any female. "Tell me about the girl he has offered for, Aunt Lou."

"He has not actually offered for Lady Cecily yet, but you will soon see her for yourself. She and her parents will come to Felversham for Christmas."

"Jasper wants your approval before he comes up to scratch?"

"If you ask me," the duchess said dryly, "it is sheer delaying tactics. Lady Cecily Barwith is Flint's daughter, and you know the earl and your uncle have been close friends since their schooldays. Her breeding is impeccable. Her fortune is large, and her expectations larger, for she is the earl's only child. That is not to be despised, though Jasper has no need of it. Add only that he describes her as well favored yet no spoiled beauty, well behaved and modest yet not tongue-tied, and amiable yet conscious of her position in the world. How can we not approve?"

Temperate praise, Iain thought. Jas was not in love. He had found a suitable bride, one to please his parents, and Lady Cecily, "conscious of her position in the world," was no doubt delighted with the bargain. A marriage of convenience on both sides, such as Society expected of them.

"As your doctor, I must approve anything that raises your spirits," he said with a smile.

"You *will* be able to stay over Christmas, will you not, Iain?" his aunt asked.

"Yes, Cranmer will be my *locum tenens* from Christmas Eve to Twelfth Night in exchange for his summer fortnight, as usual."

"Splendid!" boomed the tall, lean, gray-haired gentleman in riding dress who strode into the sitting room at that moment. "May I come in, Louisa?" the duke inquired belatedly, moderating his tone somewhat.

The duchess hid a smile. "Well, Edward, I am not sure you ought to intrude on a consultation with my physician . . ."

"Gammon, my dear, who better?" Like his nephew before him, he bent to drop a kiss on his wife's cheek. "Besides, you were talking of Christmas, not of pills and potions. Louisa's been telling you about Jasper's betrothal, Iain?"

"Yes, sir, though I gathered he is not quite betrothed yet?"

"As good as, my boy." His face, as weathered as any of his tenant farmers', took on a brooding look. "I shall let her hunt Daystar."

"Certainly not," said her grace.

"Not?" asked Pembroke in surprise. "You think the mare is still too young?"

"Now, how should I be able to express an opinion on that, Edward? I have seen her only at a distance, through the window. But I do recall your telling me Daystar is too headstrong for most females, though not up to the weight of a man. It will not do, you know, my dear, for Lady Cecily to end up as Iain's patient before ever she becomes Jasper's bride."

"You are right, as always, Louisa. Daystar is a trifle hard-mouthed too. Flint's girl shall have Veleta, at least until I have a chance to judge if she is capable of holding Daystar. It's a deuced pity though. Daystar is ready to try a good run."

"I suppose," the duchess asked gently, "Jasper has told you Lady Cecily hunts?"

"Good gad, surely my son would not wed a female who does not!"

"It is possible the question never arose during his courtship, or if it did that the answer would not influence his choice. It is even possible she does not ride."

Seeing his uncle stunned into silence, Iain said soothingly, "I daresay my sister will be glad to take Daystar out, if you will trust her, uncle."

The duke brightened. "Yes, by Jove, Elspeth's a regular

goer. A sensible girl, Elspeth. Married a neck-or-nothing fellow who ain't afraid of a rasper."

"Elspeth and Lord Sutton met on the hunting field," her grace pointed out, "not in town, like Jasper and Lady Cecily."

"If she can't ride, he can teach her."

"If she wishes, Edward. You are not to dragoon her into it."

"I never dragoon anyone," he protested, hurt. He eyed his nephew. "I have the very mount for you, Iain, a young hunter I purchased last summer, a fine gray gelding but not up to my weight, nor Jasper's. Consider him yours."

"I shan't hunt, sir."

"What? What? But, demme, you've the best seat of the family! Though, come to think of it, you've not been out with the hounds in quite a while."

"Close to ten years." Iain patiently repeated his annual explanation. "As a physician, I cannot afford to risk breaking an arm or leg and being forced to call on my patients in a sling or on crutches. I should have dowager duchesses fleeing my practice in droves."

Diverted, his lordship demanded, "Dowager duchesses? Which dowager duchesses are your patients?"

"Only one, to tell the truth, and I must not divulge her name. Actually, her grace might be amused to see me on crutches. However, I treat many elderly ladies, titled and untitled, who like to think their doctor is a careful, prudent man despite his comparative youth."

"Bath is full of aged fussbudgets," his uncle commiserated.

"And Felversham is so close to Bath, word would be bound to get about if I were to risk my neck in the hunting field. So, you see, I must regretfully decline, though I thank you for the offer of the gray."

"Well, well, much as I honor your decision to take up a profession instead of accepting an allowance, it's a sad thing that it keeps you from riding to hounds, my boy. I know, you shall teach Flint's girl to ride while Jasper hunts!"

Laughing, Iain pointed out that though Lady Cecily might not care to hunt, she very likely already rode. "And if not, Jasper will doubtless wish to teach her himself."

He was genuinely sorry to disoblige his kind and generous uncle. Pride was part of it, he admitted to himself. He did not wish to appear to his cousin's bride as a poor substitute called in to perform a task Jasper shunned. Thus it must appear to Lady Cecily, though he knew the duke had no such intention.

Pride of a different kind, added to his genuine belief that a physician owed it to his patients to stay healthy, had made him reject the offer of the young hunter. This was the pride of a man who earned his own living, reluctant to accept any more favors of the wealthy relative to whom he already owed so much. Worse, if he accepted the gift, he would have to accept stabling as well. He could not afford to keep another horse. His hack and a single carriage horse for his gig stretched his budget.

Yet when he compared his busy, useful life with his cousin's bored, pointless, fashionable existence, he could not be sorry he had chosen to study medicine.

Perhaps marriage would settle Jasper, and persuade his still-energetic father to let him take a hand in the management of Felversham and the other estates. However, that must depend to a great extent on the beneficial influence of the future Lady Avon.

Unfortunately, Lady Cecily Barwith sounded like a well-bred, conventional female without an idea in her head.

Two

The sun came out as the carriage emblazoned with the Flint coat of arms turned off the Bath road. The earl decided to ride ahead the rest of the way to Felversham, "to have a word or two with Pembroke before you ladies arrive and he has to busy himself doing the pretty," he explained. "It's only half a dozen miles."

Six miles! Within her fur muff, Cecily's hands clenched in a spasm of panic.

She forced herself to relax. It was too late now. From the moment the invitation was accepted, she had been committed to wedding Lord Avon. To rebuff him now would devastate her parents and affront not only the gentleman himself but the Duke and Duchess of Pembroke. Worse, everyone would believe he had not come up to scratch. She would never be able to hold up her head in Society again.

"I know you will behave just as you ought, dearest," said her mother as her father cantered away and the coach resumed its steady course along the well-kept lane. "Remember not to show by vain or presumptuous conduct any consciousness that you are especially favored by the Pembrokes. Modesty best becomes a young girl."

"Yes, Mama."

"Do not seek out Avon, though I shall permit you a few minutes alone with him now and then, should he appear to desire it. He is a gentleman and can be trusted not to go beyond what is acceptable."

"Yes, Mama." Her voice wavered. What was acceptable in a gentleman as good as betrothed? Would Lord Avon try to kiss her? He never had before, nor had he shown any desire to be alone with her. In fact, she had seen little of him in the past fortnight, as he had gone hunting in the shires with friends, while she and her parents spent a week at home before setting out for Felversham.

Her mother patted her arm. "Do not be uneasy, child. The Pembrokes cannot help but love my dearest girl as I do." She turned to her dresser, seated opposite with her back to the horses. "Dilson, Lady Cecily's abigail will likely not arrive for some hours. Put out the blue-and-green-striped lutestring at once, and see that the peach sarcenet is in order for this evening. Now, let me see, what shall I wear?"

While her elders embarked upon this important subject, Cecily glanced down at her deep-rose velvet carriage dress trimmed with black satin. Her Parisian bonnet was of black velvet lined with rose sarcenet and embellished with a wreath of roses about the crown. A charming ensemble, Mama had said at the inn that morning, and perfect for the occasion.

Cecily enjoyed pretty gowns. Nonetheless, now that she had been out for nearly a year, she began to find tiresome the nuances of ever-changing fashion and the fuss over wearing precisely the right clothes at the right time. One spent so much time choosing and fitting and changing one's dress. Only listen to Mama trying to decide between her straw-colored and her lavender crepe!

Wondering whether Lord Avon would want to marry her if she stopped dressing perfectly, she gazed out of the window. In the leafless hedgerow a flock of chaffinches squabbled over hips and haws and cow-parsley seeds. Smart in brown-and-white coats, pink waistcoats, and blue-gray caps, the little birds never gave a thought to their adornment. Cecily smiled at them.

The hedgerow gave way to cottages clustered around a church, a few shops, and a small inn. Hedges and fields returned for a short way, then the lane ran between woods and a sinuous wall of amber Bath stone until they came to the gates of Felversham.

The tall wrought-iron gates stood open. "I daresay dozens of relatives will arrive today and tomorrow," said Lady Flint as the gatekeeper came out of his lodge and waved them on. "And dozens of friends after Christmas. Last time your papa and I came to stay, every bedchamber was occupied, and there are upward of threescore, not counting the servants' quarters."

With so many guests, Lord Avon and the Pembrokes would surely be too busy to spare much time and attention for Cecily. She resolved to enjoy her last days of freedom before submitting like a dutiful daughter to her parents' wishes and Society's expectations. Without stooping to actual impropriety, she would ask herself "What do I choose to do?" instead of "What ought I to do?" If Lord Avon decided after all that she was not suited to be his future duchess, so be it.

The carriage drive ascended a gentle rise along an avenue flanked by bare chestnuts. From the top, Cecily saw the magnificent classical facade of a vast mansion stretching across the opposite slope of a shallow valley. Felversham eclipsed her own not unimpressive home.

A pair of riders cantering down from the house distracted her attention from the splendid view. Crossing a bridge over an ornamental water, they disappeared into a patch of woodland. When they emerged from the trees a moment later, she recognized Lord Avon on his superb black Thoroughbred, Caesar.

Signaling to the coachman to continue, Lord Avon turned his mount to trot beside the carriage as Cecily lowered the window. He was a fine figure, erect in the saddle, his blue riding coat fitting smoothly over broad shoulders. Beneath the glossy beaver, fair locks brushed forward in the modish windswept style framed his handsome, smiling face.

All in all, a sight to gladden any female's heart, Cecily acknowledged. No doubt she would come to love him in time. She stifled a sigh.

"Welcome to Felversham, ladies," he said, his light, pleasant voice raised over the sounds of hooves and wheels on gravel. "Lord Flint apprised us of your approach, so Cousin Iain and I rode out to meet you. I'll perform proper introductions when we reach the house," he added as Cecily peered past him at his companion.

"Cousin Iain" briefly raised his hat to her. A grave-looking gentleman of much the same age as Lord Avon, he had black hair cut short, with close-trimmed side whiskers, and a square chin that reminded Cecily of Papa's. She could see that he was not so tall as Lord Avon, his bottle-green coat did not fit so perfectly, and his horse, a bay gelding, was not half so fine.

"Iain Mac-something," whispered her mother. "The duchess's sister married a Scotsman, a nobody. They both died young, and the orphaned children, a boy and a girl, were brought up at Felversham. He inherited a small competence, I believe, but chose to become a lawyer. Or is it a clergyman? No matter. He is still received as one of the family, and his sister married Viscount Sutton, so be sure you do not slight him."

"Of course not, Mama." Cecily turned back to the window as Lord Avon remarked upon the mildness of the weather. "No snow for Christmas this year," she said regretfully.

"No, but for the New Year, perhaps, if you believe the old country maxim that a heavy crop of berries foretells a hard winter." He waved at a holly bush, bright with scarlet berries, standing sentinel at the edge of the now-nearby copse. "With luck we shall be able to skate on the—"

A crack, a wail, and a heavy thud interrupted him. With

a shouted "Whoa, there!" the coachman pulled up the carriage, while Caesar reared as Lord Avon reined him in. Mr. Mac-something swung down from his saddle and ran forward.

"What is it?" Cecily leaned out of the window, "What has happened?"

"A child just fell out of a tree," Lord Avon drawled, his tone amused, "right in the middle of the way."

"Oh, dear, is he hurt? Can I help?"

"Good Lord, no. A scruffy brat, and Iain is seeing to him. I am sorry you have been disturbed, ladies."

But Cecily had opened the door and jumped down, ignoring her mother's faint, reproachful "My love!" As one of the footmen in the Flint blue-and-white livery scrambled down from the back of the coach and scurried too late to let down the step, she hurried after Lord Avon's cousin Iain.

He knelt on the gravel beside a small sprawled figure and a large broken branch. Heedless of the rose velvet, Cecily sank to her knees opposite him. He glanced up, astonishment in his hazel eyes.

"Lady Cecily!"

"Is he badly hurt?" she asked anxiously.

"He's had the air knocked out of him." Mr. Mac-something's matter-of-fact voice was a rich baritone. "I don't want to move him until he's breathing more easily."

Beneath a grubby, torn jacket, the boy's skinny shoulders heaved as he gasped for breath. The man stroked the tousled head. His gloveless hand, so gently reassuring, looked strong and competent, with well-kept nails on the blunt-tipped fingers. Cecily raised her eyes to his face. Rather heavy dark brows, together with a firm mouth and the determined chin she had already noted, gave him an uncompromising air.

"Iain, move him aside so that the ladies may proceed," said Lord Avon impatiently, towering over them on horseback.

"In a moment."

Brows knit, his lordship dismounted. "Lady Cecily, allow me to hand you back into the carriage."

"Not just yet. I may be of use." She could see he was irritated and knew she was not living up to his image of her. Well, he would just have to accept her as she was.

The boy whimpered, and she turned back to see him trying to raise himself. Tears cut streaks through the grime on his face, chalky except for a red patch where the gravel had scraped his cheek. "Me arm," he moaned.

His left arm, folded beneath him, was bent at an unnatural angle. Cecily winced at the sight. She helped to shift him onto his back, then she took his other small, dirty hand in a comforting clasp.

"What a brave boy," she softly commended him.

Marveling, Iain stared at her. Jasper had described her as well favored. Just now, gazing down with compassion at the hurt child, she was the most beautiful woman in the world.

But the child needed him. He tore his eyes away from Lady Cecily's lovely face.

He had recognized the boy as his uncle's gamekeeper's son. "Ben Diver, isn't it? You have broken your arm, lad, but it will mend, never fear. Don't try to move it." He looked up at his bored cousin. "I'll have to cut his sleeve, Jas. Have you a knife on you?"

"Not I."

"My mother's maid will have scissors, sir." Lady Cecily started to rise, but the child clung to her hand.

Lady Flint's footman, coming up, had overheard Iain's request. "I've got a pocket knife, sir," he said, producing the implement from his pocket and unfolding the blade. "It's pretty sharp."

"Thank you." As he slit the threadbare sleeve, trying not to jolt the injured limb, he continued. "I shall need two straight sticks, about a foot and a half long, if you can find such."

"Her ladyship sent me to fetch my lady, sir. . . ."

"I shall go to Mama shortly, John. See if you can find what the gentleman needs."

"Very good, my lady." Reluctance and disapproval in every rigid inch, the footman moved off into the wood. He was undoubtedly destined someday to become the starchiest of butlers.

"Lord Avon," said Lady Cecily with a note of slightly apprehensive appeal in her sweet voice, "perhaps you would not mind explaining to Mama?"

Jasper bowed and said ironically, "I shall endeavor to do so, ma'am." He strode away, leading Caesar.

Iain had laid bare the crooked arm. "A simple fracture," he said, relieved. "I'll set it and splint it before we move him."

Cecily realized he was neither lawyer nor clergyman. "You must be a physician, sir? I am afraid I don't know your surname."

"Macfarlane." An unexpectedly charming smile lit up his serious face. "But Cousin Iain will do, as we shall soon be related by marriage."

She felt the heat rise in her cheeks. "That had best wait upon the event, Dr. Macfarlane," she said primly.

"As you wish, my lady."

His stiff tone and set mouth suggested he took her words to mean she considered him encroaching. Inadvertently she had offended him. Worse, he now believed her the sort of haughty, supercilious female who disdained those less favored by fate. She did not know how to explain that she simply wished neither to broadcast nor even to contemplate her approaching betrothal, still less the marriage to follow.

"Are you a lady, miss?" Round-eyed, the boy forgot his pain. "A real lady? Lor! That's why I clumb the tree, miss . . . my lady, to see the pretty ladies a-coming, an' the footmen up behind. I wants to be a footman, I does, in a fancy coat an' all, but me da says I'm to be a gamekeeper like him acos I got no brothers."

"Gamekeepers are important men," Cecily told him. "My papa, who is a real lord, often asks his gamekeeper's advice."

"Yes, his grace does too, and the lords what shoots with him, but—" Ben broke off and gazed up in alarm at the real footman, who reappeared with two sticks in his white-gloved hand and a look of distaste on his face. "Wotcher going ter do to me arm, Dr. Iain? Will it hurt?" He clutched Cecily's hand tightly.

"Yes, but you are a brave boy. Lady Cecily says so." As he spoke, Iain untied his neckcloth and unwound it till it hung loose. He took John's sticks with a nod of approval and laid them on the ground. "My lady," he said, "I'll need your footman to hold the lad still while I manipulate the bone."

John's horrified expression as he glanced down at his spotless white breeches almost made Cecily giggle. "I shall hold Ben," she said firmly.

"Oh, please do, miss—my lady," cried the frightened child. "I'll be good, honest."

Iain looked from one to the other. "Very well. It will take only a moment, I trust."

Determined not to let him despise her for squeamishness, she watched his deft hands straighten the broken bone. Ben moaned and jerked once. As the doctor wrapped his neck-cloth around the splinted limb, the boy's cheeks took on a greenish hue.

"I'm awful giddy, Dr. Iain," he whispered, closing his eyes.

Iain felt his forehead. "You'll soon feel more the thing, laddy, as long as you're not jolted about on horseback. I'll send for the gig, and in the meantime you'd best have my coat to keep you warm." He started to undo the buttons.

"Oh, no, Dr. Iain," Cecily cried, reaching out to stop him,

"we have plenty of rugs in the carriage—John, pray fetch one at once—and plenty of space to carry Ben up to the house."

Their eyes met and held. A current of heat tingled through Cecily's body to the tips of her toes. She had won back his regard. Odd that his opinion should matter so much to her, even if he was Lord Avon's favored cousin.

Moments later she was ensconced in the carriage with Ben's head in her lap. From the opposite seat, her mother gazed with shocked dismay upon a daughter run mad, whereas Dilson looked as if she contemplated giving notice. Lord Avon, however, appeared to have recovered from his pique. A slight, amused, indulgent smile hovered on his lips as he closed the door and bade the coachman drive on.

"Cecily, what in heaven's name has come over you?" Lady Flint exclaimed.

"You have always taught me, Mama, that it is a lady's duty to see to the welfare of her dependents."

"But this ragamuffin is not your dependent. . . ."

"Yet," Cecily murmured.

"And besides, two gentlemen and two footmen could surely have managed without your aid!"

"Yes, Mama. I did not think."

It was true, she had not thought before acting upon impulse, but she was not a bit sorry. All her life she had suppressed her impulses, had tried to be perfect to compensate Mama and Papa for the row of little graves in the churchyard at home. She had behaved the way they and her governess and Society ordained. Soon she would have to behave the way her husband ordained. For just a few days, the Twelve Days of Christmas, she would please herself.

Three

A frisson of nervous anticipation coursed through Cecily's veins as she descended the grand staircase at her mother's side. She was going to meet her future parents-in-law, but what really had her in a flutter was the feeling that she was going to meet herself, for the first time.

Now, in the brief no-man's-land between childhood and marriage, she hoped to learn who was this person who for nineteen years had lived the role of obedient daughter.

At the bottom of the marble stairs, in the spacious domed hall, Lord Avon and Iain Macfarlane stood chatting. Lord Avon came to greet the ladies. The look he gave Cecily she recognized as more approving than admiring—she had changed out of the soiled, crushed rose velvet and was once more neatly and appropriately clad, in blue-and-green-striped lutestring.

"My mother is eager to make your acquaintance," he said to Cecily, offering Lady Flint his arm, "and to renew her acquaintance with you, ma'am. You have both met my cousin, Dr. Macfarlane," he added mockingly.

The doctor, himself restored to decency with a fresh cravat and clean unmentionables, made his belated bow. Lady Flint nodded, gracious but with a hint of rebuke. She held him responsible for her daughter's momentary lapse. Cecily swept a low, graceful curtsy, glad to see his delightful smile in response. They followed the others across the hall.

He was not much taller than she. The short black hair

she had glimpsed when he raised his hat showed a distinct tendency to unruliness. No doubt if he wore it longer it would disport itself in ungovernable curls at odds with the self-discipline she sensed in him—and quite inappropriate to his profession.

"How is Ben, doctor?" she asked softly, picturing the poor child laid down upon his bed of pain.

"He's in the kitchen, stuffing himself with mince pies and regaling all and sundry with the tale of how he rode in a carriage with *two* real ladies."

Cecily laughed. "He has made a quick recovery!"

"Given proper care, children are remarkably resilient. I have often thought I should like . . . no matter! I don't wish to bore you."

She would have pressed him, but they entered a reception room where several small groups of people sat or stood about in quiet conversation. Perhaps a score in all, they were dwarfed by the size and splendor of the room. The walls were hung with gold-patterned red silk panels between white pilasters, and the lofty coffered ceiling was painted with scenes of classical Greece.

Lord Avon turned to find her gazing upward. "An odd conceit, I have always thought," he observed with a smile, "to make one crane one's neck to admire paintings on the ceiling."

"Was it painted by Angelica Kauffmann?" Cecily asked.

"I believe so. I did not realize you are a connoisseur of art." His tone was questioning.

"I cannot claim to know a great deal, only I am particularly interested in Angelica Kauffmann because she was a woman."

His laugh was condescending, as at a forgivable feminine foible. Dr. Macfarlane looked intrigued, but as he was about to speak, Lord Avon offered Cecily his arm.

"Come, let me make you known to my mother."

Lady Flint was already talking to a silver-haired lady who

sat near the fire on a sofa, her limbs raised on a footstool. The duchess turned her head and gave Cecily a smile of such sweetness that it almost reconciled her on the spot to her future marriage.

"My daughter Cecily, Duchess."

Cecily curtsied.

"Welcome to Felversham, my dear. Do you mind if I keep you to myself for a little while, for a comfortable coze, before Jasper bears you off to meet the rest of his relatives?"

Her greeting made it plain she regarded Cecily as virtually her son's betrothed. "Of course not, ma'am," Cecily said perforce.

The duchess cast a speaking glance at Lord Avon, who said, "Lady Flint, I believe you are acquainted with my aunt, Lady Missenden?"

As they went off—neither reluctant to leave her alone with the duchess, for was not Cecily a pretty behaved, compliant young lady?—her grace invited Cecily to sit down beside her. Dr. Macfarlane lingered a moment to adjust the shawl about his aunt's shoulders. She looked up at him, blue eyes sparkling with mischief.

"Thank you, Iain. How do you suppose I go on without you when you are in Bath?"

He grinned sheepishly. "Well enough, I daresay, but Mrs. Fredericks has gone to her brother's house for Christmas, has she not?"

"My companion, Lady Cecily," the duchess explained, adding tartly to her nephew, "I do not call upon Henrietta to rearrange my shawl, I assure you."

"No, nor to do half the things for you she ought. But I shall not scold you now for your determined independence. I must not keep you any longer from your 'comfortable coze.' " He smiled at Cecily.

"Do you not think, sir," she proposed tentatively, "that a determination to be as independent as possible may be a good thing? At least, when my old nurse 'took the rheumatiz,' as she said, she found a certain amount of exercise kept her joints from stiffening so badly."

The doctor looked at her in surprise. "In some cases, perhaps, but there is more than one type of—"

The duchess laughed. "You two may discuss my case at a later date. Just tell me, Iain, before you leave us in peace, how does that child go on, who broke his arm?"

"Famously, Aunt Lou, testimony to my brilliant medical skills."

"Dr. Macfarlane tells me Ben is in the kitchen devouring mince pies," Cecily put in. A notion struck her. Was she bold enough to suggest it? Nothing ventured, nothing gained, she told herself, regarding it as a test of her resolve to please herself. "Did you know, ma'am, that his ambition is to become a footman? I wonder if you might not find it convenient to employ him as a page, to run errands for you and to learn how to behave as an indoor servant."

Her grace was obviously startled, whether by the idea itself or by Cecily's forwardness in speaking out on such brief acquaintance.

"A splendid notion," exclaimed the doctor. "You will not hesitate to send Ben Diver running where you would not ask Mrs. Fredericks."

"Perhaps," said the duchess thoughtfully. "Once his arm has healed."

Dr. Macfarlane turned back to Cecily, hazel eyes twinkling. "But how does your suggestion accord with your approval of activity as a palliative for rheumatism, Lady Cecily?"

"Don't tease her, Iain," ordered his aunt. "Go away, do. Edward will be here any moment, wishing to further his acquaintance with Lady Cecily."

Dr. Macfarlane and the duchess exchanged slightly apprehensive glances. As the doctor bowed and departed, Cecily wondered what was the significance. Was the duke less enthusiastic about his heir's bride-to-be than she had been given to suppose?

If so, she could hardly count on him to save her. He would never offend a good friend like the Earl of Flint by hinting his daughter was unsuited to become the Marchioness of Avon.

The duchess talked to her kindly about life in town as compared with the country, and similar indifferent subjects. Nothing arose to awake in Cecily a desire to express any unconventional point of view. She liked the duchess very much. Such a mama-in-law would be some compensation for a marriage of convenience, she thought hopefully.

Her gaze sought out Lord Avon, but first found Dr. Macfarlane. He was laughing with a pretty, golden-haired young lady.

An unexpected pang shot through Cecily, a painful contraction of the heart, as though from a sudden deep disappointment. *Don't be a ninnyhammer,* she scolded herself. She had had no reason whatsoever to assume Iain Macfarlane was unattached—and still less to care.

Her carefully schooled face must not have revealed the burst of emotion, for the duchess continued to talk of the convenience of living close to the shops and amusements of Bath.

"And we are so happy that Iain was able to set up a practice close to home," she continued, "quite apart from his being the best physician I could ask for with my silly ailments. He and Jasper grew up together, you know. They are as close as any two brothers who have taken different paths in life. Now that Jasper is ready to settle down, they will doubtless be closer than ever." She patted Cecily's hand with her knotted fingers.

Cecily understood the unspoken words. Despite his profession, the doctor was a loved and respected member of the family, and the duchess was relieved by her future daughter-in-law's willingness to accept him as such.

The duke came in just then, with Cecily's papa.

"Well, Cecy, what do you think?" Lord Flint greeted her. "Pembroke and I have picked out a pretty little dapple-gray mare for you to ride while we are here."

"If you like her, she's yours," the duke announced.

Cecily curtsied, further depressed by this indication that his grace, too, considered her betrothal a settled matter. "Thank you, sir," she said, "you are too kind."

"Fiddle-faddle, my dear, she is only a hack. I had a fine young hunter ready for you, but Flint tells me you don't care to hunt. A dashed shame!"

"Edward!" said the duchess in a warning tone.

"Perhaps your papa is mistaken?" the duke said hopefully. "I daresay your hunt at home does not admit ladies, so you have no notion what you're missing?"

"I fear, sir," Cecily found herself saying, "I do not hunt because my sympathies are all with the fox."

The duke's jaw dropped. Lord Flint looked dazed. Her grace chuckled. Lord Avon, who had arrived unnoticed at Cecily's side, had that glint of mocking amusement in his gaze. Iain, also converging on the group, frankly grinned.

The two young gentlemen each offered Cecily an arm.

"Do come and meet my sisters, cousins, aunts, uncles, and their spouses," drawled Lord Avon.

"And mine," said his cousin.

Her face burning, Cecily glanced at the duchess, who nodded. A hand on each offered arm, she fled.

"You knew!" she accused her rescuers in a whisper.

"Only that my father hoped you shared the family passion for the hunt."

"Not that your sympathies lie with his prey." Dr. Macfarlane was still grinning, but with warm understanding in his eyes.

"Still less that you would tell him so. Lord, I'd not have missed his face for a monkey!"

"I cannot conceive what came over me. Pray don't tell

Mama," Cecily begged as they approached the nearest group of people. "Don't tell anyone."

"We shan't breathe a word," the doctor promised, adding challengingly, "shall we, Jas?"

"It's a deuced good story, coz," Lord Avon protested, then sighed, "but as you wish, Lady Cecily. My lips are sealed."

The introductions proceeded. Cecily was already acquainted with a few of the relatives, met in town. Plainly everyone knew or guessed she was Lord Avon's intended, though nothing specific was said. She could not but be gratified by her kind reception, even as she was embarrassed by the obvious interest with which she was regarded.

Yet afterward one particular moment stood out—the moment when she was presented to the golden-haired beauty.

She was Lord Avon's sister, Sophia, and married to Lord Garwich.

In spite of everyone's kindness, Cecily rather dreaded the time after dinner when the ladies withdrew from the dining room, leaving the gentlemen to their port. Without their restraining presence, the ladies were apt to be far more searching in their inquiries into her accomplishments.

Cecily had often enough witnessed a young lady put through her paces and dismissed as of no account. Heretofore she had escaped such an inquisition because of her father's rank. Now, among the members of a ducal house, a mere earldom was no protection.

When she discovered that the amiable duchess always retired directly after dinner, her qualms increased. It was not that she cared whether she was approved, she reminded herself, but the process was uncomfortable. Besides, Mama would be sadly disappointed if Lord Avon's female relatives persuaded him not to come up to scratch.

Entering the drawing room, she braced herself. Card tables were already set up. Cecily was competent at whist, loo, ombre, and quadrille when she managed to stop her mind wandering from boredom, but the games would probably wait for the gentlemen's reappearance. Chess men had been laid out on a checker-topped table too, she noted. Though the carved figures had always intrigued Cecily, Mama held the common opinion that chess was too difficult for the female brain.

The usual occupations for ladies immediately after dinner were conversation, needlework, and music. A spinet stood in one corner of the room. Cecily hoped she would not be invited to play or sing. Mama and Papa both fondly assured her she performed charmingly; she knew her musical skills were mediocre. Concentrating on the notes of the complicated sonatas and Italian arias expected of an accomplished young lady left her no attention to spare for phrasing or dynamics.

A voice came from behind her. "Do you play, Lady Cecily, or sing?"

Unprepared, Cecily forgot to put a guard on her tongue. "Not if I can help it," she blurted out, then added, "but Mama will expect me to if I am asked."

"Then I for one shall not ask you," the young raven-haired matron assured her with a sympathetic smile. The wayward black curls, together with the smile so like her brother's, reminded Cecily that this was Dr. Macfarlane's sister.

"Thank you, Lady Sutton, but someone is bound to," she sighed.

"Nothing is so horrid as to be forced to perform before strangers."

"Especially when one knows one's performance to be indifferent!"

Lady Sutton laughed. "Should you like to escape for a quarter of an hour? I usually go up to the nursery to make sure the children have settled down, especially their first night away from home."

"Oh, yes, let me go with you. You have several children?"

Cecily asked as they turned back toward the stairs. "You do not look old enough."

"Two, and a third on the way." She patted her still-flat abdomen. "No hunting for me this season, alas. Uncle Edward is sadly disappointed that I shall not try out Daystar, his young mare, but Iain agrees with my midwife at home that riding is unwise. He has made something of a study of pregnancy, since his particular interest is children."

"Is it? He was very good with the little boy who broke his arm, the gamekeeper's son."

"He is all praise for your assistance." Lady Sutton cast a curious glance at Cecily, who felt herself blush. Tactfully the viscountess made no comment on the eccentricity of an earl's daughter kneeling in the mud to help an urchin. "You are fond of children?"

"I . . . I hardly know. I have no brothers or sisters. Does Dr. Macfarlane have a great many children in his practice?"

"Very few, poor fellow. Bath is crammed with aged invalids, many of them wealthy, fortunately. Iain's dream is to open a clinic exclusively for children, particularly those whose parents cannot afford medical care. He saves every penny he can, and he has not touched a penny of his inheritance from our father, thanks to Uncle Edward's generosity. Here is the night nursery." She put a finger to her lips.

Following on tiptoe, Cecily gazed down at a dark-haired cherub smiling in his sleep. Young as he was, the infant looked heart-stoppingly like his maternal uncle.

Cecily decided she was exceedingly fond of children, which would explain the odd emotions churning inside her. They could not possibly have anything to do with that likeness.

Four

When Cecily and Elspeth, as she had been invited to call Lady Sutton, returned downstairs, the gentlemen were already entering the drawing room.

"All's well?" Lord Sutton asked.

"They are both fast asleep, Tom," Elspeth assured him.

"Inspecting the nurseries, eh, Lady Cecily?" inquired the duke jovially and all too loudly.

Color tinged Lord Avon's cheekbones. "Will you sing for us?" he begged in haste.

Elspeth looked in surprise from him to Cecily, obviously feeling he ought to be aware of her reluctance to perform.

"Not tonight," Cecily excused herself. As she cast about wildly for something to explain her refusal, her gaze fell on the chessboard. "If it will not inconvenience anyone, I have been longing for a chance to learn to play chess."

"Capital!" cried the duke. In view of her interest in chess and in the nurseries, her faux pas over the fox seemed to be forgiven. "I shall teach you myself. Iain, we'll have our game later."

"By all means, uncle," Dr. Macfarlane agreed with a slightly puzzled glance at Cecily.

Did he think she was deliberately toadying to his grace, even at the cost of disobliging Lord Avon? She wanted to tell him she had not known the board was set up for the duke. "I don't wish to inconvenience anyone," she repeated.

"Not at all, not at all," his grace insisted.

"You had best help teach Lady Cecily, Iain," Lord Avon proposed dryly. "My father's explanations are not always of the clearest. He so confused me in my tender youth, Lady Cecily, that I developed a terror of the game. Should you take a liking to it, however, I must try again."

Laughing, Cecily went with the duke to the chess table. The doctor pulled up a chair beside her. At first his closeness distracted her, a disturbing quiver running through her whenever her elbow chanced to brush against his sleeve. She soon found herself glad of his assistance.

The duke saw the game in terms of a fox hunt—the king was the fox; the pawns hounds; the queen the huntsman; the bishops whippers-in; the knights well-mounted riders ready to take hedge and ditch in their stride, though with a deplorable tendency to jump the hounds. The castles, inexplicably known as rooks, his grace held in scorn. They were plodding farmers on sorry nags who insisted on going around the edges of each field so as not to damage the crops.

Though a complete novice, Cecily could see how these views affected his play. With Iain's aid, she quickly grasped the basic moves and began to realize the immense complexity of strategy and tactics.

As, under the doctor's tutelage, she cornered his grace's fox-king, she said regretfully, "I doubt I shall ever devote enough time and effort to it to play well."

"Dash it, nor do I," the duke admitted, "but I enjoy a game now and then all the same, even if Iain wins every time."

"I don't claim to play well, sir, merely slightly better than you! As you say, it's agreeable as an occasional pastime."

"Much more entertaining than cards," Cecily observed. "I should like to play again sometime, and learn more, if either of you gentlemen is willing to oblige me. But now I must leave you to a proper game."

The duke demurred, saying being beaten hollow once was enough for one evening. "Won't you favor us with a song, my dear?" he requested.

Resigned, Cecily obliged.

Iain was intrigued. Lady Cecily Barwith sang her ornate Italian aria as woodenly as most well-bred young ladies, though she had a pleasant, low singing voice. Otherwise, she was not at all what he had been led to expect. Jasper's description to his mother had told only the half of it.

Despite his cousin's temperate praise, Iain had not been surprised to see a lovely young lady, for Jas would demand nothing less. But Lady Cecily was not at all a milk-and-water, compliant female without a mind of her own. Every time he recollected his uncle's stunned face when she confessed her outrageous sympathy for the fox, he felt his lips twitch. And every time he recollected her practical kindness to little Ben Diver, defying decorum, his heart swelled within him with an emotion he did not choose to identify.

Oh, yes, Lady Cecily had a mind of her own!

Yet on one point Iain had not been mistaken. Jasper was not in love, and nor, he was quite certain, was Lady Cecily. They were on easy but nothing approaching intimate terms.

She did not seek to meet his eyes, nor even follow him with her gaze. He did not attempt to be alone with her, nor even draw her aside from the others for a private word, as Iain would have if she were his . . . if he were in the same circumstances. Both were satisfied to make a suitable, indeed a splendid match applauded equally by both families and all the rest of the Beau Monde.

The aria ended to a scatter of applause, the most fervent from the least musical members of the family and those at the card tables—including Jasper—who had not listened. Watching Lady Cecily closely, Iain saw her delightful mouth turn into a scarcely perceptible moue. She was not content with her own performance, he guessed.

Someone called for another song. Lady Cecily sent a swift glance to her mother, who shook her head.

"Good," Elspeth murmured in Iain's ear.

"Pray hold me excused," said Lady Cecily with an air of relief. "I am a little tired after the journey."

Bidding the company good night, Lady Flint bore her off to bed, and several other ladies admitted to fatigue and followed. Iain caught Elspeth's arm as she rose.

"What do you mean, good?" he said. "She sang no worse than most accomplished young ladies."

"Myself, for instance! But she dislikes performing, she told me. I was glad for her that her mama decided a second song would be putting herself forward."

"Ah, I see." Driven by something within him, Iain asked, "Do you like her?"

"Cecily? Very much. One cannot be certain, of course, but I believe she may have what it takes to make Jasper settle down."

"One must hope so," Iain said, conscious of a hollow feeling, caused, he was sure, by his doubt over his cousin's readiness to settle down, even with Lady Cecily. "They don't seem particularly fond of each other."

"I daresay affection will grow once they are married. They are both likable people. Not everyone can fall desperately in love while jumping a five-barred gate side by side, as Tom and I did. Speaking of whom, he is bearing down upon me with a light in his eye which says 'Time you retired to your rest, mother of my children.' Good night, brother dear."

Iain watched them go, for the first time envious of their love.

He and Jasper were the last to go up to bed. As they mounted the stairs together, Jasper said, "Well, coz, do you approve?"

"Of Lady Cecily? She is"—*enchanting?*—"an excellent choice. Pretty and amiable, well-bred, and she will grow into the dignity required of a duchess."

"Dignity? Yes, I daresay. I confess," his cousin mused, "she has more spirit than I gave her credit for. Perhaps marriage won't be the intolerable bore I had anticipated."

Suppressing a shudder, Iain asked, "When do you mean to pop the question?"

Jasper did shudder. "I feel the jaws of parson's mousetrap closing upon me. I'll put it off as long as I decently can."

"Not so long as to embarrass the lady!"

"No, you're right. I shall go on bended knee on New Year's Day, so that Father can announce the betrothal to family, guests, servants, and tenants at the Twelfth Night revels. Good enough?"

"Good enough," Iain affirmed, while a silent voice inside him cried, *Too soon, too soon!*

They ought to have more time to get to know each other before committing themselves, he thought. But they had met last spring in London. They had had time enough.

For a marriage of convenience, all they needed was to know they did not dislike each other.

Rain fell overnight. Despite a sky threatening more rain, most of the gentlemen and several ladies went out with the hunt next morning, Christmas Eve day. Of those remaining, only Elspeth wished to ride with Cecily, and she could not.

"May I not go alone, Mama?" Cecily begged. She felt restless enough to scream if she took no exercise. "With a groom, I mean, of course."

"She will be safe enough with any of Pembroke's grooms, Lady Flint," the duchess promised. "Most have doubtless gone with the hunt, but some will have stayed behind."

"Very well, my love, but do not leave the estate. The

grounds of Felversham are quite extensive enough for a good ride, are they not, duchess?"

"Quite. Lady Cecily, you may accomplish an errand for me, if you will."

"Certainly, ma'am."

The duchess twinkled at her. "It is an errand of your own making. My physician and my husband are agreed that I shall do well to employ a page. Will you be so good as to stop at the gamekeeper's cottage and inform young Ben that I shall expect him as soon as his arm is healed?"

"Oh, yes, ma'am! I am so glad."

"The gamekeeper's cottage?" Lady Flint said dubiously.

"I need not go in, Mama. The groom may call someone out to speak to me."

Permission achieved, Cecily dashed up to her chamber to change into riding dress. Her abigail helped her into her new habit. The chestnut-brown cloth was lavishly trimmed with gold braid and frogging à la Hussar, and the matching hat was a jaunty little creation with a curled gold plume.

The duchess had sent a message to the stables, so when Cecily went down, a groom had already brought to the front door the dapple gray the duke had provided for her. Shadow was a pretty, young Thoroughbred mare, docile but with clean lines that promised a fair turn of speed. The groom was a stolid youth, mounted on a stolid dun cob. Cecily hoped he would be able to keep up if she found a good spot for a gallop.

Errand first, she decided, and asked the groom to lead the way to the gamekeeper's cottage. Incurious, he obeyed.

In a clearing in the wood where he had come to grief stood Ben Diver's home. The thatched, whitewashed cottage looked too low to possess a second story, though tiny dormer windows under shaggy brows peered from the roof. Approaching, Cecily saw a horse tied near the door. She recognized the bay gelding instantly.

So Dr. Macfarlane had not gone with the hunt, as she had assumed.

On a sudden impulse she turned to the groom. "Help me down, then you need not stay. Mr. Macfarlane will see me back to the house."

"M'lady." Unquestioning, he swung down and cupped his hands for Cecily's foot.

As he tied Shadow beside the bay, Cecily hesitated. The door stood open to the mild day, and she heard voices within. No one had observed her arrival.

She had told Mama she *need* not go in, but she had not said she would not. Surely the duchess would not have sent her if she considered it improper or unwise to enter the cottage. Cecily was curious, having never been allowed in a servant's or tenant's cottage at home. And Dr. Macfarlane was in there.

She glanced back. The groom had remounted. He tipped his hat to her and rode off.

The sound of Dr. Macfarlane's laugh decided her. Where he was she could come to no harm.

Five

The train of her riding habit looped over her arm, Cecily stepped up to the open door and raised her hand to knock. Before her gloved knuckles hit the wood, a glad cry welcomed her.

"Look, Ma, it's the lady. The lady I told you 'bout, what helped Dr. Iain do me arm and let me go in the grand carriage."

Instantly Cecily found herself bustled in, seated in a stout rocking chair by the fire, and provided with a mug of near black tea. She glanced around the room, a kitchen that was obviously also the family's main living space. All was neat and clean, from the brick floor to the iron pots hanging by the fireplace to the well-scrubbed table and the ham and braids of onions dangling from the ceiling. A door in one corner probably led to a bedchamber, and a ladder in another corner to a loft with further sleeping quarters, Cecily guessed.

Mrs. Diver, a plump body in a red gingham apron, with graying hair beneath a spotless white mobcap, beamed at Cecily. So did Ben and his older sister, and so did the doctor.

"I just dropped by to check Ben's arm," he said, his dark eyebrows raised inquiringly.

"I bring a message from the duchess."

"From her grace?" gasped Mrs. Diver. "Well, I never!" A small girl who had been hiding behind her skirts peeked out. "There's many a message my man gets from *his* grace, m'lady, 'bout the pheasants and all, but what's the duchess got to say to the likes of us?"

Cecily smiled at her. "She hopes you and Mr. Diver will be willing to allow Ben to take a post as her pageboy when his arm is healed."

Ben, his splinted arm in a sling, whooped, then asked anxiously, "Does a pageboy get to wear liv'ry?"

"I cannot promise, but usually." Cecily turned to his mother, who looked worried. "I understand your husband expects Ben to follow in his footsteps, Mrs. Diver. I hope he will at least consider letting him try an inside position for a while."

"He'll do what her grace wants, m'lady. I just hopes Ben'll behave himself proper. He's a good lad, but he don't know how to go on up the big house."

"The duchess realizes he will have a great deal to learn," Cecily reassured her.

"That he will. Anyways, it's right kindly of your ladyship to take an interest in my boy. He come home yesterday singing your ladyship's praises, he did, didn't he, Dr. Iain?"

Cecily blushed. She could not very well explain that she had been driven less by kindness than by a spirit of rebellion.

"I'll impose on your kindness again, Lady Cecily," said the doctor, a hint of challenge in his manner, as if he guessed her thoughts. He held out his hand to the little girl. "Young Annie here has the earache and will not let her mama hold her still for me to take a look. Perhaps in your lap she may stay quiet."

Rising to the challenge, Cecily smiled at the child. "Would you not like to come and see the pretty gold braid on my dress?" she invited.

Thumb in mouth, Annie allowed herself to be settled on Cecily's knee, where she gravely inspected the braiding. The doctor, kneeling beside them, parted her hair with a gentle hand and peered at the offending ear.

"It is a trifle inflamed, and there is some matter exuding. I want you to wash it out twice a day, Mrs. Diver, with some warmed rectified spirits of wine. I shall send down a bottle from the house, and I'll look in again on Boxing Day."

Making their adieus, and followed by thanks, Cecily and Dr. Macfarlane stepped out of the cottage. The doctor looked around.

"Did you come alone, Lady Cecily?"

"No, I sent the groom home, thinking to ride back with you," Cecily explained, a trifle abashed. Perhaps it was rather presumptuous of her to suppose he would wish to escort her. "Did you intend to join the hunt?"

"Not I. Less in sympathy with the fox, I fear," he added, laughing, "than for fear of an accident that might interfere with my work. I was going to ride into the village to visit a few patients, but I have plenty of time to see you back to the house first."

"I don't wish to take you out of your way. May I not go with you? The village belongs to the Felversham estate, I expect?"

"Yes, the villagers are all tenants. Why?" He frowned. "I suppose the Felversham people will be your—"

"Oh, no, I should not dream of nosing about before—" Cecily's cheeks grew hot again. "It is just that Mama told me not to ride beyond the estate. She meant the park, I daresay, but that is not what she *said.*"

"Fortunately it is not my business to see that you follow Lady Flint's orders, express or implied! However, it looks like rain."

"A wetting will not melt me, I assure you."

Iain studied her face. The ready blush had faded, leaving the roses of good health in her cheeks and slightly parted lips. Great blue eyes, an incredibly dark shade, looked up at him appealingly. Glossy brown curls peeked from beneath that ridiculous little hat.

Jasper was a lucky devil, and he didn't even seem to know it.

"I daresay you won't take a chill," Iain said gruffly, yielding to temptation, "as long as you change out of wet clothes quickly. Come with me if you wish, but first promise you will not enter where I suspect infection."

She promised. He cupped his hands to throw her up into the saddle, where she sat with the ease of a practiced horsewoman, though the dapple mare danced a little in her eagerness to be off.

"You ride well," he said, mounting Hippocrates and turning the gelding's head toward the village. "It is truly the fox's fate that deters you from hunting, then, not a dislike of the exercise."

"Oh, yes, I love to ride. I grew up in the country, and one of the frustrations of spending so much time in town this past year has been the lack of a place for a good gallop."

"I can imagine. In my hunting days, it was the ride I enjoyed, not the pursuit."

"The duke must be disappointed in you for dropping out of the hunt. I am afraid I sadly shocked him," she added with a saucy smile.

"Prodigiously, though you recovered his esteem with the chess game. You must not suppose, because he is obsessed with hunting, that my uncle is a bad landlord. Felversham and its farms are in excellent condition, and he takes good care of his dependents. With his example to follow, I'm sure Jasper will become an admirable duke."

"No doubt," Lady Cecily murmured, not noticeably impressed by his attempt to boost his cousin's standing in her eyes. "He seems to like to spend a great deal of time in London."

"And you do not care for life in town?" Iain asked, unable to stop himself, though he ought to be trying to reconcile her to Jasper's preferences. "You spoke of frustrations."

"I do not mean to complain. I enjoy balls and parties and the theater and concerts and everything. Only *not* every single night! And to be constantly changing one's dress, and endlessly standing still to try on new gowns—well, you cannot conceive how tiresome it is. I like pretty clothes, but I am sure I could do very well with not half so many."

"That's a most becoming habit you're wearing," he said, seeing not the habit but the slender, rounded, pliable figure within it. Hastily he raised his eyes to her face.

Their gazes caught and held. Which was the first to look away, Iain was not sure. Lady Cecily burst into speech.

"I daresay residing in London is pleasanter when one is not making one's come-out. As a married lady, I will surely be able to spend an occasional evening quietly at home!"

"Undoubtedly." But would Jasper stay at home with her? Doing his best to sound convinced and convincing, Iain went on. "Very likely my cousin will choose to spend more time at Felversham once he is wed."

"It is charming country," she said, looking around distractedly, as if she had scarcely noticed where they were.

The muddy lane led downhill between leafless thorn hedges. On one side a still muddier plowed field stretched to the farther hedge. On the other, dank dun grass surrounded a lightning-blasted oak overgrown with dismally dripping ivy.

Their eyes met again, and they both laughed.

"Need I remark that you are not seeing it at its best? We are nearly at the village. There's the church tower." He pointed with his riding crop.

Cecily was glad to reach the village, to have something to take her mind from the alarming disorientation she felt whenever Dr. Macfarlane looked at her. Or she at him.

With the aid of the mounting block by the lych-gate, she

descended from Shadow's back, and they tied the horses to the iron railing around the church. Cecily quickly turned her back on the building where all too soon she would wed Lord Avon, since the duchess's disability ruled out a London wedding. Tomorrow, Christmas Day, she would have to attend the morning service there. For now—sufficient unto the day was the . . . evil? No! It was a splendid match. Her parents were happy. His parents were happy. He was handsome, charming, amusing. She was the envy of every marriageable young lady in the kingdom.

She did not glance back at the church where that enviable winter wedding would soon take place.

The villagers Cecily and Dr. Macfarlane met regarded her with as much interest as had Lord Avon's family. No doubt half of them had gossiping relatives in service up at the mansion. With instinctive courtesy no one made any reference to her future connection with their landlord, or none but a child quickly hushed.

The children adored Dr. Iain, as everyone called him. He did not woo them with comfits, yet his patience, compassion, and willingness to listen won them over. Pleased to be able to help, Cecily held some of the young patients for him to examine while harried mothers kept their other children out of the way or got on with preparing midday dinner for their husbands.

Dr. Iain had older patients here too. The last of these, at the far end of the village street, was a rheumaticky old shepherd. He sat huddled under a rug by the fire, wrapped in a woolen shawl, a nightcap on his head.

The gray-muzzled black-and-white dog at his feet raised its head when his daughter ushered in the doctor and Cecily. It gave them a mournful look and subsided again.

"The poor beast do take it a'most hard as Pa that they can't get out and about these days," sighed the woman.

"I'm changing that," Iain said decisively. "Sitting around coddling yourself isn't helping, Johno, is it? I want you to start moving about as much as you can without severe pain. Take yourself over to the Pembroke Arms for a glass of cider on a fine day. Wrap up warmly, mind."

The old man brightened at once. "Down the Arms, doctor? It'll be good to see folkses again." The dog licked his hand.

"We'll see how it goes, at least. And I've brought you a ginger and willow-bark mixture which seems to help her grace." He gave the woman instructions on preparing the medicine.

Deeply gratified by the doctor's readiness to try the remedy she had suggested, Cecily wondered whether Lord Avon would ever give any weight to her opinions. She could not even imagine a situation where she might venture to advise him.

As they walked back down the village street toward the horses, Iain said ruefully, "I ought not to offer two new remedies at one time. If he improves, I shan't know which is responsible. But I cannot bear to withhold anything that may make my patients more comfortable. There is so little I can do for most of them."

"You do all you can, I can see that. I do hope exercise will help him. Did you advise the duchess to try it?" she asked diffidently.

"Yes, indeed." He gave her a teasing smile. "I'm still waiting to hear how you reconcile it with the employment of a page. Or was that advice solely for Ben's benefit?"

"Only partly. Well, perhaps mostly! But if Ben does the little necessary, everyday things for her, then she will be able to use what energy she has for pleasant things, like strolling in the garden. I doubt she will wish to go to the Pembroke Arms for a glass of cider!"

"I doubt it," he agreed, laughing. "Dash it, a drop of rain just hit my nose. Time we were going home. We'll take a shortcut across the park, and you shall have your gallop."

She mounted Shadow with the aid of the block, steadied

by his hand. While their hands touched, glove to glove, the hammering of her heart threatened to stifle her. Could she be ill? She did not dare consult him as to the meaning of her symptoms, not when he so studiously avoided her eyes.

"Hippocrates is ready for a run," he said in a constricted voice as they started off.

Exclaiming over his horse's odd name, Cecily regained her composure.

"Hippocrates was a famous Greek physician," he explained, "and it just happens *hippo* is the Greek for 'horse.' "

"What about the hippopotamus?"

" 'River horse.' You have seen pictures? When Hippocrates guzzles his oats too eagerly, I tell him that is what he will end up like."

At first their way led along a ride through a fir plantation. By the time they emerged from the trees onto an open track leading uphill across the park, the heavens had opened in good earnest. Within moments Cecily's adorable little hat dissolved about her ears and her hair started to lose its pins.

She must have looked like the veriest hoyden, but she did not care. She would cringe to have Lord Avon see her thus, but Iain—Dr. Iain—*Dr. Macfarlane,* she *must* think of him thus—would not curl his lip at her disheveled appearance.

A trickle ran down inside the neck of her habit, and she shivered. "Shall we race?"

"No. You are on unfamiliar ground and an unfamiliar mount. I will not leave you behind."

"Ha! As if your hippo could beat Shadow! Come on!"

Hooves pounding, they sped neck and neck up the hill and over the crest. The mansion spread before them. Cecily hoped anyone looking out of a window would be unable to recognize her through curtains of rain, but she could not bring herself to really mind if they did.

She exchanged a laughing glance with Iain, still matching her pace for pace whether by chance or design. He signaled to her to take the right branch at a fork in the track.

"To the stables!"

Cecily nodded. She was in no fit state to go in through the front door.

They rode under a stone arch into the deserted stable yard. Cecily walked Shadow over to a mounting block. Iain dismounted and hurried to give her a hand.

As she started to slide down, her soaked skirts tangled around her legs. She lost her balance. In spite of his steadying hand, she would have fallen, but he caught her in his arms.

For an immeasurable eon he held her, their eyes speaking to each other of dreams and wishes, of passion and tenderness.

Boot nails sounded on the cobbles. "Coming, m'lady!"

Instantly Iain released Cecily. Scooping up the train of her habit, she fled.

At the archway she paused to glance back. Through the pelting raindrops, with smarting eyes, she saw Iain staring after her. His face was a mask of yearning and despair.

Six

Cecily sat by the fire in her chamber, her chilled hands wrapped around a hot cup of tea. She was scarcely aware of her abigail moving about, tut-tutting over her sodden habit and ruined hat. Through the rising steam from the tea, in the flickering flames, she saw Iain's face.

All the tea in China could not wash away the lump in her throat.

Her parents would never let her wed a physician, despite his connection to the Duchess of Pembroke and Viscountess Sutton, even if she were not as good as promised to Lord Avon. She could not claim they had not consulted her wishes. Had she expressed the least distaste for the marquis, they would have politely declined the invitation to spend Christmas at Felversham.

She did not dislike the marquis, but she had never bargained for falling headlong in love with his cousin!

"Cecy, my love!" Lady Flint bustled into the room. "What is this I hear of your taking a wetting? I was sure you must have returned before the downpour. Wherever have you been?"

"Felversham is very large, Mama. I rode farther than I intended. The mare the duke bought for my use is a darling."

"So very kind of Pembroke! Well, child, Lord Avon is come back from the hunt and inquiring after you, but you must be sure your hair is quite dry before you come down. It will not do to be falling ill at such a time."

"No, Mama."

After a flash of hope, Cecily decided regretfully that illness was no solution. It would postpone Lord Avon's proposal, but not prevent it.

He was as committed as she was, or more. A gentleman's honor simply did not allow him to fail to come up to scratch—in the vulgar phrase Mama deplored—after such indications as he had given. Even if she succeeded in giving him a disgust of her, he was honor bound to request her hand.

What if she simply refused his offer?

She would without a second thought if she saw the slightest chance of being permitted to wed Iain. Failing that, to reject Lord Avon would open both of them to the utmost opprobrium. As a gentleman he could not expose her as a jilt. People would assume he had dishonorably failed to propose—and wonder what she had done to cause such a dereliction of duty in one whose honor was hitherto unsmirched.

So many people would be hurt. Cecily herself would have earned her disgrace, but Lord Avon had done nothing to deserve to be made the target of a thousand spiteful tongues. Nor did the duchess deserve to see her son condemned. Cecily's own mama would be cast into the depths of despair, dear, kind Mama, who wanted only what was best for her daughter.

And what was best included a titled, wealthy husband.

"Cecy, you are woolgathering, I declare. Have you heard a word I have said?"

"I must be sure to dry my hair?" Cecily hazarded.

"Yes, but since then! Well, no matter, it was nothing of importance, and I am sure a girl in your happy position is entitled to a little daydreaming! You had best wear the burgundy merino when you come down. It is warm as well as elegant."

"Yes, Mama."

Cecily's thoughts twisted and turned and found no way out, and Iain's expression had made plain his absence of hope. On top of all other obstacles, he must fear being regarded as a fortune hunter. Their love was doomed.

All that remained was to make sure no one guessed, to conceal their pain and carry on with dignity as if the world had not been rocked to its foundations.

In a spirit of gallant self-sacrifice, Cecily went downstairs as soon as her maid declared her hair dry. Lord Avon invited her to go with him to inspect his ancestors in the portrait gallery.

Afraid he meant to propose, she panicked for a moment. Her discovery of her love for Iain was too new to bear such a strain with equanimity. Time—even just a few days—must surely enable her to bear it with decent composure.

Perhaps Elspeth saw her dismay in her face, if not the reason for it, for she said brightly, "It is an age since I admired the first duke. Such a handsome, well-set-up fellow, Cecily, even in the extraordinary clothes Tudor nobles wore. May I go with you, cousin?"

Lord Avon made no demur. Together they went up to the long gallery, where the tall windows along one side admitted enough of the gray, wintry light to view the paintings on the opposite wall.

Elspeth's irreverent comments on the portraits made Cecily laugh in spite of her broken heart. They moved from the ruffs and pointed beards of the Elizabethans, past the long, curling Jacobean wigs and the last century's powdered hair—"So aging!" said Elspeth.

Coming unexpectedly face-to-face with Iain, Cecily gasped.

"Not a bad likeness, is it?" Lord Avon drawled, and she realized he too was in the picture. "At least you can recognize us. Stubbs generally did a better job of horses than of people, which was all Iain and I were concerned about at the time. Those were our first hunters."

"And this was mine," said Elspeth, moving on to the next canvas. "Dear old Pegasus. Stubbs was dead by then, much to my fury. What a figure I had in those days," she sighed.

"And still do, coz. There is a place in this life for the matronly."

"Wretch! But there, Cecily, you need not fear putting on a pound or two."

Lord Avon gave her a repressive frown, to which she responded with an irrepressible smile. Cecily felt ready to sink beneath the weight of expectations, but at least she had not given herself and Iain away with her unguarded reaction to his portrait.

She did not see him again until just before dinner, and there were enough people about to make it unnecessary for them to speak to each other. Seated between Lord Avon and one of his uncles, she was at the opposite end of the table and on the same side as Iain, so she could not even see him. Out of sight, out of mind, she told herself sternly.

It did not work. She was constantly conscious of his unseen presence, breathing the same air, eating the same dishes from the same gold-rimmed porcelain, hearing the same buzz of polite conversation. Did he try to distinguish her voice with the same involuntary eagerness as she listened for his?

Or had she imagined he cared as much as she did?

That horrid possibility struck her as she left the dining room with the other ladies. She almost looked back, but stopped herself just in time. And reminded herself that if he did not love her after all, then at least only she would be hurt.

One thing she was certain of: She could not sit through a game of chess with him that evening with any degree of calm. The prospect of a game with the duke without Iain's support was almost equally dismaying. Nor would she be able to keep her mind on cards, or find the right notes if she had to sing or play.

She might retire early with a claim of suffering the ill effects of her wetting, but what if Mama asked Iain to treat her?

The gentlemen came in while Cecily was still dithering. A brief glimpse of Iain's face before he turned away to speak to his sister was enough to reassure her of his love—and his despair.

As Lord Avon approached her, one of his brothers-in-law caught up with him and challenged him to a game of billiards.

"I want my revenge for last night's debacle," he said.

"Later, old fellow. Lady Cecily, are you going to give my father a chance for revenge at chess, or will you give us some music?"

The words popped out of Cecily's mouth. "I should like to learn to play billiards, sir, if you would be so kind as to teach me?"

His well-concealed but perceptible boredom turned to startlement. Billiards was even more of a male province than chess! What *would* Mama think of her boldness?

But Lord Avon assented with a smile of indulgent amusement. "Intent on setting us all by the ears?" he murmured sardonically.

"No!"

"Ah, just tired of being angelic all the time? Mama tells me you played the angel to the Diver boy again this morning."

"He is a nice boy, and I am sure he will make your mother an unexceptionable page."

"No doubt. Garwich," he said to his brother-in-law, "do join us in the billiard room, and be a good fellow, see if you can prevail upon Sophia to come too. She used to play before she metamorphosed from a schoolroom miss into a proper young lady."

Cecily managed to quite enjoy the evening, though unceasing heartsickness lurked behind every smile, every cry of triumph at a good shot and groan of disgust at a bad one. She could not but notice that though Lord Avon stood close behind her, his arms around her, his hands on hers as he helped her line up the cue, her senses stirred not at all.

The least touch, a mere look from Iain, was enough to set her all aflutter.

She did not see him again until the next morning, when the whole company drove down to the village church for the Christmas morning service. The church was crammed with the nobility, villagers, and farm people. Somehow Iain and the Suttons ended up in the pew just behind Cecily and her parents. Throughout the service she was acutely conscious of his gaze on the back of her neck, to the point where she lost her place in carols she had known by heart since childhood.

At the end, when she followed her parents out of the pew, she and Iain reached the aisle at the same moment. In the crowd, perforce he offered her his arm. The unnatural silence between them quivered with tension as they made their slow way from the church.

If only it were Iain who would escort her down the aisle from the altar a few short weeks hence!

Lord Avon awaited them by the church door. "Ah, you've extricated her in one piece, coz! A devilish crush. Come, I'll drive you both home in my curricle. You won't be any worse squashed."

To protest would have looked churlish on Cecily's part. She looked at Iain at last, watched him lose the battle with temptation. Intimately squeezed between two gentlemen, in love with one, bound to wed the other, she had to call upon every iota of self-discipline and self-respect to preserve a calm, ladylike demeanor.

Having survived that agony, she thought as she went up to take off her pelisse and bonnet that she need no longer seek to avoid Iain. Surely it would not be wrong to take a forlorn pleasure in his company—others present, of course—until a formal betrothal forced her to give all her loyalty to Lord Avon.

Perhaps Iain came to the same conclusion. At least, he had no chance to stay aloof, for he was in his element when the children joined the company for Christmas fun. His nieces and nephews and young cousins adored him no less than the village children.

Since even the urbane Lord Avon took part in the games of speculation, charades, lotto, jackstraws, and snapdragon, Cecily had no qualms about enjoying herself. On Christmas Day, Mama could not frown upon a bit of a romp.

The festivities ended all too soon. In the days that followed, soberer pastimes returned. Cecily continued to play billiards with Lord Avon occasionally, but she also played chess with the duke with Iain's assistance, and sometimes with Iain alone. She asked after his patients too, and they talked about life in Bath, in London, and at her country home. The weather turning crisp and fine, on hunt days he walked with her and Elspeth in the shrubbery, though they did not ride together again.

They both succeeded in maintaining a front of friendly cordiality. Cecily wondered if he found it as much of a strain as she did.

And constantly she wondered when Lord Avon was going to make his formal request for her hand.

The arrival of a stream of new guests reminded her that the New Year's ball was the next day. Quite likely Lord Avon would consider that a suitable time for a proposal of marriage.

That evening she was unable to evade taking her turn at

the spinet. Rebelling against complex sonatas and arias, she chose to play and sing a simple ballad to which she could do more justice—a Scots ballad.

" 'The king sits in Dunfermline town,' " she warbled. " 'Drinking the bloodred wine/Oh, where will I get a skillful skipper/To sail this ship of mine?' "

By the time she had drowned Sir Patrick Spens's "with the Scots lords at his feet," she was in a thoroughly mournful mood. When the hearty applause died away, she launched into "Come You Not from Newcastle?"

"Come you not there away?
"Oh, saw you not my true love,
"Riding on a bonny bay?"

As she sang, she avoided Mama's eyes, for Mama did not approve of common ballads in company. She avoided Lord Avon's eyes, for he was not her true love. She tried to avoid . . . she could not stop herself. Her gaze was drawn to Iain like a weary bird to its nest.

"Why should I not love my love?
"Why should not my love love me?
"Why should I not ride after him
"Since love to all is free?"

Iain watched her, his face stony but for his eyes, where his heart lay vulnerable, exposed for any to see whose attention was not fixed on the fair performer.

At his side Elspeth whispered, "Lud, to think I thought her singing wooden!" She looked at him and frowned. "Iain?"

He essayed a smile. "She sings well, does she not?"

Elspeth glanced at Cecily, then back at her brother. "Oh, my poor dear! I had not guessed. No hope?"

"She is titled and wealthy." Softly as he spoke, his voice cracked. "And if she were not, how could I stoop to stealing Jasper's bride?"

Seven

"Lady Cecily, I had not meant to speak for a few days yet." Lord Avon's voice was husky. "But tonight you are so enchanting, I cannot delay."

Cecily moved away from her suitor to one of the gallery's tall windows. Outside, a near-full moon sparkled on frosty gardens and, shining through the panes, gleamed on the silver net overskirt of her white satin ball gown. She shivered. The moment had come, and she had utterly lost sight of the resigned meekness she needed now.

"Sir?" she quavered.

"Cecily, you cannot be unaware of my intention. I own that I formed it in a spirit of dutiful compliance with my parents' wishes, but in the past week I have come to believe I am lucky beyond my deserts to have chosen you. Will you do me the very great honor of becoming my wife?"

Wife. If he had simply asked for her hand, she might have brought herself to say yes. If he had spoken the word "marriage," it would not have made her flinch. But *wife* was so intimate a term! She could not be his wife.

She could not bear it, and—in a flash the realization came to her—she would be cheating him. He did not deserve a wife who loved someone else.

"I cannot!" she wailed. "I meant to say yes, truly I did. I would not for the world have let you imagine I intended to say yes if I had not."

"Dutiful compliance with your parents' wishes?" he

wryly echoed himself. Hands on her shoulders, he turned her so that the light from the wall sconces fell on her face. "But when it comes to the point, you find the idea so distasteful. . . . I had thought we might deal very well together. Do you dislike me so much? No." He laid a finger on her lips. "I shall not press you for an answer."

"Indeed, sir, I don't dislike you at all," Cecily assured him. "I would gladly have done my duty, but then . . ." She faltered, but she owed him an explanation. "You see, quite unexpectedly I fell in love."

Lord Avon raised his eyebrows, his expression reflective. "I do see. Now, who . . . ? Good Lord! Forgive me if I dare hazard a guess. Is it Iain?"

She nodded, with difficulty holding back a flood of tears.

"Then you are quite right, we cannot marry. I find I have no desire whatever to be wed to my cousin's beloved." He paused. "Forgive me again, I suppose he does love you?"

"I . . . I think so. He has not said."

"No, he wouldn't, knowing of the understanding between us—between our families, perhaps I should say. I'll tell him that is at an end."

"Th-thank you, but it won't h-help! Mama and Papa will never let me marry a d-doctor."

"And Iain is too proud to press his suit so far above his rank and fortune," Lord Avon said thoughtfully. "Now, don't cry, Cecily, I beg of you." He pressed a handkerchief into her hand. "We must return to the ballroom looking well pleased with each other if we are to baffle the gossipmongers."

"There is b-bound to be the horridest gossip anyway. Everyone believes we are practically b-betrothed."

He put on his haughtiest air. "You and I, my dear Lady Cecily, are of too exalted a station to care for the bibble-babble of the prattle-boxes."

Cecily produced a watery giggle, marred by a sniff. "I daresay it will not be half so bad if neither of us appears mortified, but I shall find it very hard to seem ch-cheerful."

"You shan't, my dear, because you have my promise I shall find a way out of this maze. I shall make it impossible for Iain not to ask for your hand, and impossible for your father to refuse it."

"Only . . . only if he truly loves me."

"Oh, I believe you may count on that," said Lord Avon dryly. "Now I come to think of it, it would explain why he has spent the past week looking as if half a dozen of his wealthiest patients just dropped dead. But, if you have no objection, I shall consult Cousin Elspeth. She's bound to know what's going on in her brother's head."

"I do not mind. I like Elspeth very much. Lord Avon—"

"Cousin Jasper."

"Not yet! Lord Avon, I am very sorry to have disappointed your expectations."

He took her hand and raised it to his lips. "My dear child, I am only sorry my admittedly somewhat cold-blooded approach to matrimony put you to such . . . inconvenience. I hope we shall be friends as well as cousins."

"Oh, yes!" Cecily had never in all the months of courtship liked him half so well.

They returned to the ballroom just in time for him to sweep her into a waltz. No one—including Iain—seeing Lady Cecily smiling up at Lord Avon could possibly have guessed that they had just come to an agreement to part.

Later on, standing up with Iain for a country dance, Cecily tried to cheer him up, to let him see how her hopes had risen. Even had the figures of the dance allowed private conversation, she could not actually tell him what had happened lest it ruin Lord Avon's plans. Though he smiled at her gaiety and inconsequential chatter, his eyes remained somber.

Perhaps he thought she had heartlessly resigned herself to her fate and resolved to renounce their love.

No, he would not so misjudge her. He must imagine she was putting on a show to deceive the world, hiding her breaking heart as he endeavored to do. If only she dared assure him that their future was secure!

Not until Cecily retired to bed in the early hours of the New Year did doubts begin to creep in. She could not imagine how Lord Avon intended to carry out his promise.

If he failed to bring Iain up to scratch, she would be utterly humiliated, and if Iain applied to her father for her hand and was refused, *he* would be utterly humiliated. Lord Avon could not hope to persuade both his cousin and her parents. He had set himself an impossible task, and her life was ruined forever.

Cecily woke late the next morning. She was dressing in her riding habit when Lady Flint came into her chamber and dismissed the maid.

"Well, my love, you and Lord Avon were missing from the ballroom for an age last night. Have you something to tell your mama?"

"No, Mama. We were not gone so very long. We were just talking." She kept her eyes on her reflection in the pier glass, and so saw as well as felt her cheeks grow pink.

The blush reassured her mother. "No matter, child. I expect he will wait until just before the Twelfth Night masquerade. Most guests will leave the next day, so he will not have to put up with a great to-do for days and days. Gentlemen abhor a fuss. Does he ride with you today?"

"I believe not, Mama. He spoke of the New Year's Day hunt."

"Oh, yes, it is something special, I collect. Your papa went off hours ago. Do not ride too far, Cecy, after dancing all night. You must not overtire yourself."

"I shall not, Mama, and the sun is shining, so there is no fear of a wetting." She kissed her mother's cheek, feeling horridly guilty for her deception.

But if she revealed that Lord Avon no longer intended

to make her his bride, she would be whisked away from Felversham before his plot reached fruition. After all, there was always a chance he might succeed.

As Cecily's doubts and fears came and went, her spirits rose and fell like a shuttlecock. Far from feeling tired, she was filled with a restless energy. She had company on her ride, for the bright sunshine and crisp air called forth several ladies and two or three nonhunting gentlemen. They turned toward the village, where some of the ladies wished to purchase ribbons to trim their Twelfth Night costumes or dominoes.

"What is your costume to be, Lady Cecilia?" someone asked.

"I shall just wear a domino," she said with regret. "Mama does not wish me to dress up." Tactfully she did not add that Lady Flint considered masquerade costumes to be beneath the dignity of an earl's daughter, smacking of the stage.

The tiny haberdasher's shop had scarce room enough for everyone. Cecily, not wishing to make any purchase, decided to go outside and wait with the gentlemen, but when she stepped out, they were trotting off up the street. Unwilling to stand alone in the street, she was about to go back inside, when she saw Iain come out of old Johno's cottage a few doors down on the other side.

"Dr. Macfarlane!" she called impulsively.

His face lit and he came toward her, smiling. "Happy New Year, Lady Cecily."

"Happy New Year." She was suddenly breathless. "How . . . how does Johno go on?"

"Quite nicely, though whether it is due to exercise or the ginger and willow-bark tea, I cannot tell. He puts down the improvement to a daily mug of cider."

Cecily laughed. "Mulled, in this weather, I trust."

"The weather may be responsible, come to that. Cold

and dry is better than dampness for some rheumatic complaints. But you must be chilled, standing here."

"I just came out of the shop." And his very presence warmed her. "In spite of the frosty air, the sunshine is delightful."

"Yes, on a day like this, one notices the snowdrops and winter aconites and Christmas roses, not the leafless branches. On a day like this, it's almost possible to believe in the future."

How she wanted to tell him his cousin was working for their future! "You must never lose hope," she said seriously.

"That's what I tell my patients. Come, I don't want you to join their number. Go back inside—or ride home with me."

"A race? I know the lie of the land now, and Shadow's ways."

"A race! Yes, why not?"

They retrieved Shadow from the groom who was walking the ladies' mounts, and Hippocrates from the church railings. As they rode down the lane toward the fir plantation, Cecily felt as if she had known Iain forever and could talk to him about anything in the world—except for a direct reference to their love and Lord Avon's plans.

She wanted him to know why she had been prepared to settle for a loveless marriage, to make sure he understood she was not influenced by his cousin's rank and wealth, only by her parents' wishes.

She told him about the stillborn babies, about the little brothers and sisters who had died in infancy. "Only I survived," she said, "so I have tried to make it up to Mama and Papa, to be just what they wanted me to be."

"A very paragon of all the virtues, and the graces, too. Don't tell me they are dissatisfied?"

"Oh, no! They are all that is loving, and I love them dearly as well. Mama has not even chided me for playing chess and billiards, and romping with the children on

Christmas Day, and only a little for helping Ben Diver the day we arrived."

"Shocking sins, indeed!"

"She did not say a word when I sang those ballads instead of an aria, though she considers them ungenteel."

"They were deservedly popular with your audience. Your singing was admirable." Softly he sang, " 'Why should I not love my love?' "

Cecily glanced at him, but his gaze was fixed straight ahead.

"One cannot always live one's life to please others," she said, the broadest hint she dared give.

"No, else I had not become a physician, but it must ever be an object to strive not to grieve one's nearest and dearest."

Did he mean her, or himself? Was he saying she must marry Lord Avon so as not to grieve her parents? Or that he must renounce her so as not to grieve his cousin, his uncle, and his aunt? Either way or both, Cecily honored him for the sentiment, though she vehemently disagreed.

Vehemently but silently. She was unaccustomed to argument, and no rebuttal came readily to her tongue.

They turned in among the firs. In the shade the air struck cold, and by wordless mutual consent they urged their mounts to a canter. A few minutes brought them back into the sun, where they drew rein on the edge of the wood.

"A race to the stables?" Iain asked with a somewhat forced smile, his eyes shadowed by the brim of his hat. "Or, rather, since it will not do to gallop into the yard, to where this track meets the carriage drive?"

"Yes. Come on, Shadow!"

Again they galloped neck and neck. Cecily urged Shadow on but failed to gain an inch. As they approached the crest of the hill, she asked herself why she was trying to outpace Hippocrates. Suppose Lord Avon's plan failed and this was the last time she would ever be alone with Iain? To shorten it thus was sheer folly!

She slowed Shadow to a walk. Iain and Hippocrates promptly fell back beside them.

"I thought I felt Shadow stumble. I was afraid she might be lamed."

Iain studied the mare's gait for a moment. "I cannot see any limp, but perhaps you had best walk her the rest of the way."

Thankful, Cecily nodded. "Do you count horse-doctoring among your skills?" she inquired archly.

He laughed. "Not I, but I can spot a limp as well as any farrier, if not diagnose the cause."

"Elspeth told me your chief interest is in treating children." She had not spoken of it before, since it touched too closely on the painful subject of his plans for the future.

She was glad she had asked. Eagerly he expounded on his hopes for founding a clinic and investigating the way various remedies affected children differently from adults.

"You should not have got me started," he said ruefully as they rode under the stable yard arch. "My friends avoid the topic, for I can go on for hours."

"It is all fascinating," Cecily assured him. "If you had started thirty years ago, perhaps I should have half a dozen brothers and sisters now."

"Perhaps." Reminded of the reason for her compliance with her parents' every wish, Iain fell silent.

He handed her down from the saddle without mishap this time, without any excuse to take her in his arms—just as well, as grooms and stable boys were about. Nonetheless, their eyes met.

Cecily read love, sorrow, and understanding in his gaze. He thought she still meant to marry Lord Avon! How could she explain he had misinterpreted the purpose behind her words?

As a groom approached, Iain said hurriedly in a low voice, "We may still be friends when you are Lady Avon?"

"We shall always be friends, I hope, whatever may happen!"

"Then I must be satisfied. Excuse me, pray, I have to drive into Bath this afternoon to see a few patients who do not trust my *locum tenens*."

He turned away. Cecily trailed alone and disconsolate into the house.

She loved him more than ever, and she no longer had the least doubt that he loved her. If Lord Avon failed, she would just have to find a way to abduct Iain and get herself so thoroughly compromised, there was no choice but for them to wed.

Resolute, yet shaken at the prospect of such outrageous behavior, she fervently prayed Lord Avon would succeed.

Eight

For the next three days Cecily was on tenterhooks. Twelfth Night was nearly upon them. If she was not betrothed to Lord Avon by then, everyone would be all agog for explanations. He said nothing to the purpose, and they were never alone together. The only assurance she had that he had neither forgotten nor neglected his promise was his response to a pleading look: a murmured "Have faith!"

Since the phrase was accompanied by a teasing smile, she was far from reassured.

Twelfth Night at Felversham was a democratic occasion in the ancient tradition. Under a king and queen chosen by lot, high and low, young and old, mingled in disguise to dance and feast in the ballroom, the portrait gallery, and various nearby apartments.

Decorum was preserved by the knowledge that the duke's democratic principles were not so enlightened that he would hesitate to dismiss any dependent who stepped across the line. Masks were no excuse for license.

Though Cecily was not in costume, her mama had permitted her to have tiny star-shaped spangles sewn all over her gown, which was the intense blue of the evening sky when stars first appear. It was the color of her eyes, visible through the black silk mask concealing the upper part of her face. Most of her hair was hidden by the hood of her watered-silk domino. As she moved, the changeable silk revealed the shades of sunset: pink, peach, and flame.

"The Queen of the Night," said a highwayman, materializing beside her as she entered the ballroom.

"She was a villain," Cecily protested, laughing, as she recognized Lord Avon.

"What better match for a villainous Gentleman of the Road?" His eyes gleamed mockingly through the holes in his mask. "Meet me by the first duke at the stroke of midnight, fair queen. I shall wave my magic flute and turn into a fairy godmother. Or perhaps a pumpkin or a pirate, who can guess?"

The crowd swirled around them, and he was gone.

As partner succeeded partner, known and unknown, Cecily watched for Lord Avon, but there were several highwaymen present and the one who danced with her now was not he. What was he going to do? Surely he did not expect to force her parents' and Iain's hands with a public announcement that she and Iain were engaged to marry?

They would deny it. Nothing but public humiliation lay that way.

Iain stood up with her, sober in a plain black domino. Cecily was too agitated to enjoy the dance, and his hazel eyes were anguished. Clearly he expected to hear this night that she was betrothed to his cousin. When the music ended, he pressed her hand and whispered "Courage!" before relinquishing her to a waiting Harlequin—whom she promptly abandoned.

"Do you know the time?" she asked him.

"Nearly midnight."

"I am sorry, I must . . . I am engaged for the next set." She slipped away through the throng.

The Highwayman awaited her by the first duke's portrait. He took her hand. "Come, down the back stairs. Quiet, and hurry."

"What . . . ? Where . . . ?"

"The child—the gamekeeper's brat—has hurt himself

and is crying for you." Lord Avon's eyes glinted with deviltry behind his mask.

Cecily refused to believe Ben had come to grief just at the time when the marquis had arranged to meet her. She recalled her father's mention of Lord Avon's youthful peccadilloes, and tales she had heard of the riot and rumpus kicked up by young blades with nothing better to do. What was he up to?

"Don't turn missish on me now!" he said impatiently. "Do you or don't you wish—"

"Yes, yes, I am coming."

He rushed her down a narrow, dark stairway. At the bottom he took a warm cloak from a hook on the wall and placed it around her shoulders.

"Where are we going? Where is Ben?"

"He stayed at home. I'll take you there. You can go up before me on Caesar."

The black Thoroughbred was already saddled and waiting by the side door. Cecily decided she had no choice but to trust Lord Avon. She let him toss her up onto Caesar's withers. He swung into the saddle behind her, and they set off into the night.

The frost had broken, and a mild, blustery wind, such as breathes a balmy promise of spring even in January, tossed diaphanous rags of cloud across the haloed moon. The canter across the moonlit park would have been almost unbearably romantic if only the hard chest Cecily leaned against was Iain's, not Lord Avon's.

With a chuckle he said, "You will have to claim you were abducted by a masked highwayman."

Iain tore himself away from Cecily and went to find a punch bowl to drown his sorrows, to dim the vision of her eyes full of love and hope.

What did she expect of him, that he would toss her over

his saddle bow and carry her off like the knight in one of her beloved ballads? Did she not understand that would be a betrayal that would damn him forever in his own as well as the world's eyes?

Why the deuce was not Jasper with her? He must intend to announce their betrothal at midnight, the witching hour—unless he had shied off at the eleventh hour. Was Cecily to suffer the public humiliation of his failing to come up to scratch?

Iain gulped a glass of punch. As he turned to pour another, a Goddess of the Hunt, all in green with bow and quiver, accosted him.

Of the several Dianas present at the hunt-mad duke's entertainment, this one turned out to be Elspeth. Drawing him aside, she said urgently, "Iain, the little boy has hurt himself, the gamekeeper's son. He has broke his splints and injured his arm again, I collect. You must go to the rescue."

"Oh, Lord! Where is he?"

"I am told he was left at home with his elder sister for fear of just such an accident in the crowds." She scurried along beside him as he thrust through the crush toward the stairs. "He climbed a ladder, I believe, and fell forward when he caught his foot in the top rung. I am not perfectly sure. It sounds odd, but his sister brought the message and doubtless she was out of breath and in a fright."

"There is a ladder to their attic room. Tell his parents I'm on my way, Elspeth."

"If I can find them in this squeeze!"

The stables were deserted, but he was used to saddling Hippocrates for himself. A few minutes later he trotted under the archway.

Despite flying clouds, the moonlight was bright enough to risk a canter once he had ripped off his mask for better vision. As he rode, uncomfortable on horseback in evening dress, Iain tried to fix his mind on the medical problem ahead of him. His thoughts kept drifting back to the revelry he had left behind.

Even now Jasper and Lady Cecily must be receiving the congratulations of well-wishers, for the Marquis of Avon was an honorable gentleman and would never cry off at this late stage. Iain did not see how he could bear to go back to add his felicitations. Perhaps he would ride on from the gamekeeper's cottage to his home in Bath and write to Jasper from there.

Cecily, secure in the knowledge that she had done her duty, would understand. She would be grateful to be spared facing him until she had forgotten. . . .

"No," he cried aloud, "she cannot *forget!*" She would mourn their love, though she let it die and—as duty and honor demanded—turned her affections to her husband.

Between the bare trees he saw lights in the cottage windows, upstairs and down. At last his thoughts turned toward the child lying frightened and in pain, awaiting his coming. He hoped Ben had done his arm no permanent damage.

Hippocrates tied, Iain hurried into the cottage and scrambled up the ladder in the corner of the kitchen. Stepping over the top rung, he straightened as far as he could.

The long loft, with its low, sloping ceiling, was lit by a single lantern. Near it, on a straw-filled mattress covered by a colorful counterpane, sat Lady Cecily.

"What the deuce are you doing here?"

He looked appalled. Wondering what his cousin's plot would bring next, Cecily said with fragile composure, "Lord Avon brought me."

"Jasper? What has my cousin got into his noggin?"

"He told me Ben was hurt and in need of whatever comfort I could bring."

"Jasper?" Iain asked incredulously. "Concerned for the gamekeeper's brat? But never mind that. I have come to see to his injury." He glanced down the length of the loft. "Where is he?"

"Up here, I gathered, but I cannot find him."

Stooping, the doctor moved a few steps, peering at the beds laid out in a neat row on the floor. "Nor can I. Where's Jasper? Surely he did not leave you here alone?"

The immediate answer was a scraping noise followed by a crash. The ladder disappeared. A moment later the door below slammed.

As Iain and Cecily stared at each other, hooves drummed, fading into the distance.

Cecily closed her eyes. She should have guessed from the glint in Lord Avon's eye that he was going to do something drastic like this. By the time the Divers came home from the Twelfth Night celebrations, she would be thoroughly compromised. Iain would feel obliged to marry her whether he really wanted to or not.

He *did* want to, she told herself. Had she not contemplated doing something of the same sort? She opened her eyes and held out her hand.

"It would seem we are stuck. Come and sit down."

Iain's incredulous look faded. His lips twitched. "You don't appear desperately surprised . . . nor distressed," he said dryly as the mattress crunched beneath his weight.

She blushed. "I am not very surprised. The story about Ben was not at all convincing, and Lord Avon had promised me—"

"Good Lord, this is a plot between the two of you?"

"I did not know precisely what he would do. But if it succeeds, how can I be distressed?"

"Truly?" He took her hand. "Life as a doctor's wife is very different from anything you have known, and I shall not give up my profession."

"Of course not! Iain, you will not do anything idiotically noble like refusing my fortune?"

"What makes you suppose you will not be cut off without a penny for making such a mésalliance?"

"Papa would never be so petty. He wants me to be happy.

Besides," Cecily added frankly, "he does not care for my cousin, who will inherit the title and the entailed property. And even if he leaves the unentailed property to the Society for the Suppression of Vice—which I cannot think likely!— I shall have my mother's dowry. It is irrevocably settled on me. I should think fifty thousand pounds will be enough to found a children's clinic, will it not?"

Iain laughed a trifle shakily. "More than enough, beloved. You don't believe that's why I want to marry you?"

"You do want to marry me?" she faltered. "I could not bear it if you were trapped into—"

He pulled her into his arms, and her last doubts fled as their lips met. His kiss was full of tenderness, with a promise of passion to come. It ended all too soon for Cecily.

"My dearest love," he murmured into her hair, "I want nothing more in the world than to make you my wife. However—"

"However?" She sat bolt upright, staring at him in indignation.

"However, there is bound to be a vast amount of talk, and I see no need to add a touch of genuine scandal to what will otherwise be a nine days' wonder."

Crossing to the ladder hole, he lowered himself and dropped to the floor below.

"Iain!" Cecily knelt by the hole, gazing down at his upturned, grinning face. "You mean we are not stuck after all?"

"We are not. Jasper is far too clever for that! We shall return to the house before we are missed, and I'll request your hand of your father in due form. With Jasper no longer your suitor, I daresay Lord Flint will make the best of my offer."

"I hope so," Cecily said doubtfully.

"Come."

He reached up, and Cecily slid down trustfully into his arms.

After another loving kiss, they headed for the door. Iain opened it and followed Cecily out.

"What the deuce?" he swore. "Jas has taken Hippocrates! I'm afraid it looks as if he does want us to be away long enough to make certain of the business. We shall have to walk."

Cecily held out a foot clad in a dainty satin dancing slipper. "Not in these."

"Oh, Lord!" He looked down at his own somewhat sturdier leather shoes. "I'll go and fetch a mount."

"It seems Lord Avon has left you another way to escape, if you choose."

"You know I don't! But—"

"Iain, I had much rather not wait all alone here in the woods." She glanced around at the leafless trees, towering darkly, their wind-tossed branches casting restless, eerie moon-shadows. Any tree trunk could conceal a *real* highwayman. "Stay with me. Lord Avon cannot want a scandal any more than we do. Let us see what his ingenuity brings next!"

In the ballroom, in the course of a country dance, Diana the Huntress met a tall pirate with a black beard and a velvet eye patch. As they promenaded together, she hissed, "It *is* you! I have been looking for you everywhere. You were a—"

"Shhh. I am a pirate," Jasper said with a grin. "I have always been a pirate, don't forget it. Mama has retired to bed at last."

"Thank heaven. Aunt Louisa has by far too knowing an eye."

"Yes, a fait accompli is the only thing for Mama. Time for act three of this little comedy. I wish I could have rehearsed Iain and Lady Cecily. You know your lines?"

"Word perfect," Elspeth promised over her shoulder, rejoining her partner.

The dance soon ended. Through crowds thinned at this late hour, Elspeth hurried to where she had remarked Lord and Lady Flint conferring worriedly in a corner. They must be wondering what had happened to the expected betrothal, she thought with a touch of pity for their coming disillusionment.

"Lord Flint? It is you? At last!"

"Who . . . ?"

"Elspeth Sutton. May I speak to you privately?" She glanced at Lady Flint as if uncertain of her identity.

"This is my wife. What is it? Is something wrong?"

"Cecily?" asked Lady Flint, hands clasped in anguish.

"She is quite safe now, I assure you. I have only a rather garbled account, but this is what happened as far as I can gather. It seems my brother saw Cecily abducted by a highwayman, whether real or in costume I cannot guess, some hours since. He rode after them and somehow rescued her."

"My poor child," moaned Lady Flint.

"Where is she?" Lord Flint inquired more practically.

"They were near the gamekeeper's cottage, so he took her there. She was quite frightened, I collect, and in no case to walk any distance—Iain's horse had run off at some point. A farm laborer on his way home saw the lights and called in to say hello to Diver. Iain sent him back here to look for me, hoping I might somehow avert a scandal. Unluckily, I was with Cousin Jasper when the man found me and told the tale."

"Lord Avon knows?" they asked in dismayed unison.

"He sent me to search for you, while he has a gig harnessed to fetch them. I expect you will want to go with him, Lord Flint? I shall stay with Lady Flint. Take heart, dear ma'am," she said soothingly as his lordship strode away. "The man swears Cecily is not hurt, and in comparison, what is the ruin of the match of the Season?"

Lady Flint groaned, but, Elspeth noted, did not contradict her.

* * *

Cecily stopped in the middle of her sentence as Iain held up his hand. Listening, she heard hooves, jingling harness, the creak of wheels.

"I believe we are about to discover the rest of Jasper's plot," he said in a voice filled with misgiving. "I trust he has not brought a crowd to witness our unmasking."

Lord Flint strode into the cottage.

"Papa!" Cecily jumped up and ran to him.

He folded her in his arms. "The brute did not hurt you, Cecy?"

Lord Avon's words came back to her: *You will have to claim you were abducted by a masked highwayman.* She had thought he was joking!

"No, Papa. Iain—Mr. Macfarlane—rescued me before the highwayman had a chance to work his wicked wiles."

"I confess I cannot quite make out exactly what happened."

"Do not make me talk about it, Papa, I beg of you. Until Iain came, it was perfectly horrid!" She turned, still encircled by one of his arms, and held out her hand to Iain, who took it in a warm clasp. "He is a hero, Papa!"

"My thanks, doctor." Lord Flint shook hands heartily with his daughter's rescuer.

"Oh, Papa, when may we be married?"

Her father looked grimly resigned. He glanced at Lord Avon, who leaned against the doorpost wearing a pirate costume, his most sardonic expression on what was visible of his face above a huge black beard.

"I suppose . . . ?" said Lord Flint unhopefully.

Lord Avon shook his head. "They have been alone together for several hours," he pointed out. "I trust we may avert a scandal, but you cannot expect, my dear sir—"

"I suppose not." The earl heaved a sigh and shook hands reluctantly with his future son-in-law. "Forgive me, my dear fellow, if I say you're not quite what I'd hoped for for my girl. But needs must when the devil drives, eh?"

"I drove the gig here," said Lord Avon, laughing devils in his eyes, "but I brought Caesar, and Lord Flint rode, so you may drive Lady Cecily home, Iain. I'll be groomsman at your wedding."

"Good of you, Avon," Lord Flint conceded. "Come along, Cecily. What your mama is going to think of this night's work I dare not guess." He stumped out.

Lord Avon smiled. "Never fear, Elspeth's seen to Lady Flint, and I shall handle my mother and father," he said softly, and turning his back, he warned, "don't be too long about it."

So Iain swept Cecily into his arms for a swift, joyful kiss, and they went out together into the moonlit night.

Epilogue

Frost sparkled in the sun that February day as the cream of Society crammed into the village church. The Earl of Flint's daughter was to marry a physician! He was the Duchess of Pembroke's nephew though, and duke and duchess would attend the wedding. No one who was anyone had refused the coveted invitation.

Everyone had expected Lady Cecily Barwith to wed the Marquis of Avon. Yet rumor had it he was to stand up with his cousin, the bridegroom. That certainly put paid to any hint of scandal, but what a delicious tidbit of gossip!

Dr. Iain Macfarlane and Lord Avon arrived together. His lordship was acknowledged to appear perfectly content with his supporting role in the affair.

Thus most eyes were on the bride as she walked up the aisle on her father's arm, her face radiant behind her veil. A few glanced at the fortunate bridegroom waiting at the altar, his expression serious but his eyes bright.

Fewer still spared a glance for the groomsman. Those who did were surprised to note a triumphant grin, directed at some member of the congregation. And heavens above, was that a wink?

Seated at her husband's side, her face a picture of quiet smugness, Elspeth, Lady Sutton, winked back.

Three Nights at a Country Inn

Monique Ellis

Paving the Road to Hell

"You've got to rescue me!" Archer Huntleigh-Bowes shouted through the closed door, neatly dodging the man-servant attempting to stop him, and burst into his former comrade-in-arms' icy bedchamber at the unreasonable hour of nine in the morning shortly after 1816 slid unlamented into 1817. "Instanter, or I'm for it, Charlie!"

A hearty snore greeted him.

"I was summoned to dine with my godfather yesterday evening," Archer rattled on, "and was treated to his usual bear-garden jaw. Dammit, Charlie, something must be done!"

The former captain tore open the dusty velvet draperies, caring not in the least that more than one form occupied the rumpled bed and ignoring the fanciful forests of frost decorating the panes and the clouding of his breath in the air.

"If you can't rescue me, or at least come up with a sensible suggestion as to how I may rescue myself, then you must accompany me to Brevett-on-Chipple—which happens to be at the back of beyond. You wouldn't care for that in the least, so you'd best come up with a solution," he grumbled, turning to the bed. "It's a damnable thing when one's six and twenty, or as close as makes no difference, and has seen service on the Peninsula and at Waterloo, and *still* can't call one's soul one's own."

Charles Moreland's batman seized Archer's arm and attempted to pull him to the door, winking and nodding at the bed. "Sir, ah, the captain, ah—"

"Has company? 'Course he does, Fellowes. Were I not in this fix, I'd be similarly companioned. Well, she'll have to take herself off, whoever she is. It's morning, isn't it? Time she was gone anyway. Who's he been making merry sport with this time—Meg Quarrel or Dulcie Ducroix? Or did he finally manage to convince Fanny Bliss to dally with him?"

"Ah—er—"

Archer strode across the room, seized the covers, and pulled them back.

"Bloody hell," Fellowes muttered behind him, "we're for it now."

"Well, I'll be damned," Archer laughed, brows rising. "Lady Carlotta Leighton, I do believe. At your service as always, my lady."

The frowzled and improbably blond head burrowed in the nearer pillow turned, china-blue eyes glaring at him blearily as the notorious viscountess struggled to cover what the club wags called her best points.

"I'll thank you to take yourself off, Archie," she snapped. "No sense of couth—none. Breaking in on a gentleman before he's prepared to receive you, indeed! At the very least you could make up the fire and offer me your greatcoat. It's cold as an Alpine peak in here."

"More like you're the one's not prepared."

Which she wasn't. Harsh morning didn't treat Lottie Leighton's more than forty mature years kindly, for all she appeared well enough preserved by candlelight. Instead of taking himself off Archer sat on the edge of the bed, the better to admire the generous pink charms exposed to his view.

"And here I understood from your note that you were incapacitated yesterday evening, for which reason you couldn't accompany me to the theater," he chided, twirling a brassy curl around his fingers, then giving it a firm tug. "You'd best be rousing yourself, madam. I encountered your husband not ten minutes ago in Brook Street, swearing you'd been abducted and threatening to call in the Runners."

"Oh, piss-pots," the blowzy viscountess groaned. "You're certain?"

"Absolutely and positively. There was smoke pouring from his lordship's ears and fire from his nostrils. Indeed, he was swearing vengeance on whoever it was had encouraged you to stray from your marital vows once again."

"Was there ever such a troublesome man," she yawned, plump charms fading to blue now that her cozy nest was disturbed. "Swinard does it often enough, heaven knows. Why shouldn't I indulge myself similarly? I wonder what has him in a pet this time."

"Haven't the foggiest, though he did give me the fish eye. Fortunately I was able to tell him I hadn't seen you in days, and referred him to my godfather had he any doubt as to where I'd spent last evening—which is what brings me here, Charlie."

A muffled groan was his crony's only response.

"Drat the man." Carlotta Leighton—dubbed "Harlotta" by Sally Jersey in one of her more puckish moods—pushed her tangled curls from her eyes. "His latest convenient must've turned him off, and he's doubtless feeling the inconvenience of it."

"Which one? He has a gross at least," Archer grinned as Captain Charles Moreland began to show signs of rousing. "Hear you, Charlie," he teased, leaning across Lottie Leighton's rump to shake the half-pay officer's shoulder, "I won't have you poaching in my preserve again, you understand? This time I'll overlook it, of course."

"I'm not in any man's preserve," Lady Leighton yawned. She slapped Archer away as she sat and pulled the covers to her chin.

"Certainly not in mine or your husband's," Archer chuckled good-naturedly. "Not in Charlie's either, come to that. Only fellow I've seen you with regularly is Bertie Scanlon—though what you see in the bounder escapes me, for his cockloft's as empty as his pockets and his eyes protrude like a toad's."

"He has other attractions," the woman murmured absently, "one of which also protrudes most wonderfully when properly encouraged. You over there, Fellowes—that's your name, isn't it—fetch my gown and cape. I believe I abandoned them in the captain's sitting room. Archie, gather up my stays and petticoats. And will one of you make up the fire? I've no desire to catch my death."

Less than half an hour saw Carlotta Leighton on her way in a hired chaise, still grumbling over the irrationality of husbands believing they could disport themselves in any manner they pleased while insisting their wives adhere to both the letter and the spirit of their marital vows. Archer watched the carriage turn the corner, scowling at the gray buildings across the way as he ran powerful fingers through his unruly dark hair.

Behind him Charles lolled by the sitting room fire in an ancient wing chair whose cracked leather upholstery bore a strong resemblance to a map of the Nile estuary, his nakedness covered by a quilted and fur-trimmed scarlet dressing gown, his feet thrust in tapestry slippers. Charles—of an age with him and blessed, or cursed, with a similar baggage of experience—grinned wryly as he set aside the tankard of restorative concocted by Fellowes before he departed in search of a carriage for the viscountess and some provender with which to break their fasts.

"You're in a pickle apparently, but there's no sense going off like one of Winyate's rockets," Charles rumbled. "Not the least productive. Neither's dashing about town half dressed. Y'look rather more dilapidated than usual, in case you don't realize it. Doesn't do the least good, you know— not always appearing at one's best."

"To blazes with my toggery!"

"Besides, one never can, my father tells me—call one's soul one's own, that is."

Archer's shoulders stiffened. The half-pay captain laughed good-humoredly.

"Oh yes, I heard you in there," he said. "Was only pretending to sleep in hopes Harlotta'd take herself off before I had to behold her in all her matutinal glory. She's well enough when the lights're out, but the rest of the time? Deliver me! Even the Portugee hoors were better favored, for all taking a turn with her's quite the fashion.

"No, first one's soul belongs to one's parents, m'father says, then to one's schoolfellows, and then to one's wife once one's of an age to acquire one and is forced to it. The pater's warned me away from the ladies, bless him. Females're another matter," he grinned salaciously. "Says being seen with *la* Leighton will increase my stock, believe it or not. He has the right of that at least, even if she does have a nasty habit of lightening my already shallow pockets. Perniciously expensive female, that one. Can't afford her often. Always demanding some trinket or another. The trinkets she favors tend to sapphires and diamonds, unfortunately."

"Wish it was your father instead of Sir Evrard controlling my purse strings." Archer sighed.

"No, you don't. What little's left of one's soul once everyone else's taken their share belongs to one's sisters and female cousins. I have it on the best authority they relinquish their mite most reluctantly when a fellow takes it into his head to wed. Causes no end of disharmony."

"Had to do the pretty last night?" Archer inquired more as a matter of form than from genuine curiosity, turning from the soot-stained window.

"At a concert of sacred music, of all miserable things."

"Poor fellow."

"The pater'd already made good his escape, intuiting what was to come. Most excellent sense of preservation, the pater. Mine's not nearly so well developed. Of course, he's had a few years to tune his perceptions."

"Ain't interested in your father's perceptions—not unless he can turn them to good account in the preservation of mine."

"Wasn't much I could do once my mother summoned me," Charles explained with a wry smile, "and started nattering about it's being unseemly for them to gad about without male escort. Eldest cousin's got her eye on an anemic curate, and's convinced she must play prunes-and-prisms at every turn if she's to land her underfed trout."

"Y'don't say," Archer murmured, resuming his pacing. "When one considers I've seen service on the Continent, and was even mentioned favorably in a dispatch or two, and managed to achieve the rank of captain without having it purchased for me, it makes my godfather's maunderings all the more ridiculous. I'm not a feckless idiot bent on a course of determined self-destruction, blast it!"

" 'Course you're not, but don't be a bore, there's a good fellow," Charles soothed. "You've said it all before. I'm a younger son. My being a scapegrace is accepted form. Indeed, an' if I weren't there're those who'd claim I wasn't doing my duty by hallowed tradition. Dreadful thing—if the younger son turned out more sensible than the elder. You, on the other hand, are all that's left of your family.

"For pity's sake, stop treating my carpets like a race track. You're making me decidedly queasy given I didn't waste all my evening at that deuced concert."

"Obvious you didn't." Archer grinned, taking the place across the fire from his friend. "Where'd you join forces with Harlotta?"

"A hell—the Tinker's Bum. I was winning until she

turned up. That's one female definitely doesn't bring a gentleman luck, or at least she didn't me."

"And she'll bring you even less if you don't have a care. The viscount was threatening to call out whoever she's been favoring of late, and the law be damned."

"Y'don't say? Then he'll have to face half of London one morning, and the rest the following dawn. Didn't have a chance with her until Bertie Scanlon sank sodden beneath the table. Now, let's have it. You're accustomed enough to Sir Evrard's lectures, so it must be more'n that's set you off."

"I'm ordered to marry," Archer groaned, burying his head in his hands.

"Could be worse," Charles returned with the sangfroid of one not faced with the problem. "Find a complaisant chit, jump over the broomstick, and then—"

"Y'don't understand. I'm ordered to marry specifically, not generally. One Miss Sarah Timmons."

"Who the devil is Sarah Timmons?"

"A fubsy-faced, on-the-shelf country chit with a tradesman father and a runaway *ton* mother. She's a considerable heiress and Sir Evrard's great-granddaughter into the bargain, and therefore some sort of distant connection of mine."

"Good God!"

"Precisely. Why Sir Evrard would want me for her I haven't the slightest notion given his opinion of me, but he does and he's sworn he'll see us wed or dead. I'm to present myself at the home of Mr. John Timmons of Brevett-on-Chipple within the week, there to woo the fair damsel and her father's brass. I'm ordered to win both."

"Perhaps she won't have you," Charles suggested hopefully.

"A butter-toothed ape-leader—for that's what she must be—refuse an offer?"

"There's that, of course."

"Indeed there is. To listen to the old fellow, you'd think I was still in leading strings, or else bent on a course of dissipation such as hasn't been seen since Nero."

"Well, you have been having rather a carefree time of it since you sold out. Hedonism, I believe it's called."

"So have you," Archer roared, incensed. "I'm not a libertine and a wastrel, no matter what the old man says!"

"Consorting with a demi-rep the likes of Harlotta Leighton? He threw her up to you, didn't he? And Meg Quarrel and Dulcie Ducroix, delightful armfuls though they may be, aren't precisely the sort to raise his estimation of your taste in female companions. Opera dancers, after all— when they're earning their keep on their feet rather than on their backs."

Archer nodded, jaws clenched.

"And frequenting hells like the Tinker's Bum, which you've done often enough of late. And risking your neck in that curricle race to Brighton in a snowstorm. And—"

"There's no need to enumerate my sins. You can't manage the necessary tone of repugnance. I haven't outrun the constable, nor do I intend to, blast it! Neither do I intend to end my days with a broken neck in a ditch—not after surviving the best and the worst Nappy could throw at us. It was barely a flurry, and you know it—a matter of a few paltry flakes."

"Doesn't matter. Snow was falling, and the road in deplorable condition. Skinny Rutledge got himself a broken arm and had to shoot his pair. Sir Evrard was bound to hear of it given he and Rutledge's father belong to the same clubs. Come to that, I rather suspect the old gentleman threw me in your face. He did, didn't he?"

Archer nodded, flushing furiously. "Told him you're the most solid of fellows under it all," he protested. "Told him he'd no right to cast aspersions on your character."

"For pity's sake, the only miracle would've been if he

hadn't. Told you before it's different for me. I'm a younger son. The point is, what do you do now?"

"I present myself as ordered unless you can come up with something. No choice. The old fellow currently holds the purse strings, you know that. Generous enough when I was in the Peninsula. Now? While I'm not precisely in dun territory, I'm not particularly deep in the pockets either."

"Oh, Lord—you fool! I suspected you'd been dipping a bit deep, but I'd no idea you were at point-non-plus."

Archer shrugged, then colored up like a steamed lobster. "I wrote my godfather a note requesting an advance on next quarter's allowance as it took most of this quarter's to clear last quarter's more pressing debts," he admitted. "I was summoned to dine, and presented with this."

He pulled an oblong document from his coat pocket and thrust it at Charles. The stocky young man unfolded it.

"But this is—"

"A special license. All perfectly legal, with only the names to be filled in. Sir Evrard listened to me with his usual courtesy once Aunt Melodie left us to our port and cigarillos. When I'd had my say, he had his."

"Rather heavy-handed, that. Not like him in the least."

"No, it isn't, but it's the tone he's taking now. It's not that I'm not fond of Sir Evrard, for I am, but a country miss of no breeding and less education who's never set foot beyond a town so insignificant I'd never heard of it until yesterday evening? Good Lord, what will I have to say to the woman, or she to me? But, 'She's a fine, sensible young woman,' my godfather claims. Yes, in those precise words. She'll steady me, and I'll liven her up. Heaven deliver me!"

"You might give her a disgust of you."

"How? If they're so desperate to wed her off, there must be something horribly wrong with her. I could have a crooked back or six toes on each foot—or no toes at all, for that matter—and she'd probably present me to all her acquaintance as the most desirable of bridegrooms."

"We change places, then."

"To what good? Oh, it'd be a fine enough lark, but once we'd had our fun I'd be in worse case than ever."

"At least you wouldn't be trotting to the slaughter meek as a lamb, and extending the dagger—or whatever it is butchers use—to your executioner."

"It won't wash. You know females. The sainted Sarah'd devil me with it for the rest of my life."

"There's that, of course. Still, it would be amusing."

"For you, perhaps. Not for me," Archer insisted. "She'd be bad enough. Just think of what Sir Evrard'd say—and with justification. His great-granddaughter, after all. I can't insult him in such a fashion, or her either, no matter what she is. Can't you come up with a sensible suggestion?"

"Run away to sea. It'd be for only what—nine years? Then he has to turn the whole over to you, wed or not."

"You're mad!"

"Offer for her governess or companion. She's sure to have one."

"Worse yet," Archer groaned. "Bombazine and camphor for the rest of my life? And my knuckles rapped at every turn? I thank you, no."

"Take the king's shilling then, as you've sold out. Or scurry to the Antipodes. Or hide out in Paris—that's a pleasant enough little town when all's said and done. Or one of those German watering places. There's sure to be one where you can live on the cheap so long as you eschew the petticoats and the tables. Or escape to India and make your fortune and laugh in your godfather's face. That's a traditional resource of black sheep when too hotly importuned by their nearest and dearest."

"Blast it, I have my fortune! It's just that I can't touch it at the moment. Will you be serious?"

"I am. Lacking those remedies, you've no choice, you see. Playing lack-wit won't fadge, for Sir Evrard's certain to have reported on you. Your chosen bride's pater knows every one of your good points, and every one of your faults—of that you may be sure. A lack of furniture in your attic isn't one of 'em, except at times like these."

"Lack-wit? Now, there's a sterling notion! No, don't laugh. I'd have to be subtle, but combine that failing with a few others—such as a tendency to inappropriate light-mindedness and a certain libertine bent, add recklessness when driving the young lady about, and I should be able to force her to turn tail. She's certain to be a dried-up stick, and bridle at the very thought of a stolen kiss or two. If all else fails, advances in the direction of her abigail should get me chased from the place. We'll travel in my racing curricle, leave grooms and valets behind."

"Cawker!" Charles spluttered. "In January?"

"Won't be so bad. We'll bundle up and travel light, and take our time about it. Lots of good inns along the way. Weather's more like March just now. Besides, a traveling carriage would imply serious intent. A racing curricle sends a different message. With any luck, she'll refuse me on the spot. I'll be able to depart as free as I arrive, and with equal dispatch."

"I'm not haring off to God-knows-where in a curricle at this season," Charles insisted.

"Brevett-on-Chipple. Lord Leighton's on the warpath, and your name was mentioned."

"Damn and blast! By you?"

"Lord, no! I'm a better friend than that. Chuffy Binkerton. Never been your friend, Chuffy—not since that time after Ciudad Rodrigo when you stopped him from raping a schoolgirl."

Fellowes returned, followed by a train of servers from the local tavern. The unpleasant topic was abandoned as a gateleg table was pulled before the fire, covers set, dishes from which floated the aromas of grilled beefsteak, kedgeree, and pork pie placed on the dresser. That afternoon, portmanteaux containing only the essentials for a brief repairing lease, and

sporting their oldest—and warmest—toggery, Charles Moreland and Archer Huntleigh-Bowes departed for that northern
hinterland known as Brevett-on-Chipple, armed against the
bitter cold by flasks containing Charles's famous revivifying
blend of brandy, blue ruin, and black Barbados rum.

Sarah Timmons's father cornered her in the entry that
same morning as she was tying the strings of her warmest
cloak, the express that arrived while they were at the breakfast table in his hand.

"It's too cold for you to walk," he said, smiling down at
her. "Ride with me. The carriage will be at the door in a
moment."

He stuffed the letter in his pocket, donned his greatcoat
and accepted his hat, gloves, and malacca cane from the
hovering butler as he rattled on about the atlas and globe
she and her mother had agreed were needed at the little
school established for the children of his workers where
Sarah had taught since her nineteenth birthday. One thing
had led to another. Now she oversaw the school, just as her
mother had before her—something he accepted even if such
employment for an heiress was slightly unusual.

His smile didn't quite reach his eyes, and those canny
gray orbs never quite met hers. Whatever the letter con-
tained—and Sarah had her suspicions given she'd recognized the hand as her great-grandfather's—her father didn't
want witnesses when he imparted its contents. So, it was
to begin again.

And it did. Once the carriage door was closed, he extolled
the sterling qualities of one Archer Huntleigh-Bowes, late
of His Majesty's forces, with a rapid-fire delivery that left
the topic exhausted by the time they reached the end of the
chestnut-lined drive.

"You understand me, lass?" he said sharply when he'd

done. "I'm only asking you to meet the fellow. If he's not as reported, we'll send him packing."

She nodded, not trusting herself to speak. At least this time her father was admitting his game rather than attempting to claim an unknown eligible had appeared on their doorstep by chance. That was progress of a sort, she supposed.

"He'll arrive tomorrow, or possibly the day after. Your mother's grandfather's godson, after all," he persisted, toying with his cane. "You may find you like him."

Again Sarah nodded. Unfortunately, mild though his manner, her father's tone was the one he employed when he would countenance no opposition.

"And what of my visit to Miss Saunders?" she managed to ask, close to strangling on the words. "It's been projected since August, and I'm to leave day after tomorrow."

"That can easily be put off until spring. If young Huntleigh-Bowes is all Sir Evrard claims, mayhap you'll stop to see her on your bride journey. Besides, the roads'll be in better condition then," her father insisted with another smile as forced as it was fond. "I've never been pleased by the notion of your traveling alone so far from home at this time of year in any case."

"Alone? With my abigail, a footman, a coachman, two outriders, a courier, and a groom accompanying me? Especially as you've already sent another courier ahead to arrange for changes of teams and accommodations? That's hardly traveling alone, Papa."

It was amazing how unforced her laugh sounded—at least to her own ears.

"Far more sensible for Miss Saunders to come to us, especially at this season. She's a sensible woman. All governesses are—even retired ones. She'll understand." He scowled, still eyeing her dubiously. "Not playing games with me, are you?"

"Of course not, Papa."

He continued to watch her narrowly as they proceeded toward Brevett-on-Chipple. It was barely more than dawn given the season, the thin light as cold as the air, the carriage wheels jouncing across the frozen ruts and cracking the ice of what, at yesterday's high noon, had been puddles of snow melt. Sarah shivered despite the hot bricks at her feet, clinging to the strap and bracing for the next lurch. There were too many potholes for the coachman to avoid them all.

"I'd expected a tad more opposition," he said at last.

"So I can still surprise you? That's nice."

"None of this is to be repeated to your mother, if you please. She'd not understand."

"You might listen to her counsels on occasion. It would save you a deal of bother, and me a deal of discomfort. How will you explain my not departing for Kent as planned?" she said after drawing a deep breath. "You'll have to tell Mama something."

"Simplest thing in the world," he said, relaxing against the squabs. "Young Huntleigh-Bowes will stop by with some reports as a favor to Sir Evrard. I'll prevail upon him to linger a bit, and upon you to put off your trip. Nothing in the least out of the way in that. Your mother won't suspect a thing."

"She won't? I doubt you've ever played a game of which she wasn't completely aware, no matter what she pretends."

"Minx!" Then her father's expression sobered. "If young Huntleigh-Bowes's arrival is delayed, you merely need claim a minor indisposition. I'm afraid I must insist, Sarah, if you push me to it. I'll not have Sir Evrard offered the insult of your absenting yourself just now. It's he who arranged the visit."

"And doubtless held a pistol to his candidate's head, just as you are to mine. Is that how we came to be cursed with Mr. Broome in August? Certainly he was delivering letters, and certainly you prevailed upon him to linger—which meant I had to endure yet another gentleman casting calf's eyes on your coffers while considering my existence an inconvenience to be borne with stalwart fortitude when it couldn't be ignored."

"Robert Broome was of excellent family, outstanding prospects, and superior intelligence," John Timmons blustered, coloring slightly. "What you can have found in him to take in such dislike I shall never know."

"Why, precisely those attributes of which he had such an excessively elevated opinion, Papa. You mistook bombastic self-importance for worth, which surprised me greatly at the time. It was his tailor and barber were superior—not his understanding. Certainly Mama would never've countenanced such a nodcock for a husband."

"Ah, but then your mother is beyond compare."

"So are you, Papa," she murmured too softly to be heard, "both in your good points and your bad."

Had there ever been such a muddle? Yes, frequently—whenever her father, with the best intentions in the world, attempted to ensure her future. He should keep to his manufactories and leave her future to her; but there, he never had and he never would.

"And our situation is, ah, unique," he murmured, smiling fondly.

"It is indeed. Better to remain a spinster than to be chained to an arrogant, self-important, worthless lump of flesh who finds no value in me beyond the attractions of my eventual inheritance. We've discussed this before."

"Why you insist upon undervaluing yourself so I shall never understand," her father sighed.

"I'm passably well-acquainted with my looking glass."

"Then you should be able to read what it tells you," he snapped. "No, you're not in the latest style, but—"

"Papa, I'm a country sparrow—in miniature. My features are too sharp, my chin too definite, my nose too small, my eyes too assessing, my manner too assertive and unmissish.

Beyond those faults, should we wish to be charitable we may term me slender. I overheard a more candid description at my come-out: 'A scrawny plucked chicken with ice in her veins, but a wealthy one.' That was Mortimer Chudley: no chin and less intelligence; spots; shoulders of buckram and calves of sawdust. One popped. He left a trail. Surely you remember him?"

At least her father had the grace to flush. Endearing—that so elegant a gentleman could, on occasion, have the air of a stripling caught in an idiocy.

"He asked for my hand not two days later," she forged on, determined to put an end to the foolishness regarding Mr. Archer Huntleigh-Bowes, Esquire. "Is it any wonder I laughed in his face when he called me the fairest damsel he'd ever beheld? Yet you encouraged me to accept him."

"Why did you never tell me any of this before?"

"Because it didn't seem worth it. One way or another, every gentleman who has presented himself to date has proved as venal an opportunist as Mortimer Chudley. This one will be their twin, believe me." She sighed, gazing at her father imploringly. "Cancel this visit, or else don't invite the fellow to stay. Please, Papa."

"Archer Huntleigh-Bowes may surprise you," John Timmons insisted uneasily. "A former officer in Wellington's army, after all."

"You believe so? Why? None of the others have, and certainly forming part of the duke's 'infamous army' doesn't indicate he's ready for a pair of wings and a halo. Rather the opposite, in all likelihood."

"It's gonna snow ternight," the moppet trudging beside Sarah declared, inspecting a sky of so raw and clear a blue the color slashed the eyes like a knife. The late afternoon sun barely topped the hills, casting long shadows across the countryside and turning the rutted lane into a model of miniature mountains and valleys so ruggedly primordial they could have symbolized Earth on the first day. "Me gram said so."

" 'My grandmother,' Lucy," Sarah corrected absently, giving the child's hand a squeeze. " 'Tonight.' 'It will snow.' "

"That's what I said, ain't it? 'Portant thing isn't how you says a thing, but what you says. Leastways that's what Gram tol' me, an' she's old as the hills an's seen a hunnert times as much. Been smelling it coming fer two days now."

"She has?"

"Yes, miss. Lots o'snow. Wind too. It's in how the birds is acting, and the mice. Says now we live in town, we've forgetted how t'read the signs. She ain't forgot."

"No, I don't suppose she has," Sarah agreed, giving up on grammar lessons for the day.

They'd left the sturdy stone building converted for use as a school well behind, and were approaching the village. The time for being concerned with the irregularities of the verb "to forget" was over. It didn't do to press the children too hard. She'd learned that within days of taking over the school. Education had to be amusing or they balked.

Boots crunching on the crusted snow from an earlier storm, well bundled against the chill, the pair strode on, breaths clouding the air. Some yards ahead the other children raced and doubled back, shouting and laughing in their game of tag.

"S'warmer today, miss," Lucy continued, adroitly avoiding the potholes. "Allus gets warmer when it's coming on t'snow, Gram says. See how the water's running out from under the banks an' leaving little ledges? An' every place there's a rock or a bush there's a holler now."

"There is indeed."

"Puddles'll ice over t'night though. Be dangerous traveling by t'morrow. Maybe you oughtn'a be going down way past Lunnon t'visit your old governess just now?" The child didn't look at her directly, but Sarah could feel those bright dark eyes on her even so. "Take you two whole days t'get there, an' that's if there weren't no storm coming. Maybe you oughta bide here an' teach us instead just like allus, and wait until spring. We'll be missing you something fierce."

"It's only for a month," Sarah explained for the dozenth time that day, crossing her fingers in their thick mittens as the irony of it quirked her lips. Her father wasn't the only one attempting to delay her journey. "And you know how much you all enjoy it when the vicar or his sister assist with lessons."

"Won't be the same," Lucy insisted stubbornly.

"And then, my mama has promised to stop by. Think of all the new things you'll have to tell me when I return! She knows all sorts of wonderful games. And you can write me while I'm there, just as I'll write to you all every week. I've left the funds to pay for my letters with Miss Quade." A splendid notion, that had been. Excellent practice in composition and penmanship, let alone spelling. "Besides, if I didn't go what should I do with the lovely picture book you all made for me to while away the hours in Papa's carriage?"

"You could look at it at home nights."

"And Miss Saunders would be so disappointed," Sarah continued, going over some of the same ground she'd covered with her father that morning, and eliminating only more personal considerations. "She hasn't been well, you know."

"I suppose you gots to go, then."

"I do, indeed."

One by one the children scattered to their homes as they passed through the village. Then Sarah was alone on the lane leading to her father's house with only her thoughts and the little parcel containing the picture book for company. Those thoughts weren't pleasant ones any more than the few minutes in her father's carriage had been. But her mind was made up. She had just the remainder of the afternoon to get through, and then the evening, without betraying herself.

As the hands of clocks approached midnight of the day Archer Huntleigh-Bowes and Charles Moreland quitted London and John Timmons issued his orders regarding her visit to her former governess, Sarah gazed about her bedchamber, torn between the desire to laugh and the necessity to weep.

Packing for oneself wasn't a simple matter, especially if one had never been anywhere but Bath for a year at an exclusive seminary to give one a touch of Town bronze, and once—when one was quite young—into the Lake District to marvel at the durable wonders of nature rather than the ephemeral handiwork of man.

That those journeys had been made in one's father's luxurious traveling carriage, every need and whim seen to by others, was proving disastrous. That one's mother—and one's father as well—had accompanied one to render everything yet more agreeable helped not in the least.

She had been, Sarah decided with a wry grimace, unconscionably spoiled—a notion that had never before occurred to her. What a complacent, self-satisfied, arrogant, heedless little prig she was! The welter of belongings strewn on her canopied bed and the velvet settee by the fireplace was proof enough of that. Never had the room appeared in such disarray. Never had such a salutary lesson been so well merited.

She'd always believed herself the soul of organization. Compared to her, the lowliest scullery maid was a pattern card of forethought, she an infant still drooling down the bib of its pinafore.

One had to decide which items were absolutely essential, which frivolities not to be considered.

One had to take only what one could carry oneself, as one would be traveling by common stage and would have to walk to the crossroads just beyond Whittelsy—a full five miles in the bitter cold of a windy, moonlit winter night—to board that stage.

One had to ponder the appearance one would present as a traveler. That of the pampered daughter of a wealthy mill owner from the Midlands was quite the opposite of what was required. Unfortunately, no matter how restrained one's customary garb, it still more than hinted at one's origins.

Sarah turned her back on the mess and parted the draperies, leaning her head against a windowpane in hopes the chill would ease the throbbing of her temples. She had much rather not be quitting Brevett-on-Chipple on a forbidding January night, but her father had left her no choice. Archer Huntleigh-Bowes was little more than an expensive fribble, given his description. A rattle, a reckless top-sawyer who amused himself racing his curricle when the inclination struck him, a dedicated gamester, a confirmed rake and, given all the rest, a gazetted fortune hunter. It was as much in what her father'd claimed for Huntleigh-Bowes as what he hadn't.

Dear heaven—what was he about, ordering her to chain herself to such a wastrel? That the man was a distant connection of her mother's, a member of the *ton,* and a former officer who'd seen honorable service made his presence in her life not one whit more acceptable than if he'd sprung from the stews of London, the scion of a cutpurse and the darling of a slattern.

Certainly when she'd rejected Mr. Broome's offer, made in form in August, her father had listed the proposals she'd turned down—eleven since she turned nineteen and reluctantly made her bows to the limited society to be found in the environs of Brevett-on-Chipple. That—as her father had pointed out again only hours before, calling her into his study for still another conference concerning Mr. Huntleigh-Bowes's advent—amounted to two and three-quarters gentlemen per year who hadn't met her exacting standards. He'd threatened in August to find her a husband if she didn't find one herself by the first of the year. She'd never believed he'd carry out his threat. The notion was preposterous—that her beloved and adoring father would force her to something she held in repugnance. She'd had the wrong of it. That he claimed it was for her own good made not the least difference.

She sighed, let the draperies drop, glancing at the writing table where she customarily planned lessons. She'd cleared away the books and papers. The simple brass standish, for once neatly centered, called attention to the folded sheet of paper containing a note to her father.

Hers was admittedly an odd sort of running away. One didn't customarily inform those whom one was fleeing of one's destination, let alone the period one anticipated being absent. But, as she'd strongly hinted to her father, someone else could rescue Archer Huntleigh-Bowes from the consequences of his undoubted profligacy. Filial duty and maidenly obedience had their limits.

She slipped card case, well-provisioned purse, and handkerchief into her oldest reticule, then began tossing random items into the battered portmanteau she'd unearthed in the attics. Moments later a quick heft proved it would be far too heavy to carry to the end of the drive, let alone to the crossroads beyond Whittelsy.

She frowned, then pulled the old shawl in which she customarily carried books and papers from the portmanteau and spread it on the bed. When ordinary people traveled they didn't have expensive luggage, not even antiquated expensive luggage. At best they might have a wicker hamper or a pasteboard valise and a bundle or two. And women's bundles? They were invariably tied up in shawls past their prime. Sometimes necessity had the air of cleverness. Given the depth of her purse, she could replace in Kent anything she lacked. She wasn't going there to cut a dash.

Not half an hour later, garbed in her plainest winter

gown, a spencer of thick wool, a quilted gray pelisse, and her oldest mantle and bonnet, clutching the clumsy bundle she'd contrived, Sarah slipped from a side door and gazed about her.

The half moon sailing in the midnight sky might not give much light, partly veiled as it was by scudding clouds and haloed by higher thin wisps, but the reflections from the snow-covered ground doubled and tripled its meager glow. She could see well enough not to lose her way or twist an ankle. That was what counted.

As she reached the first bend in the drive she turned, looking back at the sleeping house. She wasn't certain even her mother would understand what she was about, supportive though she had been when Sarah sent previous suitors packing. Rejecting nonentities was one thing. Taking matters into her own hands in this manner might be viewed by even Georgiana Timmons as a trifle extreme, for all she'd come close to committing what the world viewed as a worse solecism when she wed. That her mother, and not the world, had had the right of it then just as Sarah did now might not help.

And then she shrank into the shadows cast by one of the soaring chestnuts lining the drive, heart pounding. Was that a figure at her parents' bedchamber window? To be stopped now, caught like a child with a forbidden sweet in its mouth, would be unbearable. But no, trick of the light or guilty imagination, whatever the flash of white had been seemed to melt into nothingness. She waited to see if it reappeared. When it didn't she sighed and squared her shoulders.

Slipping as her boots broke through the hard crust of the week-old snow, Sarah turned her back on the securities of hearth and home and trudged down the curving drive toward the lane leading in one direction to Brevett-on-Chipple, in the other to the Whittelsy crossroads where she would catch the stage. The frozen ridges left by carriage wheels and carts were making her progress slower than she'd anticipated. It was a good thing she'd allowed more than enough time.

The Best-laid Plans

John Timmons descended late to breakfast the next morning, lulled into oversleeping by the sigh of snow against the windows and the soughing of the wind about the eaves. A peek from his bedchamber window when hushed night eased into hushed dawn had convinced him neither he nor his workers would reach the manufactory that day. The storm's sibilant whispers only emphasized the underlying preternatural silence, a ghostly sort of waiting in which time seemed suspended. A time of magic when all things were possible.

And then he chuckled at his unaccustomed fancifulness. A pragmatic designer of more efficient and safer manufacturing devices, a man charmed by numbers who found a smoothly functioning machine more beautiful than the fairest woman, speak of the preternatural or consider magic? Ridiculous!

It was merely a good day to be at home. He would, he decided as he entered the breakfast parlor and gave the bellpull a sharp tug, have another talk with Sarah regarding young Huntleigh-Bowes. Oh, she'd been accepting enough when he insisted she give the fellow a chance. The problem was, she'd been too accepting. Either she planned mischief, or she didn't care. Either way, he didn't like it.

Only Parkins appeared, coffee pot in hand. Odd, that. He gave the man a genial nod as he glanced at the spot beside his place where the early post and London journals customarily waited. That morning, given the weather, there should have been nothing, but there was. A note. Addressed to him in Sarah's hand. Neatly folded and primly sealed.

Timmons stared at the thing with a sinking heart, willing it to vanish. It didn't.

"Where did that come from?" he managed, pointing.

"Miss Timmons's abigail found it on her worktable when she delivered a can of hot water at the usual hour."

"And Betty brought you the letter, and you brought it here."

"Yes, sir."

Timmons nodded, dreading the obvious next question and already knowing the answer. "Has my daughter's bed been slept in?"

"No, sir. Betty is in the housekeeper's room, sir. I've told her to say nothing, and I set Mrs. Twiddy to inventorying the stillroom to keep them separate."

"I see. Excellent thinking. Thank you. Coffee, Parkins. Nothing else just yet. And," he sighed, "if you'd send word to Mrs. Timmons that I'd appreciate her joining me as soon as possible?"

He sat after Parkins vanished, staring at Sarah's note as if even touching it would set in train events he didn't want to contemplate, determinedly sipping the scalding black brew and trying not to think. It didn't work. He picked the damned thing up. He cursed all independent misses with more intelligence than was good for them. He even wondered, if only briefly, if the wealth he'd amassed over the years might be more bane than boon. And then, sighing once more, he broke the wax seal and opened the thing.

As ever with Sarah, it was short and to the point—if hardly sweet. She was making her visit to Miss Saunders as planned, and intended to extend that visit until he came to his senses regarding Archer Huntleigh-Bowes and her own spinster state. He was not to worry—she had sufficient funds to defray the expenses of her journey. He could tell Mama anything he wished. She was, she insisted with a firm underscoring of the words, his most dutiful and obedient daughter in most things, but not in this. The final words—*I'm sorry, Papa, and would have preferred not to displease you in anything, but you've forced me to it*—brought a lump to his throat. *Had you wanted a mindless ninny for a daughter, you should've raised me differently.*

He rose then, going to the windows to stare out into the winter storm.

The wind, after merely flirting with the prettily tumbling flakes at dawn, had become a driving force during the last minutes. He could swear it had. And the snow was heavier, a white curtain hiding all but the nearest landmarks. The drifts must be horrendous in less sheltered spots, capable of swallowing a coach and team.

Where was she? Traveling how? And in what circumstances? She was nothing but a green girl, an innocent, easy prey for plausible rascals and chousing innkeepers, and those were the most honest sorts she was likely to encounter. He had to mount a search party. He had to find her. Blast it, he'd never've insisted she actually marry the fellow!

"John? Is something wrong?"

He turned from the window at the soft voice behind him. "She's bolted," he blurted without a thought as to how his gentle wife would receive the news.

"Sarah?" Georgiana smiled at him from the door, then came over to the window, slipping her hand in his. Together they stared at the storm. "Yes, I know. She left about midnight, carrying what looked to be a bundle wrapped in an old shawl. I couldn't sleep, and was watching the moon and the clouds, and so I saw her."

"You didn't stop her?" he roared, whirling to face his wife.

"Of course not. Sarah's infinitely sensible. If she felt called upon to begin a journey in the middle of the night, she must have had a compelling reason. Don't scowl so—you'll give yourself the headache."

He stared at her, eyes narrowing. "She hasn't been complaining to you, has she?"

"Sarah never complains. What have you done to cause her to run off in this impetuous manner? Impetuosity isn't her long suit."

He sighed, turning back to the window.

"She's out in that mess," he said softly. "I must go after her."

"What have you done, John?"

"Nothing."

"Sarah would never behave in such a fashion without extreme provocation."

"Nothing, I tell you!" he exploded.

"John?"

Her hand was resting on his arm now, her face turned up to his.

"I invited Huntleigh-Bowes to come visit," he muttered after a moment. "He should arrive in the next day or two."

"I'm sorry, my dear, but I don't understand. Why would Sarah flee Sir Evrard? She's been pleading for him to come to us since his first letter. I know she'd've put off her departure for Kent on the instant, then traveled back to London with him."

"Not Sir Evrard."

"Who, then?"

"The young one. You know—former ward. The military fellow who's sold out."

"Oh, dear heaven—not again?" she sighed.

"He needs settling down and Sarah needs livening up," Timmons insisted.

"And I suppose you and my grandfather concocted this scheme between the two of you, and kept it secret from Lady Huntleigh-Bowes as well."

"Sarah wants a husband."

"No, my dear—you want her to have one. There's a deal of difference."

"She's out in that maelstrom," he said, returning to the main point as he knew his position on the other was untenable, at least in his wife's eyes.

"Yes, she is. You might consider the probable results the next time you decide to concoct another of your ill-conceived plots. The feckless popinjays and self-important nonentities you've paraded before her would be enough to turn any rational young woman's stomach. Little wonder she wanted to avoid another such encounter."

"Georgiana," he began.

She cut him off, informing him that standing before the window staring at the snow served no one, and in the meantime their breakfast was getting cold. They'd put it about that Sarah had left for Kent a day early because of the opportunity to make the journey with friends who'd stopped by briefly in the middle of the night, racing to beat the storm. She'd been awake and given Sarah permission.

"But look at it out there," he protested.

"She's traveling ahead of the storm. Sarah will be just fine."

"And if she hasn't managed to stay ahead of it?"

"No matter what port she finds, you may be sure it's a safe and secure one. If it's not, she'll make it so."

"Damme, but it's cold!" Charles Moreland gasped into the wind somewhat later that same day, then drained the last of their remaining flask of brandy down his throat. "That's the end of it," he sighed. "Should've brought a cask with us."

"There's a fur robe under the seat."

"A robe ain't what I need. Shelter is."

"Stubble it." Archer Huntleigh-Bowes clenched his chattering teeth, pulled the brim of his hat lower over his eyes, then drew his neck into his coat like a turtle as he squinted through the driving flakes. "I'm as m-much of an iceberg as you are."

What had been merely the most decorous of flurries when they departed the inn that morning was rapidly transforming itself into a storm to be reckoned with. Unconscionable—for such a glorious lark to turn sour without so much as a by-your-leave. The curricle wheels, now heavily caked with snow, dragged in the thick blanket covering everything in sight. That that sight often didn't extend more than a few yards on either side and barely more than that ahead was hardly encouraging. As for his prized bays, they were plodding like spavined breakdowns rather than the valuable bits of blood and bone they were, heads hanging low, ears plastered against their skulls.

Beside him, Charles shivered. Occasional hedgerows offered no shelter from the wind. Drifts filled the ditches and threatened the road. Traveling via the back lanes recommended by the ostler where they stopped the night before had proved as serious an error in judgment as Charles predicted.

"It's no worse than the Corunna retreat," Archer said, more to reassure himself than Charles. "Bivouacked under worse conditions many a time."

"We were more or less equipped for it then." Charles retrieved the robe and bundled it about them any which way he could. "And we were expecting it, you'll remember, and there was no help for it in any case. Had plenty of choice this time. Should've stayed in London."

"Guess you liked the notion of old Leighton making a sieve of you?"

"I'd've avoided it. Not such a bad shot myself, come to that. Besides, that's not what I meant, and you know it."

"So you say. We'll stop at the next inn, no matter what its sort."

"Inn?" Charles snorted. "Probably nothing better than a hedgerow tavern. We could be trapped for days."

"Prefer being trapped in this? Or a barn?"

"Dear Lord, no! I've bunked with enough bovines to last me a lifetime."

"Chickens're worse, except when they're in a pot. At least there'll be no question of our continuing to Brevett-on-Chipple, for which I dearly thank providence. Could be delayed a month, and I wouldn't mind in the least. Maybe some other poor sod'll please in the interim, and I'll escape. We're sure to come upon something soon."

"Don't want it to get about I've stayed in a place of the sort we're likely to stumble across out here though," Charles grumbled.

"So concerned with your consequence? Didn't seem to matter in the Peninsula."

"This isn't the Peninsula. It gets about I've permitted you to tumble me into another bumblebroth, I'll never hear the end of it. Fellows're beginning to call me a noddy as it is."

"Go by an assumed name, then. Wouldn't much care for the tale to get about m'self, and they have the nastiest habit of doing so."

"An assumed name? Now, there's a fine notion," Charles retorted, tone wandering between despair and amusement.

"I think so. Excellent solution to all our problems. Who'll you be?"

"There's no hope for it, I suppose. This gets about, I'll be in worse case than ever. Charles Moore, then," his companion suggested. "Close enough that I won't forget who I am if someone says it, and you won't forget what to call me."

"And I'd best do the same. I have my reputation to consider as well, what's left of it—or Sir Evrard's. Wouldn't want it getting about his godson mired himself in this sort of scrape," Archer agreed with a chuckle. "Wouldn't dare show my face in Town for a month of Sundays. Besides, it'll be rather a lark—being someone else for a change, and with no fear it'll get back to my undeviatingly conventional godfather. Wouldn't mind being someone else permanently, come to that. How does Archibald Dozier strike you?"

"Will you be serious!"

"No, I don't like it either. Makes me sound like a hairless vicar in need of a nap. Archimedes Leigh's too schoolmasterish. Arcturus LeBeau? No, he's a caper merchant who sprang from the stews and ought to get himself back there."

Charles chuckled in spite of himself. "Keep it simple. Arthur—that's close enough I can get my tongue around it. Arthur Hunt. Neither of us'll forget that one."

In the event "soon" proved to be something over an hour, by which time Archer was leading his team, their portmanteaux buckled to the harness, his crippled curricle abandoned in a ditch. Charles forged ahead, testing the road for more hidden potholes with what remained of the axle, the carriage robe flapping from his shoulders like a pilgrim's cape, the fur turned inward. It wasn't the most prepossessing of hamlets they happened on, but at least the well-kept little church indicated it probably wasn't a thieves' hideaway, and the inn—little more than a tavern, just as Charles had predicted—appeared tidy and had an adequate stable. While Archer saw to his cattle, Charles hired the only two bedchambers the place offered, instructed the beds be aired and fires lit to take off the chill. He then repaired to the taproom where he ordered a restorative bowl of punch, genially offering a cup to the pair of ancients huddling at a table near the fire.

It wasn't a bad place of its sort, Archer agreed when he stumbled into the low-beamed room, knocking the snow from his boots, unwinding the scarves shielding his neck and ears, and divesting himself of his greatcoat, hat, and gloves. The place was scrupulously clean, the fire was hot, and the tempting aromas of roasting chicken and simmering stew floating from the kitchen boded well for their supper.

More to the point, his pair was snugly stabled and the ostler seemed to know what he was about.

Archer helped himself to a liberal portion of the steaming punch, gratefully breathing in vapors redolent of lemons and cinnamon and heavy dark rum, and something else infinitely attractive but damnably elusive.

"Wish you'd give me the method for preparing this," he grumbled, sipping it carefully to avoid burning his tongue after introducing himself to the taciturn pair at the table. "Best order up another bowl, as you insist on sharing," he added.

The antiquated, ill-sprung coach lurched through another pothole, tossing the luckless passengers like dice in a cup. The portly, backward-facing commercial traveler across from Sarah uttered a groan and clutched the shoulder of the tetchy solicitor beside him. The rest sorted themselves out in resigned silence. Such dislodgings were too frequent to merit comment or protest.

Little Lucy Potts had been correct: There'd been snow. Lots of it. There still was, and wind, and all sorts of unpleasantness—especially when one considered the unheated common conveyance filled with strangers who didn't necessarily bathe as often as they should, and the refusal of the coachman to stop at an inn to wait out the storm. No amount of reasoning had touched him, not even citing the pitiful condition of the children traveling alone to join their parents at a beloved aunt's deathbed. He'd been as deaf to her words as he was blind to the weather, insisting he had a schedule to keep—a most unusual experience for the sole offspring of Brevett-on-Chipple's premier employer and wealthiest resident. Of course, Sarah sighed, it was reasonable enough when one considered she journeyed as Sally Bowen of Nowhere-in-Particular rather than Miss Timmons of Brevett-on-Chipple.

Bad as it was within, it must have been many times worse on the roof where two gentlemen of uncertain occupation and tippling habits and the stolid abigail of the widow next to her clung for dear life.

Sarah sneezed, blew her nose—which must be as red as a cherry, and certainly had grown as raw as an open wound over the past hours—then settled the diminutive pair against her more comfortably. Timmy and Alice Clarke were all pointed elbows, sharp shoulders, and heavy heads, poor mites. She must be a mass of bruises, but at least they were dozing rather than suffering through this endless purgatory.

The woman directly across from her, a brassy-curled actress garbed in scarlet returning to her troupe following a special engagement in York, gave her a halfhearted smile. Sarah nodded, closed her eyes.

Sleep might be impossible, but the semblance of it yielded a modicum of privacy in which to suffer. Privacy, she'd discovered that day, was a luxury she had never sufficiently prized, having been blessed with it all her life. The deep-voiced widow who shared the forward-facing banquette with her and the children had seemed to feel owed her life history, along with the life histories, destinations, and reason for traveling of every other passenger, dispensing peppermints and opinions with equal liberality. Strange, to suddenly become one of the "lower orders," forced to explain oneself—and into a multitude of prevarications and half-truths in the process.

It had been for Sarah that Mrs. Tizzet reserved her primary scold, however. A young woman shouldn't travel alone. No, not even to her new post. She should be accompanied by an abigail at the least. Such carelessness, Mrs. Tizzet prophesied darkly, could lead to ruin and worse. She would even lend Miss Bowen the services of her own dear Hettie, were it not that to do so would prove exceedingly inconvenient.

Nothing had served to stem the wearisome flood of remonstrances and cautions. Only the prying widow's attempt to take up a collection for the purpose of providing Sarah with a suitable traveling companion brought it to an end, and then only when a mortified Sarah proved she had no need of such largesse—at which point Mrs. Tizzet reproved her for permitting them to ascertain the exact depth of her pockets while eyeing the horde of shillings and guineas with considerable surprise.

The coach was merely creeping now. Sarah stifled an involuntary gasp as it plummeted into a particularly deep hole, lurching like a top at the end of its spin. It jounced back onto the snow-covered road, swaying ever more violently as the passengers slid one way and then the other. The coachman howled something into the teeth of the storm. There was a breathless moment. Then, with a groan of protesting wood, the decrepit conveyance slued and teetered and gave up the fight, sliding into a snowy ditch with the far side door resting in the broken branches of a hedgerow.

There were sighs of resignation from the passengers. Another delay to go with all the others. The women and the two children would huddle by the side of the road after assisting to unload the boot. The men would push and the horses pull. It would take a bit, but eventually they'd be on their way again, boots filled with snow, fingers numbed, and with no hope of rest until the coachman decided he'd had enough.

Sarah lowered the window. The guard was already at the team's head, soothing the shuddering beasts. The coachman shook his fist as he limped toward a farm wagon blocking the road.

"Oh, dear," she murmured.

"What d'you see?" Mrs. Tizzet tugged Sarah's sleeve. "Come now, Miss Bowen—it isn't kind to keep us in suspense."

"While we're suspending ourselves by straps, in any case," the actress, a Mrs. Selena Montague, murmured.

"There's a problem," Sarah admitted.

"Naturally," the wiry solicitor sniffed. "Been a problem ever since I boarded this dreadful contraption."

"Always the same when a coach's carrying females," Mr. Peabody, the commercial traveler, grumbled in agreement. "Even worse when there're children. Come to grief every time. Shouldn't be allowed to step outside the door, females and children shouldn't. There ought to be a law against it."

Selena Montague's silvery laugh went no further toward settling ruffled cock's feathers than did Mrs. Tizzet's incensed, "This is *not* the Dark Ages. Why, even Good Queen Bess traveled about."

"What need've you to go anywhere?" Peabody retorted. "Just enjoying yourself, that's all you're doing. You hadn't been here, I could've had two places to myself."

"*I* should forego a visit to my dearest sister so *you* could lollygag?"

The children unwisely tittered, then shrank back at the commercial traveler's malevolent glare.

"And what of Miss Bowen," Mrs. Tizzet fumed on, "who's traveling to her new post?"

"Wonder what sort of employment it may be if she's so deep in the pocket," Peabody mumbled, then reddened at Sarah's gasp.

"More likely, it's precisely the sort of thing you imply that's sent her searching for a new position," Selena Montague sneered.

"Stop this bickering on the instant!" Sarah snapped.

Six heads spun in her direction.

"And if that doesn't prove she's the schoolmistress she claims to be," Mrs. Montague chuckled with sudden good humor, "nothing will."

Sarah sorted them out. She scolded and cajoled and comforted and quelled, and bundled the children in her own cloak because they were shivering uncontrollably.

She convinced the farmer that the carriage horses could free his wagon, the coachman to lend his horses, commandeered the farmer's wagon to ferry them to the country inn he said lay two miles farther along, paying him for his trouble from her own purse as the coachman insisted it wasn't his responsibility, and begged stabling for the coach team in the farmer's barn when he insisted the inn stables would be inadequate.

She convinced the travelers to take only the essentials for a stay of a night or two, and ignored Selena Montague's amusement at the sight of her own bundle and the actress's soft-spoken, "What sort of wheedle d'you think you're cutting, my dear? It won't wash with any who take a look at your hands or hear your voice, you know."

She assigned them places in the farmer's wagon and ignored the solicitor's acid comments regarding being forced to ride in the same wagon as servants. Then, duty done, she collapsed in the wagon and pulled the children against her, suspecting it might almost have been better to remain in Brevett-on-Chipple and endure Mr. Huntleigh-Bowes's attentions than flee them.

Charles and Archer were well into their third bowl of punch, not noticeably more than a trifle above par, and had been commenting only moments before on how pleasant it was to have such a cozy place to themselves—for the storm had worsened, the tavern habitués long since departed—when pounding at the taproom door roused them from their pleasantly somnolent state.

Charles slitted one dark eye, watching with foreboding as the serving girl—a buxom wench married to the innkeeper's son who played at ostler when he wasn't sleeping by the kitchen fire—bustled across the room, drying her hands on her apron.

"I'm acoming," she shouted. "Haven't got but two feet to last me my life, y'know. No sense wearing 'em out ahead of time."

As she hoisted the bar—which had been lowered when the village venerables made their departure—Charles prodded Archer's leg with the toe of his boot.

"Best wake up," he murmured. "We're about to be invaded."

" 'Nother cup?" Archer mumbled. "Don't mind if I do. Excellent punch, Charles. Wish you'd tell me the secret of it."

"Day you wed's the day I'll tell you," Charles yawned. "Soften the blow."

That brought Archer rigidly erect.

"Thought you were shamming it," his friend grinned.

Archer turned at the blast of cold air. "Close that door!" he roared. Then, "Oh, Lord, this tears it. Knew it was too good to last."

Through the door was straggling a motley company of travelers, knocking the snow from their boots and shaking it from their shoulders.

"There're even *children*," he came close to whimpering as a prim sort lacking so much as a cloak drew a pair of snow-crusted ragamuffins before the fire and began untangling them from a haphazard assortment of outerwear. "Here, you—boy, don't drip all over m'boots," he protested. "They're in sad enough case as it is."

The look their mother turned on him would've frozen hell.

"Remove yourselves from the fire," she commanded as if they were a pair of subalterns and she a captain at the least. "Timmy and Alice are chilled to the bone. And if you could see to something warm for them to drink, that wouldn't be amiss either."

By damn, the reason the woman had no cloak was that she'd wrapped hers around her children. He had to admire that. Without thinking, Archer took the sodden garment from her and extended his cup of punch. She took it, sniffed delicately.

"Not for the children, I think, though a very small bit might be what's called for, even for them."

Her sudden amused smile was a surprise.

"Of course. Hot barley water, perhaps, or hot lemonade?"

"We're permitted tea on special occasions," the little girl with the wistful eyes of a spaniel suggested.

"You are, Alice?" the bedraggled female said.

The boy nodded. "Especially when we're wet."

"Tea it shall be then, or cambric tea at the least."

"No, real tea," the boy insisted, then conceded, "though Nurse does water it and puts in lots of sugar and milk."

"Fine lad, ma'am," Archer said under cover of the cacophony. "Honest to the core, and your Alice's something special. You must be proud of them both."

The young woman's face flamed as if he'd painted it red. "I, ah, they—"

"Miss Bowen, perhaps you'd like to wrap them in these." A statuesque female in red sauntered up, extending a pair of comforters. "The children really need to be gotten out of those wet clothes."

"Thank you, Mrs. Montague."

"Think nothing of it, my dear," the older woman murmured, eyes twinkling as the syllables rolled from her tongue with the penetrating sonority of fine organ music.

Archer glanced from one to the other. Mistress and servant? The one he'd taken to be the children's mother was their governess, perhaps, or a new nurserymaid?

"Here now, I want one of those," a florid-complexioned, portly fellow protested, his plaid waistcoat screaming of failed attempts at dandyism and sloppy eating habits. "I was the one asked for 'em, after all."

"And can wait your turn," the woman in red retorted. "You're a grown man, Mr. Peabody. The children come first."

"I'll have my coverlet," the fellow roared, lunging for the little governess.

Only swift action on the part of a robust, strong-featured female in black wielding a battered bandbox kept the lout from his prey. Archer spared Charles a quick glance. His back was turned, his shoulders convulsing. Fine friend Charles was, abandoning him to deal with this lot! There must be a dozen at the least. If one of them didn't step lively, their fine dinner bid fair to vanish down the gullets of those not nearly so deserving.

"I say," Archer sputtered, "what d'you think you're doing, assaulting a lady?"

"She ain't no lady. Besides, what business has she, worrying about those brats? Aren't hers, after all. Do her a sight more good to see to me."

The fellow who wanted a coverlet threw Archer a significant glance, eyes sliding from the woman in red to her employee. Archer took a second look, brows rising.

So that's the way it was: experienced hen escorting tender young pullet. A little long in the tooth for a neophyte, perhaps, but "Miss Bowen" had a ladylike air about her that would appeal to those who didn't demand wanton children in their beds, and she certainly was untouched. She'd flinched as if scorched when their hands accidentally met moments before, blushing like a schoolgirl.

What had been a dammed inconvenience began to take on pleasanter possibilities. With a slight bow, he sidled over to Charles.

"Tempting filly, that one," he said, forcing back a hiccough.

Charles looked him up and down, then glanced at Miss Bowen.

"You're all about in your head," he murmured. "She's a schoolmistress, or something of the sort. Reminds me of the woman had charge of m'sisters."

"Not a bit of it. Joining the profession. Had it from one of the passengers. Female in red's her abbess."

"And I'm the Prince Regent. Lay you a guinea."

"Ten to one, and make it a monkey." Archer grinned, certain of his ground. "Probably found country life dull. It is!"

"Y'can't afford such odds. A single guinea, even money, and I'll win."

"You think so? I'll have her in my bed before we leave this inn."

"Y'won't so much as steal a kiss," Charles chuckled.

Sarah sighed, glancing around the smoke-filled taproom after wiping Alice's hands and face with a damp cloth, then nodded at the child's wide-eyed glance at the plate of Turkish delight the innkeeper's wife had brought out as a treat for the children. Across the way Mr. Moore was performing similar services for Timmy while Mrs. Tizzet continued to play Grand Inquisitress regarding the Londoners' origins (modestly *ton*nish), service in the Peninsula (dreadful food, delightful señoritas), and reasons for travel at this season (an essential repairing lease).

The weary travelers were still at table, the gentlemen indulging in brandy and cigarillos, the ladies sipping tea. They were all fed at last—a copious enough meal, even if the innkeeper's wife had been forced to overburden the stew with turnips and potatoes so there'd be enough for all. Soon they'd be retiring for the night. The moment couldn't come soon enough, though things had finally sorted themselves out despite acerbic quarrels between the put-upon travelers that culminated in a bout of fisticuffs between the coachman and an outmatched Mr. Peabody, and ended only when Sarah threatened to pour the last of the Londoners' punch over the combatants. Then Mr. Moore had obligingly separated them, though only after he'd spent several moments bent over laughing—a total waste of time and energy, as she'd informed him in no uncertain terms.

And then there'd been Mr. Hunt's reprehensible behavior. Sarah shuddered, not even wanting to consider that unpleasant little episode.

At least she'd shamed the London wastrels into sacrificing their bedchambers for the common good. Unfortunately there would be only an attic pallet for her and the children, for Mrs. Tizzet indulged in a case of the vapors when faced with the prospect of disrobing in the presence of a male, no matter how young. The Londoners would doss down in the taproom. They'd bivouacked in far less pleasant surroundings, the stocky, superficially more courteous Mr. Moore had insisted.

Mr. Hunt—taller, with eyes that were strangely haunted when he thought no one watched—currently sat in a corner nursing his ringing ears and sore head, and indulging in a case of the sulks. Well, he and his insulting words could stay right there as far as Sarah was concerned. Permanently. Mr. Moore was at least civil, no matter what his suspicions regarding her current or future employment. Mr. Hunt, on the other hand, had clearly imbibed more punch than was good for him and behaved accordingly. Beyond that detail there wasn't much to choose between the pair, typical of the breed as they were from their elegantly cropped heads to their heavy gold fobs and doubtless valuable antique signet rings.

Sarah buried a sneeze in the handkerchief earlier lent her by Mr. Moore, then smiled reassuringly at Alice.

"We'll go upstairs to bed in a moment," she whispered hoarsely under cover of the desultory conversations being carried on around the table. "You must be about to crumble. I know I am."

"But our mama always tells us a story before we go to bed. By the nursery fire." Alice's lower lip quivered. "She rocks and rocks, and her voice goes lower and lower, and then Papa puts me in bed and tucks me in, and tells me I'm his bonny lass. I miss Mama and Papa," she said.

"And would have been with them today were it not for this dreadful storm. I know you do, and I'm sure they miss you too. Perhaps the snow'll stop tomorrow."

"I don't think so," Timmy said from across the table. "Maybe you'd better tell Alice a story, Miss Bowen. It won't be the same as Mama doing it, but Alice gets dreadful upset when things aren't as usual. She cries."

Sarah sighed at Mr. Moore's encouraging nod. There was clearly no help for it. A story there must be, and she was the one elected to tell it. They moved to the fire, and she made quick work of "The Frog Prince," dropping her voice as Alice's head rested ever more heavily against her shoulder. She ignored the protests that it wasn't a charming frog who was transformed into an obnoxious prince nor a lovely girl frog who transformed him back, merely informing those still at the table she was the one telling the tale. She gave but one pointed glance at the still-sulking Mr. Hunt and even more carefully ignored Mr. Moore's delighted chuckles and meaningful glances at his friend.

Once the tale was done—to a round of soft applause that embarrassed Sarah and caused Mr. Moore to give her another of his saucy grins—the two young men carried the drowsy children to the attics and helped her settle them down. As the gentlemen descended the stairs, Mr. Moore's murmured, *"Now* will you admit she's a governess?" floated back to her clearly.

"After that tale?" Mr. Hunt's chuckle was as rueful as it was amused. "Willingly. Whenever I went beyond what was acceptable, my own nurse used to tell a similar one of which I was also the butt."

And then the gentlemen's footsteps faded. Sarah joined the children on the pallet without undressing, choking back yet another bout of sneezes, and ignoring the uncomfortable lump of the reticule whose strings were firmly twisted around her wrist for safekeeping.

It was just as she was drifting off that Alice, apparently believing her to be already asleep, whispered, "Timmy?"

"Mmm?"

"I like Miss Bowen."

"Mmm."

"And I like the barmy one."

"Shouldn' use that word, Allie. Mama wouldn' like it."

"He's nice."

"Mmm."

"But the bonny one has sad eyes. Tomorrow I'm going to try to make him smile." The moppet snuggled closer and yawned. "I like him too."

Slowly her breathing stilled. Beside her Sarah stared at the darkness, now fully awake. Perhaps she, too, should attempt to make the bonny one smile on the morrow. There'd been no need to box his ears quite so forcefully, no matter what he'd said or done. Her own mama had always claimed one needed to make allowances for gentlemen who were slightly above par, and had lost the capacity for correct behavior.

Sarah awoke the next morning numbed to the core. The rough uneven attic floor had caused aches in all sorts of unlikely places—aches reinforced by the fierce head cold she'd developed during the night and the heaviness in her chest. Her throat was rough. Her watering eyes felt as if sand had been ground in them, and her face was at once burning hot and freezing cold. Her hands and feet were blocks of ice. The rest of her seemed afire for all she shivered uncontrollably.

She wanted nothing more than she wanted her own bed, her abigail to stoke the fire and bring her drafts of hot lemonade and bowls of chicken broth, her mother to bathe her temples with lavender water and send to the apothecary for headache powders. Certainly she had need of some! And to bury her head in her own soft pillows and close her eyes and shut out the world. Above all she wanted an unending supply of clean, fresh handkerchiefs in which to blow her nose, and no one to require anything of her—not even civility.

But the children were stirring. For the past quarter hour Timmy had been claiming he smelled sizzling bacon and fresh muffins. It could be true, for all she knew. She couldn't smell a thing, but they wanted their breakfast. Their faces and hands needed washing, their hair untangling, their wrinkled, slept-in clothes brushing.

So this was what being a mother meant, Sarah groaned as she dragged herself to her feet, fastened her boots, twitched her skirts, and then untied her bundle. Cramming comb and brush into her reticule, she decided motherhood was a state, like marriage, to be avoided as long as possible. All the lovely things said about it were propaganda on the part of gentlemen who didn't involve themselves in its more unpleasant details.

She piled her possessions—the picture book her students had made, a chemise, a spare gown now so crumpled that the one she'd slept in seemed fresh by comparison, a nightgown, a pair of stockings—neatly by the pallet, then pulled the old shawl around her shoulders.

Finally they descended the stairs and entered the empty taproom. Gratefully Sarah settled at the table and sent the children to the kitchen to wash their hands and faces. Perhaps someone else would brush their clothes and comb their hair. She simply wasn't up to the effort. A body could stand only so much, she conceded, blowing her nose repeatedly in Mr. Moore's borrowed handkerchief.

She closed her eyes, making herself as small as possible, clutching her reticule and praying the world would go away. It didn't. First came a blast of frigid air as the door to the exterior opened, along with hearty laughter that could come only from the London wastrels. Then the serving girl was at her side with a pot of scalding tea, inquiring as to what she and the children wanted to eat.

Dry toast for herself, Sarah told the young woman, wanting to box her ears for being so unnaturally cheerful, and porridge for the children, and eggs and muffins, and bacon, and whatever else they fancied that was to hand. Sarah pulled her purse from her reticule.

"Oh, that's been taken care of, miss," the girl said with a grin and a wink. "By Mr. Hunt."

Sarah glanced across the taproom to where the ne'er-do-wells stood by the door, unwinding scarves and watching her carefully.

"But that's entirely unnecessary," she protested, flushing. "I have the wherewithal to meet my own shot."

"And the tikes' too? Not charging you but half the value of a bedchamber for the attic and half o' that for the children, but you could all three eat like Goliath and not make a dent in what Mr. Hunt's given my pa-in-law," the serving girl grinned. "Don't worry yourself about Alice and Timmy neither. My mam-in-law has 'em patting out tarts. They're getting floury, but a quick brush'll set 'em to rights before I bring 'em in."

And then she was gone in a swirl of flannel petticoats and twinkle of sturdy ankles.

It was inconvenient, but there was no help for it. Sarah pulled Mr. Moore's handkerchief from her wristband and sneezed into it repeatedly, then blew her nose as the two gentlemen watched. What an appearance she must present! Nose red, eyes streaming, shawl sprinkled with darns and mends, gown creased. There was no help for any of that either.

"I am fully capable of paying my own shot," she croaked as the children came into the taproom, "and must insist that you inform me precisely how much—"

"Don't think a thing about it, Miss Bowen," Mr. Moore returned.

"Easy for you to say," Mr. Hunt muttered. "I want her to think about it." Then, "See here," he said, striding over to the table, "I'd like to apologize for our, ah, misunderstanding last night. Trifle under the weather."

"How much, Mr. Hunt?" she said, opening her purse.

"Well above par, if y'must know," he admitted, "not that ladies generally inquire regarding the details."

"Schoolmistresses aren't considered ladies—not in any manner the *ton* comprehends, but I meant how much have you paid the innkeeper."

"None of your concern. See here, won't you accept my apology?"

Faced with him, it was far more difficult to remember the eyes that never quite laughed even when he did, the wretchedness that lurked in their depths. There was something about him that made her bristle.

"I'm not certain I should, Mr. Hunt," she said stiffly, then spoiled the effect with an explosive sneeze.

Wordlessly he handed her a fresh handkerchief, waiting in silence while she made a sodden mess of it. Then, "Why, if I may be so bold?" he asked.

"That is none of your concern, sir." She slipped the wad of damp linen up her sleeve. "Now, if you will please tell me—"

"Blast it, will you forget pounds and pence? It's a small matter."

"We females of the lower orders must see to both, sir, or be forced to earn our keep in precisely the manner you assumed I earn mine yesterday evening."

"Well, I'm not going to tell you how much it was."

Knowing she should accept his kindness with thanks, an evil demon prompted her to hold out ten pounds.

"I come a trifle dearer than that," he snapped, spinning on his heel and stalking over to his friend.

"Children, children," Mr. Moore murmured, "what an example you're setting the infantry."

"Miss Bowen," Timmy threw in, compounding her mortification, "Mama says if one apologizes handsomely, one's apology must be accepted no matter how naughty one's been. And I say, sir, thank you for paying our shot. Wasn't sure what I should do, for we were supposed to be with Mama and Papa last night, and I've but five and six with me, which was to pay for our lunch."

"Naughty?" Mr. Moore chuckled. "Yes, I suppose you were naughty at that, Arch—*Artie.*"

Close to tears, head aching beyond all that was bearable, Sarah stumbled over an awkward apology of her own, telling Timmy his mama had the right of it. And then, choking on the words, she thanked Mr. Hunt for paying her shot as well. She truly never should've left home, she admitted silently. Even the unpleasantness of being faced with another self-serving suitor would've been preferable to this.

Wearily she set her reticule and purse aside as the serving girl arrived with their breakfast. The gentlemen joined them without being asked, efficiently taking over on the children so she could consume her tea and toast in silent misery compounded of equal parts of emotional and physical misery.

The rest of the travelers began to straggle in, a half-kempt band that yawned and stretched and complained of stiff necks and impossible accommodations. Sarah reached for her purse, intending to tie its strings and return it to her reticule. Mr. Peabody crashed against Mrs. Tizzet in his rush to appropriate the only remaining place near the fire. Mrs. Tizzet in her turn crashed into Sarah's elbow. Reticule, card case, purse, comb, brush—all went flying. The children scrambled after the coins as Mr. Moore knelt to gather the spilled cards. He hesitated, hands stilling. Then he neatly flipped the stack so only the backs showed, slipped them in their case, snapped it shut, stood, and handed it to Sarah.

"That's all of them, I believe," he said smoothly.

And then the children were handing the coins to Mrs. Tizzet, who was replacing them in the purse and then tying its strings in a firm knot.

"And now, Miss Bowen," Mr. Moore said once the rest had settled at the table and were calling for their breakfast, "why don't you permit Arthur and me to see to the children for the rest of the morning? There's sure to be a game we can invent to amuse them, and I'm certain they'd enjoy a romp in the snow. *Faute de mieux,* we'll tell 'em tales of the Peninsula—merely geography lessons, naturally."

Ears ringing, head spinning, suddenly Sarah found herself being carried to the settle Mr. Peabody had reluctantly abandoned when the serving girl refused to bring him his breakfast there. A folded jacket was being placed beneath her head, a gentleman's greatcoat spread over her aching limbs.

"A nap'll set you right," Mr. Moore murmured over her halfhearted protests. "Arthur and I are entirely capable of playing nursemaid for a few hours. Excellent odds—two grown men against two children."

Then he was sending Alice and Timmy for their wraps, and cautioning the rest of the company to moderate their tone as Miss Bowen was extremely unwell. The voices faded to a meaningless drone. She closed her eyes. The little inn's taproom became a ballroom. She was draped in gossamer shawls, whirling in a dizzying waltz with a partner's whose haunted eyes were the only sure thing in the room.

"Speak up, Evrard—I can hardly hear you," Melodie Huntleigh-Bowes protested from the other side of the hearth, raising her eyes from her embroidery as Sir Evrard watched warily, holding his breath.

Contrary as ever, and as sharp-eared and eyed as a feral cat—that was his wife. Generally it was an advantage given his career in the diplomatic corps, for her understanding was superior and she never failed to recognize the occasional valuable scrap carelessly dropped in her vicinity. He'd hoped this time she hadn't been paying attention when he'd stumbled into a paragraph not intended for her ears. Timmons was generally more circumspect, signaling his private messages well ahead. Not this time, unfortunately.

"It's nothing, my dear," Sir Evrard returned, hoping it would suffice. "Merely possible plans for this summer. Rather boring, actually. My granddaughter's husband does tend to run on, sound though he is in other respects," and the dear Lord forgive him, for Timmons never ran on about anything.

"Archer is expected in Brevett-on-Chipple even as we speak—I caught that much." Melodie's eyes were boring into him, her brows puckered by the slightest of frowns. "For what reason, however, disintegrated into incomprehensible babble. On purpose, I assume," she added tartly, "for your diction is customarily perfection itself. Well, out with it, Evrard. With what have you been plaguing the poor boy this time?"

"He's not a boy, drat it. He's a man."

"Then treat him like one."

"I do when it's possible, and insist he act like one when it isn't—to which you can hardly object."

"If you mean behaving like a misogynic septuagenarian— which is what you require of him these days—yes, I do," she returned mildly. "What is more, I'll continue to object until you learn the error of your ways. More flies are caught with honey than vinegar, as the saying goes."

The mildness was a surprise. They'd been over this

ground many times, and rough ground it had proved on every other occasion.

"What have you done this time, Evrard," she repeated.

He glanced at the windows. It was still afternoon, the draperies yet to be pulled and the lamps lit. Flakes of snow flitted from clouds pressing down on Mayfair—and the rest of London, he assumed. The entire metropolis generally shared in such dubious treats. He wondered if Archer had made it to Brevett-on-Chipple before the storm, or if he was trapped somewhere along the road.

"Archer's, ah, taking reports regarding the plight of children in certain northern manufactories to Mr. Timmons. Was getting bored in town and wanted employment. I offered him the opportunity the other night."

How Melodie managed such a ladylike snort he would never know. When other women attempted it, they sounded like sows with head colds. Then she wove her needle into the heavy canvas, set her tambour frame aside, and simply stared at him. He cautioned himself not to squirm, but the caution was as futile as ever.

What a magnificent mother Mel would have made—especially of neck-or-nothing lads with more bottom than sense—if only his second marriage had been blessed with children. The closest they'd come was Archer, and the boy'd been half grown when his parents died. Besides, guardianship wasn't the same as parenthood. Parents, he'd heard, were loved, if only out of duty. Guardians were resented. At least he was.

Lord knows, he'd tried to convince his first wife's family to send him his half-orphaned daughter—born when he was half a world away—for him and Mel to raise when eventually he remarried, but they wouldn't hear of uprooting the child. Possession, as in so many things, had proved nine-tenths of the law—especially given he'd been in India at the time.

Of course there might've been his granddaughter, had he

learned she'd been orphaned when it happened rather than being informed years later that she died in a carriage accident on her honeymoon, following marriage to a man supposedly so far beneath her that his first wife's starchy family would've been forced to cut the acquaintance had she survived. Lies, all of it, of course. That was what they'd ever specialized in when they weren't arrogantly closed-mouthed. John Timmons might not have a handle to his name, but he could buy and sell most in the *ton,* and was better read and spoken than many an Oxford don.

It had been purest accident he learned Georgiana still lived—a chance remark by one of her former schoolmates at a diplomatic reception only months before. He'd insisted establishing contact would be a delicate matter, dithered for weeks over how best to go about it. Then Mel had taken the matter into her infinitely capable hands. The result had been all he could've wished beyond the fact that so far it had proved impossible for them to meet because of his schedule and Georgiana's refusal to come to London without her husband.

"Evrard!"

He jumped, then smiled ruefully.

"It won't do, you know," his wife said. "Sooner or later you'll have to tell me. Sooner is better."

He shrugged, nodded. "All right. Timmons and I've decided to bring Sarah and Archer together. Perfect match."

"Oh, dear heaven! And ordered them to fall in love and wed, I suppose?"

"Of course not! We're not flats, either of us. Surest way to queer it."

Strange—that she could make him flush even after all these years.

"Well, not precisely," he amended.

"Deliver me from matchmaking gentlemen," she moaned. "Georgiana and I had all well in hand. They were to meet by accident this spring. Georgiana was going to claim a need to consult a Harley Street physician, and I was going to suggest they visit us then. Archer and Sarah would've been taken entirely by surprise."

"And recognized the ruse on the instant for what it was— or at least Archer would. Better to be straightforward about the matter. He knows what I expect of him, and he'd best produce it," Sir Evrard blustered.

"You've ordered him to marry her?"

"If he wants control of his inheritance before the age of thirty-five."

"And have been keeping him so illiberally supplied he constantly skirts dun territory, I don't doubt." She stood, staring at him in disgust. "Well, there's nothing for it," she said, covering her embroidery with a protective cloth. "We must pack our bags and get ourselves to Brevett-on-Chipple. I'll not have those poor lambs forced in this manner."

"But it's snowing out," Sir Evrard protested, making a great fuss of refolding Timmons's letter. "Sure to be a considerable storm to the north, and we'll be traveling right into its teeth."

"You should've considered that before sending Archer off. Better yet, you should've consulted me. We'll hire a sled if necessary. Won't be the first time we've traveled in that manner."

"I have meetings every morning for the next two weeks, and then there're the receptions for—"

"Send our regrets." Mel tugged the bellpull beside the chimney breast. "We've been called to the bedside of a seriously ill relative. If you don't bestir yourself on the instant, you'll be that seriously ill relative!"

"We can write. That'll do, won't it?"

"That's what got you in this pickle—letters. Well-meaning ones, that I grant you, but of all the muddle-headed, dotty notions! Matchmaking is an art best left to women, who have far more to gain or lose by it. Archer will come around without your making his life miserable. So will

Sarah. I'd've thought better of you than this, given the way you handled Prince Metternich in Vienna. There you showed considerable finesse."

"Mel," he pleaded, "stop pretending you're Général Martinet. We're well beyond the age of Louis XIV, and I'm not about to march in close-order drill. Besides, it doesn't become you."

"I'm going, with or without you. Which is it to be?"

"With me," he sighed. "Oh, with me, of course."

At the inn day slipped into night. The snow still drifted from the sky, filling the tracks left earlier by the children in their play, and the angels they'd created by falling on their backs and then swinging their arms and legs in great arcs. Now they slept on the settle across from Miss Bowen, tucked in Charles's greatcoat after consuming cup after cup of undiluted tea and mountains of bread and butter.

"Where did they put it all?" Charles murmured under cover of the game of vingt-et-un being played for dried peas at the big table in the center of the room.

Something had had to be done about the bickering prisoners of the storm. Only the solicitor had refused the suggestion, retreating to a corner table in high dudgeon at the notion of participating in a game of chance, even with dried peas the only stakes. Mr. Burridge had since attempted and discarded the inn's entire library—three Minerva Press offerings, all with missing pages—and was now stubbornly perusing a week-old journal.

"And should we let them sleep much longer?" Charles continued. "We do, and they'll keep us up half the night. I don't think they'll take to vingt-et-un the way the others have—Alice is too young—and there's no way I'm going back out in that snow."

"Keep *us* up? Why the devil should the infantry be our concern?"

Charles nodded to where the children's self-appointed protectress, shivering beneath Archer's greatcoat, dozed fitfully on the other settle. "D'you think Miss Bowen should stay in that cold attic tonight?"

"No," Archer agreed, not liking it. The only other place for Miss Bowen was the taproom, for the innkeeping family had refused to give up their bedchambers.

"She's quite a plucky little thing," Charles said pensively.

"That she is," Archer agreed, eyes softening. "Reminds me of that surgeon's daughter at Waterloo who seemed to be everywhere at once when the battle was over, giving us water and sending her brothers to find her father whenever she came upon one of us he could help, and comforting the rest. Little more than a child, but pluck to the backbone. Saved more than one man's life that night, and more than one man's sanity. This one's the same sort. I wonder what's sent her haring off in the middle of the school year. Not a customary time for a teacher to be changing positions."

"No, it's not."

"Obviously of good family too. One has only to look at her hands."

"How observant you are where she's concerned," Charles agreed with a crooked grin. "Could do worse, y'know."

"Worse than what?"

"Miss Sally Bowen, pluck to the backbone, instead of Miss Sarah Timmons, unappetizing spinster."

"You've an odd look, Charles. What're you about?"

"Well, y'say you don't want to be driven to the altar."

"Lord, no! The longer this storm continues, the better. Dreading Brevett-on-Chipple. You would be too if it was you about to stick your neck in the noose."

"Lower your voice, y'fool," Charles hissed as Miss Bowen stirred uneasily. "Y'don't want to wake the poor girl, do you?"

"No, of course not," Archer murmured, "but what the devil are you suggesting? That I marry Miss Bowen?"

"If she'll have you. Think what a joke it'd be, arriving with your bride on your arm."

"Couldn't do it."

"Certainly you could, and there's not a word your god-father could say. Besides, this one's pretty—hair like gold and eyes like sapphires."

"And a nose like a carbuncle."

"Some face cream and a few days without sneezing, and it'll be precisely the hue a nose should. Pert little nose too. And look how she sorted that lot out when they arrived. She'd manage your household to perfection. Sir Evrard's sure to approve of her once he knows her, and she'd be more than presentable with a few decent gowns."

"You're all about in your head," Archer said, chuckling, "though I will admit it'd be a grand lark—showing up already wed, and not a thing they could do or say about it without rendering themselves ridiculous."

"And she'd make the very best sort of mother. Saw to Timmy and Alice before she saw to herself, and gave up her cloak for them on the way here even though they're not her own. All the right instincts, you see. Devoted and self-less, just like the girl at Waterloo. And," Charles concluded on a note of triumph, "you've got a special license right there in your pocket. What a glorious irony that is."

"I don't like being managed," Archer admitted, casting a considering glance at little Miss Bowen, who was in the throes of a convulsive sneezing fit, "even by Sir Evrard. Perhaps most especially by Sir Evrard."

"Of course you don't," Charles agreed, grinning. "No man worth his salt does. You'll do what you want, but you'll admit the notion has a certain merit."

"It's totally mad," Archer murmured, but there was a speculative gleam in his eye as he continued to stare across the room at the little schoolteacher.

Charles turned the subject to what they might expect for dinner given the aromas floating in from the kitchen, and whether the innkeeper's wife had made up some chicken broth and barley water for Miss Bowen as she'd promised.

The game at the big table was breaking up, Mr. Burridge setting aside the journal behind which he'd hidden for the past two hours. Mrs. Tizzet, apparently the grand winner, was counting her spoils with glee while bemoaning they were only peas and not pounds or shillings as Mr. Peabody watched, ill-naturedly insisting she'd won by luck rather than skill. The serving girl was bringing in plates and cutlery. Charles yawned, drained the last of his ale, and stood.

"Time to wake the children and visit the necessary," he said. "I'm glad these joys of fatherhood are temporary. I'm not suited to 'em, while you seem to take to 'em like my sisters to trinkets. Which'll you convoy this time—Alice or Tim?"

There was no escaping the monotonous drone of voices weaving in and out of her fading dream like the buzz of mosquitoes on a summer night. And it had been such a lovely dream! Why did they have to spoil it?

The snow had entered the ballroom, marble pillars changing to frosted saplings whose branches met in graceful arches sparkling with leaves of crystal and nacre. And yet it had been warm, so very warm, as if a bonfire had been lit in the center of the floor. The flakes had swelled and taken wing, becoming flowers whose delicate petals spread as they soared. Beneath them she and her cavalier whirled, clad in glossy spiderwebs and rosy dawn clouds while rivulets of champagne trickled from silver fountains, the bubbles rising in the perfumed air to tickle her nose, and in her hair shone all the stars in the midnight sky. Everyone had applauded while his eyes smiled and hers smiled back.

But it was growing hotter. Everything was fading, melting, becoming a foul black ooze from which rose bloated mosquitoes, millions of them, biting and stinging and setting the flowers to flight. And then she was alone, her gown in tatters, her handsome cavalier dissolving into the ooze, the purple lips of his death's-head drawn back over yellowed teeth in the final rictus. She pulled away, but still his skeleton hand gripped her wrist, dragging her toward a sulfurous darkness in which chains clattered and butterflies screamed as the stars were extinguished one by one.

Sarah opened her eyes, shivering and staring about her in bewilderment.

It was hot, so very hot. The taproom fire had been built up. The travelers were at the table in what had become their individual spots, like a family in which orders of precedence are set by unspoken custom. The serving girl was setting platters and tureens before them, then turned to fetch tankards of ale for the gentlemen, watered wine for the ladies, and lemonade for the children.

Attempting to rise was a grievous error. The room swung as if on gimbals. She was still dizzy, and every joint ached. Even her fingers and toes ached, while in her skull a demented blacksmith slammed hammer against anvil.

She sank against the settle's high back with a whimper. Closed eyes, open eyes—it didn't matter. The room cavorted just as she had moments before in the dream that ended so unpleasantly. Daymares were the worst, hinting at truths one would rather leave buried but which one remembered only too clearly upon rousing.

In rational moments she despised even the country versions of the great *ton* balls of London. As for a handsome partner with admiration flaming in his eyes, something yet more ardent and enduring in their previously haunted depths, the notion was laughable. And yet there it was. Beneath all her vaunted practicality lurked a silly schoolgirl who longed for things that didn't exist in the real world—or at least her world.

The London gentlemen were overseeing little Alice and Timmy with the genial assistance of Mrs. Montague. Still garbed in crumpled scarlet, her curls perhaps a trifle less soigné than earlier in the day, the actress was regaling Alice with tales of all the grand folk she'd met, slipping spoonfuls of watery gray stew into the entranced moppet's mouth, ogling Mr. Moore with outrageous boldness, and coyly fluttering her lashes at the rest of the gentlemen in a hilarious parody of flirtation. Mrs. Tizzet clearly was not amused—that, or she was suffering from a massive case of indigestion. As for Mr. Burridge, the high-in-the-instep solicitor had distanced himself from the rest, and was once more pretending to read in order to show his contempt for company so far beneath him as to be invisible.

Once the room had more or less ceased its gyrations, Sarah dragged herself to her feet. Mr. Hunt was at her side on the instant, steadying her stumbling steps as she sought her empty place at the table.

"Peg would've brought you something," he murmured under cover of the laughter of the others. "Mrs. Short made you some broth."

"Mrs. Short? Peg?"

"The innkeeper's wife and her daughter-in-law. It's always wise to be aware of the troops' names and particulars. In the army it ensured loyalty. Here it ensures good service. Same thing in the end, I suppose." He eased her into her seat, scowling. "You've a raging fever."

"A small one, perhaps. I was close to the fire."

"Not close enough to be broiled alive." A cool hand pressed against her forehead, lingering there perhaps a trifle longer than was necessary to determine the state of her health. Then that same hand brushed a few stray tendrils from her eyes. "Some broth with the heat taken off, and some lemonade. Does the notion of lemonade appeal to you?"

"I'd prefer something hot," she complained. She was cold, blast it, as well as hot, and her throat felt as if it had been used for polishing silver.

"What you want and what's good for you at the moment differ. Cool is better."

"And now you're a sickroom nurse?" Dear heaven—she sounded not just peevish, but sarcastic into the bargain. She did her best to soften the words with a halfhearted smile.

"A taproom one anyway. As there're no others to assume the duty, yes."

She sniffed, broke into a fit of coughing and sneezing that left her weak, and with the blacksmith on the attack. Mr. Hunt handed her yet another handkerchief from what must be an inexhaustible store.

"Picked up a thing or two here and there," he said almost apologetically. "One of the things I learned was when one has a high fever, encouraging it with hot fluids isn't wise. Discouraging it, on the other hand, is infinitely wise."

"How interesting," she murmured. "I must remember to employ you should I ever stand in need of a taproom nurse."

His delighted chuckle had her smiling weakly.

Goodness, but the man had a keen sense of the ridiculous. He must have been a veritable devil as a boy, if a good-hearted one. For that matter, he was probably still something of a devil. At least he didn't take himself seriously, puffing himself up like a toad to make others seem smaller by comparison.

And then she giggled helplessly. The notion of how Robert Broome or Mortimer Chudley would've behaved marooned at a country inn, entertaining a pair of children and catering to a spinster with a head cold, was beyond amusing. Whoever or whatever he was, Mr. Arthur Hunt had a great deal to recommend him. So did his crony, Mr. Moore.

Then the other travelers were asking how she did, and sounding genuinely concerned. She accepted their well-wishes gratefully, and reassured them as best she could. It was, after all, nothing but a head cold, no matter how disagreeable.

Her lemonade and the cooled broth arrived, the lemonade poured over firmly compacted snow so that she imagined it must be rather like one of the ices she'd read of concocted by Gunter's, the famous London confectioner's shop. The smile she gave Mr. Hunt after the first spoonful was compounded of genuine delight and infinite gratitude. A rough nurse, and a taproom one at that, but the gentleman was both imaginative and tenacious. The lemonade tasted slightly odd and had an unusual pale amber tinge to it, but it slid down her aching throat without the least effort, as soothing as it was delicious.

As ever, his answering grin had a touch of the unrepentant scamp. She shivered, and lowered her eyes to her lemonaded snow.

"It wasn't glass—it was fur."

Archer managed to keep from groaning aloud. That might not be her hundredth interruption of his attempt to recount the tale of Cinderella, but it certainly felt like it. Little Miss Bowen had taken an intensely contrary turn during the past hour, occasionally mumbling to herself, more often quarreling with him. Perhaps the whiff of rum he'd asked Mrs. Short to add to her lemonade to encourage sleep hadn't been the wisest notion he'd ever had.

"I beg your pardon?" he said. For a miracle, his voice didn't betray his irritation. At least he hoped it didn't. Ill as she was, it wasn't her fault.

"The word is *vair*—squirrel fur, a term used in heraldry, and not *verre*, glass," Miss Bowen said in her teaching voice, huddling under his greatcoat. He'd gotten very well acquainted with that voice since he'd capitulated to the children's pleas for a nighttime story. "They're homophones—words with different spellings having identical pronunciations. Timmy, can you give us another example?"

"Deer, d-e-e-r, meaning doe or stag," the lad sighed,

"and dear, d-e-a-r, meaning either it costs a lot or one loves it. Bow, b-o-w, meaning to bend at the waist, and bough, b-o-u-g-h, meaning branch of a tree. What happened next, Mr. Hunt?"

At least the child had gotten it right—and given two examples so she wouldn't call on each of the company in turn. Otherwise they'd've been treated to another endless lesson. Archer was certain poor Miss Bowen didn't realize only she cared what sort of slipper Cinderella had worn when, gowned to perfection, the girl was about to mount into a magical coach and depart for the ball, barely acknowledging the warning that all would crumble to dust on the last stroke of midnight.

"A careless translation is the problem," Miss Sally Bowen forged on without regard to his audience's desires. "Young ladies didn't wear glass slippers then any more than we do now. Much too dangerous. They wore fur slippers. Consult any authority you wish, or return to the original if you trust no one but yourself."

"My French doesn't extend to female fripperies of the current century, let alone the previous one," Archer snapped, then flushed as the others stared at him. "My apologies," he muttered, then tore pell-mell through the rest of the tale, highly annoying little Alice—who kept demanding details and expansions—and overriding each of Miss Bowen's corrections in a voice that swelled and rushed.

He was at his wits' end, and that was the truth of it. Playing nursemaid to a pair of children wasn't how he'd anticipated spending his last hours of freedom—not that they weren't engaging creatures, but a fellow had his limits.

And that's what they were, curse it. Sometime during the day he'd forced himself to admit that, if only to himself. His blasted godfather had him precisely where he wanted him: on the block, and about to be sold to the high-bidding daughter of a bumptious Midlands industrialist. Little Miss

Bowen, with her fire and her courage and her unfailing kindness and warmth, was an impossible dream.

He rounded out the tale with a list of Cinderella's children—detail omitted by Perrault, but greatly appreciated by Alice as he gave one of his inventions her name, another Timmy's, and told of how they loved to make angels in the snow.

Then he turned the children over to Charles, quashing Miss Bowen's protests that it wouldn't be at all the thing for her to remain in the taproom with an unattached gentleman, hissing, "Which do you prefer: a touch of impropriety no one who matters to you will ever learn of, or an early death? You spend another night in that attic, and you risk an inflammation of the lungs." It was ground they had gone over in excruciating detail earlier, and he wouldn't countenance a repetition.

It proved to be perhaps the longest night of former captain Archer Huntleigh-Bowes's life. Even waiting in the rain and mud for dawn near the little village of Waterloo hadn't been its equal. Then death had been abstract, not something he battled hand to hand. Perhaps he hadn't even battled it this night, but if he hadn't then he knew far less about the body's frailties than he'd assumed. He should have realized how it would be, he admitted when he finally was able to lie down. Miss Bowen did nothing by halves. When well, she probably made the healthiest female seem ill by comparison.

Fighting the soaring fever hadn't been the worst of it, though that had been bad enough. He'd been forced to employ the rough-and-ready method he'd seen an army surgeon use on the Corunna retreat when Charlie's eyes were rolling in his skull, stripping her to her shift after prying her reticule from her fingers and tucking it behind one of the brasses on the mantel, unbarring the door and then laying her in a snowbank to cool her burning flesh. It had been that, or let her slip deeper into an incoherence from which her mind might never surface even if her body survived.

As with Charlie, the desperate measure worked. The fever had broken, but not before she'd torn his heart with her helpless whimpers.

Now, with the settles shoved together before the fire, her clothing once more in place—and please heaven, let her not remember his stripping her of spencer, gown, and petticoats—he cradled her deeply sleeping form against him, permitting it the warmth that would have been her death only hours before.

And thought.

What had seemed a lighthearted solution to all his problems the afternoon before, a glorious prank to exceed every other prank he'd ever played, had turned into the only possible outcome of this long night. He was, he knew in every fiber of his being, going to be cradling this slender, trusting form in his arms every night for the rest of his life. And, he suspected, adoring the indomitable spirit it sheltered more than he had ever believed it possible to love anyone or anything.

If he ever discovered the identity of the scoundrel who'd driven her to fly for her life, he'd kill the man. Coldly and dispassionately, ridding the world of a verminous slug who had no right to existence. It had become laceratingly clear as the hours passed. The rotter who supported the charity school where she'd been employed had attempted to turn her into a whore, insisting she bed with some deep-pocketed wastrel for his own gain. That was why she'd fled toward an uncertain future, for no employment awaited her where she traveled, merely a temporary haven with a former colleague now fallen on hard times and cursed with ill health.

He shuddered. On the identity of her persecutor she'd remained silent, no matter how far her mind wandered. Not the most careful questioning had loosened her tongue. But he'd learn it. Oh yes, one day he'd know. Then he'd rob the rotter of whatever it was he cherished most in the world. And then he'd kill him.

As for Sarah Timmons, she could see to her own future. Miss Timmons didn't need him. Sally Bowen did. He also suspected that he needed her very much indeed. The notion of her disappearing from his life, of never knowing Cinderella's slippers had been of fur rather than glass, was more than distressing. More to the point, she lit rooms with her smile and gladdened his heart with her gentle ways. Her more didactic tendencies would soften with time.

They would, he decided, be married on the morrow in the very room in which they now lay as if their vows had already been spoken, the blessing given. After all, he had his godfather's special license in his pocket. Serve the old meddler right to have it used where he hadn't directed.

Pulling the slight form more firmly against him, smiling at her gentle sigh and ridding his mind of the unpleasant distant prospect of facing down Sir Evrard in favor of the delightful nearer one, Archer Huntleigh-Bowes at last sank into well-earned sleep with his bride-to-be clasped in his arms.

The Unwatched Pot Boils

It wasn't dawn yet. That didn't matter. The blasted storm was over. Above, stars glimmered in the icy blackness as the waning moon slipped below the horizon.

"It's stopped," John Timmons said, turning from his post by the window of the bedchamber he shared with his wife.

"Come to bed, John," Georgiana said, yawning. "You've been pacing half the night."

"I wanted to know when it ceased." He jerked the bell-pull by his dressing room door, then strode within, pulling his nightshirt over his head.

"John, what are you about?"

"Getting ready."

"Ready? Ready for what? Do you intend to wake the entire household at this ungodly hour?"

"If need be. Most of it, at any rate. I'll be wanting my breakfast before I leave."

"Oh, dear." Georgiana thrust the cocoon of warm covers aside and sat, searching for her slippers with her toes as she lit the lamp on the night table. "You're going nowhere, John. The roads'll be impassable."

"Not for a man on horseback."

"You intend to search for Sarah?"

"Obviously."

Slippers at last located and donned, she stood and pulled

on the warm dressing gown draped over the blanket rail. "Then I'm coming with you, John."

"Not likely," he snorted, appearing at the door in a white wool shirt and heavy tweed unmentionables, carrying his top boots in one hand and a waistcoat with padded lining in the other. "You'd never make it."

"If the roads'll be passable for a man astride, then they'll be passable for a lady riding sidesaddle. No, John—I'll not have you mortify Sarah by treating her like a child when you find her, and that's what you'll do if I'm not there."

"She'll get what she deserves, running off half-cocked. As for scenes, there'll be none. I simply intend to wring her neck. Then I'll bring her home where she belongs."

"Without so much as a by-your-leave?"

"I'm her father!" he roared.

If the household wasn't already awake, that was sure to have done it. "And I'm her mother," Georgiana returned, "and I say you shan't. I know you're worried, but—"

"Only too right, I'm worried. Out of my mind, if you want to know," he said more evenly as his valet scurried in with a can of hot water, "and have been since yesterday morning." Then he added, "I didn't like the look of her friend's coachman," maintaining the fiction they'd concocted to explain Sarah's absence. "Pour it out, Wilton. No, I'll shave myself. Send to the stables for Devil's Spawn and order up breakfast. Then pack me a bag for a two-day journey."

"You're taking the black?" Georgiana's brows soared as Wilton retreated discreetly.

The great Watford Stud hunter was John's most treasured mount, and his strongest. Devil's Spawn would never be stopped by the inconvenience of a bit of snow, that was certain. Well, she had her own hunter, and of Watford breeding as well.

"How do you intend to bring Sarah back when you find her? Slung across the cantle like a sack of corn?"

"I'll send for the carriage as soon as possible."

"And sleep where in the interim? Whatever shelter Sarah's found, it's sure to be crammed to the rafters with other luckless travelers."

"In a taproom if I must, or the stable. It won't be the first time I've roughed it."

Georgiana wasted no more breath on protest, merely commenting as she went into her dressing room, "You may be sure of it: Sarah's having a grand adventure, organizing everyone and making friends wherever she turns. I don't doubt it'll do her a world of good, for we keep her entirely too sequestered here."

"We keep her entirely too little sequestered," John mumbled around the lather covering his face.

"And she won't thank you for coming."

"Doesn't matter whether she does or not, though as she's been traveling by common stage I suspect my appearing to make all comfortable won't sit badly."

"Like a frog on hot coals," Georgiana murmured. "What about young Huntleigh-Bowes?" she called, pulling on several divided wool petticoats, then taking down her winter habit from where it hung on the far side of her dressing room.

"He's sure to have been delayed by the snow. If he hasn't, tell him Sarah was called to the bedside of a stricken relative."

"Stricken with what? And whose bedside? You've no family beyond your parents. They're both deceased, and he's sure to know I have none beyond Sir Evrard."

"Make up anything you like. That's what women're best at—inventing excuses."

She let it pass, though she'd've dearly loved to inform him that if he and her grandfather had left well enough alone they wouldn't be in this spot. Bludgeoning young people left bludgeoners as bloodied as their victims, and with those same victims imbued with determination to resist at all costs no matter where their best interests lay.

"What the devil d'you think you're doing," John growled as she came back into their bedchamber, the train of her riding habit draped over her arm.

"Getting dressed."

"I mean what d'you mean by donning a habit?" he specified, toweling his face.

She took the towel, dipped it in the basin, and removed a trace of lather hiding behind his ear.

"Well?"

"I'm going with you, John. I've already told you that."

They glared at each other. It was, she decided, one of the best battles of the eyes in which they'd ever indulged. They stood there, neither moving, shoulders rigid, nostrils flaring, lips thinned. It ended in laughter, just as such battles always did, the pair of them clinging to each other like children made dizzy dancing around the Maypole.

"You'll wear one of my greatcoats over your habit, and tie your shako down with a shawl or a scarf," John managed to gasp.

"Of course, my dear."

"And wear your fur-lined gloves."

"Naturally."

"And wool stockings. Three pairs."

She lifted her split skirt then, extending a shapely limb clad in several layers of dark wool. "As you say, John."

"Anticipating me at every turn?"

"Attempting it, at the very least," she murmured, smiling at him and swearing that come what might, he would never drive an unwilling Sarah to the altar.

There was a crick in her back and her head felt twice its normal size, but it was the pressure below her belly that finally roused Sarah just after dawn. She lay on the settle, head pillowed on a gentleman's jacket, staring at the smoke-stained ceiling and trying to remember. The few images were tenuous—intense heat, numbing cold, a voice that cajoled while hands coerced. There had been a snow angel, and a devil in black. Strong arms cradling her. A rough voice crooning a lullaby. None of it made sense.

She struggled to sit, pushing aside the greatcoat whose long tails tangled in her skirts. Dear heaven, but she was weak and light-headed. Coats weren't that heavy, not even gentlemen's greatcoats. On the settle across from her Mr. Hunt snored peacefully, his back turned. That wasn't how she remembered it, but what she did remember caused her to blush until she felt her face would set the room on fire.

At last she was on her feet, stumbling to the windows in stocking feet, pushing aside the crisp muslin curtains.

The snow had ceased. The world was palest rose, the most delicate of violet shadows stretching toward the horizon. Road, inn yard, village outskirts—all had vanished beneath a blanket that stretched as far as the eye could see. The sun, as its fiery rim broke above the distant surges of white, was the most beautiful sight she'd ever beheld.

Blaming the wetness in her eyes on the blinding brightness after what felt like days of gloom, Sarah slipped on her boots and retrieved her old winter pelisse from the settle's back, shoving her arms in the sleeves and buttoning it to the neck. The inn door was already unbarred. She stepped outside. There were footprints, one set rather large, one smaller. Stepping carefully in the larger, she followed them to the necessary.

She was just settling her skirts after rising when a furious shouting and pounding came at the door.

"What the *devil* d'you think you're doing out here alone? You didn't even make use of my greatcoat!"

It was Mr. Hunt, of course.

"You know perfectly well," she managed. "Necessaries are occasionally, well, *necessary*."

"Why didn't you at least take my coat if you weren't willing to wake me?"

"No need of either. I'm not a child, and hardly in need of escort."

There was a brief silence she employed to slow her thudding heart and cool her flaming face.

"Are you done?" Mr. Hunt inquired more mildly.

It appeared he wasn't going to permit her to emerge unobserved. Mr. Hunt was clearly a gentleman who could entertain only one notion at a time—no doubt a legacy of his military years. Right now chivalry had no place in his pantheon.

"Yes," she returned, raising her chin. She was blessed if she'd permit him to see how entirely he'd overset her.

And then the ludicrous nature of the encounter struck her, and she began to giggle. She and Mr. Hunt had certainly cut through the social niceties. No artifice or pretense of any sort for them. That might be mortifying on occasion, but it was also rather delightful, just as his forging through the snow to her rescue was infinitely considerate for all it smacked of precisely the reverse. Her well-being apparently mattered to him—and he a London gentleman while she was merely an impoverished educator, at least so far as he knew. She weighed the probable behavior of Messrs. Broome and Chudley under similar circumstances, and her giggles redoubled.

"Well? Are you coming out?"

It wasn't a question. It was a command. She opened the door. He stood in the snow garbed in top boots and shirtsleeves, dark hair on end, chin stubbled, gray greatcoat over his arm. She stepped into the snow, pulling the door closed behind her.

"Good morning, sir," she quavered, knowing she probably didn't present a very prepossessing appearance herself.

And then his greatcoat was wrapped tightly around her,

and she was in his arms as he plowed back to the inn through the heavy drifts.

"What the devil d'you mean, coming out here by yourself?" he snapped.

"And what do you mean, coming out here in the cold without a coat?"

"Didn't want to waste the time. You've been ill, blast it. Very ill."

"And so shall you be if you don't have a care."

He looked down at her, pausing in the chill morning, his breath clouding the air.

"Truly, I'm not as fragile as you believe me," she said after a breathless moment. "Indeed, I'm quite recovered. You may put me down, sir."

"And just what were you last night?" he returned, his arms tightening.

"That was an aberration."

"Then God deliver me from ever witnessing such an aberration again, for it scared me out of my wits and I don't frighten easily."

"No, I wouldn't suppose you do. Truly, sir, it's perfectly safe to put me down. I shan't break, or fall over in a faint. I'm feeling stronger by the minute."

His dark eyes bored into hers just as they'd done in her dream the day before, and with precisely the same expression in their depths. Then he threw back his head and laughed, a merry sound that would have lifted the spirits of any who heard it.

"You might not," he chuckled, "but I surely would, for you're the only thing that's keeping me from freezing to death."

She followed his eyes as he glanced toward the stable where the footprints she'd followed minutes before led from the necessary.

"What the devil?" he muttered, then shrugged and forged back to the inn, breaking his own path.

That was probably how he went through life, breaking his own path even if there were easier, clearly marked ones he might've followed. Like so many of the other things she'd discovered about Mr. Hunt over the past day and a half, Sarah rather liked that. It might make things a trifle difficult on occasion, but it also ensured life could never be dull for one who traveled at his side.

And then she gasped, blushing furiously at the wayward turn of her thoughts.

He grinned down at her, gave her a roguish schoolboy's wink. Then he was stamping his feet and unlatching the taproom door. They were within. He was setting her down and disencumbering her of his greatcoat. His low chuckle couldn't mean he'd followed her thoughts. It couldn't!

"Ah, there you are," Charles said, to one side Alice, on the other Timmy.

Archer set Miss Bowen on her feet, suppressing a shiver that had very little to do with the frigid air he'd brought in with them, somehow keeping his eyes on the trio at the table while he unbundled her. He desperately needed a moment in which to catch his breath or his voice would squeak like a pubescent boy's. "Divine madness" indeed. If he wasn't careful, he'd make a mull of it—and the rest of his life into the bargain.

"Yes, here we are," he managed. "Beautiful morning."

Either Charles had stronger paternal instincts than he admitted to, or he'd enlisted someone's aid. The children's hair was neatly brushed and combed, their faces washed, their hands sparkling clean.

"Good morning, Miss Bowen," they chorused, for all the world as if they were in a schoolroom.

"Are you feeling better?" Alice added hopefully.

"Much better, thank you."

"And what did we agree you should call Miss Bowen—

with her permission—in the interests of friendliness?"
Charles chided, a wicked gleam in his eye.

"Aunt Sally," the children said, staring up at her.

"I—ah—"

"Surely you've no objection," Charles grinned. "You
have stood rather in the nature of a favorite aunt to them
since you joined them just beyond Whittelsy."

"Was that the name of the town?"

"So they say."

The woman colored up and mumbled something about
supposing it would be perfectly correct. Then her eyes nar-
rowed. "And you, sir—what do they call you?"

"Oh, I remain plain Mr. Moore. Nothing the least special
about me."

And then Miss Bowen was across the room, thank heavens, joining them at table and chattering away as if the
world hadn't just spun off its axis, and Archer had a moment
in which to catch his breath. Carrying her about in the snow
had been a grievous error with disastrously visible results.

Making a great business of shaking out his greatcoat and
hanging it on one of the pegs provided for regulars, Archer
willed "things" to return to normal. He hadn't had any such
problems during the long night, blast it.

Of course then Miss Bowen had been so ill he feared
for her life. She was anything but now, and apparently his
more chivalrous instincts were on holiday. That was as
currently inconvenient as it boded well for future wedded
bliss. And it wasn't just propinquity—on that he would
wager his inheritance. Or if it was, it was propinquity to
this specific, irritating, delightful, unpredictable scrap of
femininity, no matter how countrified her gown and red
her nose. As Charles had said, the one he could replace,
and the other would rectify itself without his lifting a finger.

More or less under control once more, Archer joined the
others, ordering up a mammoth breakfast that shrank to

porridge, bread, cheese, and pickled onions. The inn's supplies were dwindling, Peg informed him when he protested. There was nothing left but turnips, cabbages, and potatoes, and no hope of more given the condition of the roads unless the farmer who deposited them at the inn could be convinced to part with some turkeys or butcher a hog—on which errand her husband had just departed. Archer apologized—he'd already suspected the problem—and privately swore that, come what might, they'd have a true dinner that night even if he had to go poaching in the woods behind the stable and make his peace with the local landowner later.

One by one the other guests straggled in, tempers frayed and spirits low. Soon all but Mrs. Tizzet and her abigail sprawled dejectedly around the taproom table, poking at their porridge—or, in Mrs. Montague's case, toast fingers dipped in tea.

This lady, once she had been served, smiled at Miss Bowen. "All recovered?" she said.

Miss Bowen returned her smile with one that was as unaffected as it was genuine. "Indeed I am, thank you for inquiring. Apparently one of those violent things that comes upon one suddenly, and as suddenly departs."

"How fortunate for you. I did offer to have you take my place, but Mrs. Tizzet claimed she had a delicate constitution and couldn't risk infection, and of course Mr. Hunt would hear of no one nursing you but himself. So unusual in a gentleman."

Her words hung in the air, causing Archer to flush and Charles to choke on his ale. Then the actress glanced about in apparent puzzlement.

"Where is Mrs. Tizzet? She and her maid were already gone when I awakened, and I expected to find them here."

A quick survey of the company proved that no one had seen the voluble widow or her close-mouthed abigail since the night before. Archer scowled, thinking of the footprints leading from the necessary to the stable, then summoned Peg from the bar where she was polishing glasses.

"Have you seen Mrs. Tizzet?" he said.

"Not a hair on her head. Come down real early, I expect, and's already left—how I don't know. Paid her shot ahead, so it don't matter."

"But her gown and nightrail are still in our bedchamber," the actress protested. "Only her cloak's gone. Perhaps she's visiting, the, ah—"

"And her maid? I suggest you check your till and strong-box," Archer snapped, springing from the table and dashing across the room, "and you, Mrs. Montague, had best see if any jewels you had with you are where you hid them."

"Only my pearls, and they're on my person," the actress called after him, hand rising to her bosom, "where none would ever find 'em."

More than gown and nightrail had been abandoned in the inn's smaller bedchamber. Crammed in the chamber pot was a lady's gray wig.

Roaring imprecations, Archer pelted back down the stairs with Charles hot on his heels. The rest of the company pulled on outerwear and streamed after them as they slogged through the snow to the stables. There were three sets of hoofprints. One, Peg informed them, led toward the farm where her husband had gone. The other two led to the road. On the stable door was pinned a note in a scholarly hand.

Mr. Hunt—My thanks for the loan of your steeds, it said. *I shall take excellent care of them, having a great appreciation for fine horseflesh. You will find them at the next respectable inn, where doubtless you will be glad to buy them back as such beautifully matched pairs are not easily come by. And my thanks for the gift of your watch. I shall take excellent care of that as well, though I am afraid you shall not find it waiting for you as I have developed a distinct fondness for it.*

Ah, la commedia deliziosa della vita! Addio, mio caro Signor Buffone.

It was signed *William T. Fitzmorris, Esq.*, with a grandiloquent flourish.

So the blackguard considered life a comedy, did he? And he a clown? And in shaky guidebook Italian at that, as if he were about to burst into some incomprehensible aria? The impudence of it! The unmitigated gall!

Archer threw his head back and roared wordlessly at the beautiful morning sky. The vocabulary that sprang to mind simply couldn't be uttered in decent company.

"Don't worry," he heard Charlie murmur to the children, "Uncle Arthur will be himself again in a moment."

"No, I shan't," he muttered, but he knew it to be a lie. If he wasn't careful, he'd burst into laughter and they'd all believe him mad.

They traipsed back to the inn, Mrs. Montague bemoaning the loss of her pearls, Mr. Peabody claiming he'd suspected there was something havey-cavey about the widow all along, and had taken precautions not to be parted from his brass. Sheepishly, Mrs. Montague admitted she had wondered at the "lady's" insistence on privacy when she disrobed, and sleeping on a pallet with her maid rather than sharing the bed with a stranger. Mr. Burridge, after examining his purse, suggested Mr. Peabody might do well to inspect his own, no matter how many precautions he'd taken.

Mr. Hunt ignored their natterings, gripping Sarah by the arm as she insisted she could get back on her own feet, grimly lifting her over the deepest drifts despite her protests. Mr. Moore forged behind them, one member of the infantry riding on his shoulders, the other on his hip, both chattering like magpies about the excitement of having spent two entire days with a thief, all the while thinking him a lady.

In the event, a few shillings remained in each purse. Neither had trinkets of personal value been pilfered. As for the contents of till and strongbox, the innkeeper was poorer by only one pound in three. William Fitzmorris, Esquire, clearly had a kind heart in addition to his light fingers and wicked sense of humor. Sarah listened and watched from her place beside Mr. Hunt, absently rubbing her wrist.

"What did you do with it?" she whispered under the babel.

"Do? Do with what?"

"My reticule."

"Oh, Lord! Just a moment—I'll fetch it."

He strode over to the fireplace, picked up one of the brasses. She could see his frown from where she still stood by the door.

"Oh, dear," she murmured. "Papa will skin me alive for being so careless."

And then, still frowning, Mr. Hunt was glancing along the mantel, retrieving a limp, sacklike object. He strode back across the taproom, handed it to her silently. She untied the strings, certain of what she would find, opened it. Except for a folded piece of paper and several clean handkerchiefs she had never seen before, it was as empty as it appeared. Even her purse and card case were gone.

"Oh, bother!" she murmured.

"Cleaned you out, did he?"

"Entirely, unlike the rest of you, but he left me some fresh handkerchiefs."

"And another of his notes, apparently. You'd best see what he has to say."

"I suppose I had," she sighed.

"You don't seem in the least overset."

"What use is it to bemoan the tipping of the pail when

the milk has already seeped into the ground? Especially when one has knocked it over oneself?"

She retreated to one of the window seats, retrieved Mr. Fitzmorris's letter, and unfolded it as if she were about to read a jury's verdict. Well, in a sense she was.

My dear Miss Timmons, it began.

"Oh, no!" she whispered, crumpling the thing. Then, teeth clenched, she smoothed it and read on.

I hope this finds you recovered from your recent indisposition. On the chance the reverse might be true, I am leaving you a small gift you will no doubt find more useful than mere guineas. A fair exchange, wouldn't you say? You, after all, may be resupplied with those at the stroke of your pen. A deal more effort is required of me to achieve the same effect, and a deal more imagination. Your servant, William Tiberius Fitzmorris, Esq.

She burst into laughter as she folded the note and slipped it in her reticule. She couldn't help it. She laughed until her sides ached as the others turned to stare. Then she laughed some more, tears running down her cheeks.

"Never mind," she gasped between paroxysms. "I'm all right, truly I am."

Mr. Hunt was sitting beside her now, his arm most improperly cradling her shoulders. And she in her turn? She most improperly laid her head on his broad shoulder as if doing so were the most natural thing in the world.

"Dear me, I don't believe I've ever laughed so before. What a spectacle I've made of myself," she gulped at last, wiping her eyes with one of her new handkerchiefs. "I wonder who he truly is."

"My supposition would be an out-of-favor provincial actor of light-fingered ancestry. What did he say?"

"That I have more need of his linen than my pounds," she chuckled.

"Up the River Tick, Miss Bowen?"

"Not a farthing to my name at the moment." And then she blushed, remembering that wasn't her name at all.

"I'll see you through," he murmured, taking her hand in his. "Don't worry. You can always depend on me, both now and in the future."

"With your pockets considerably lightened, and your pair to be ransomed?" she said, trying to make light of his preposterous promise and serious expression.

"I'll get 'em back," he returned, mouth thinning. "Rather fond of that pair. The rest doesn't matter. We'll muddle through."

It was, Archer admitted as he seated Miss Bowen and then took his place beside her, automatically accepting Alice on his lap, a pretty mess. The company, originally merely petulant regarding their uncomfortable circumstances, now had serious reason for ill humor. For the moment each was nursing his private discontent in silence, bickering forgotten in shared disaster. That wouldn't last—not unless he did something to ensure the continuation of at least superficial harmony. The pair who'd been riding on the coach roof were barely a step short of ruffians, the one a racetrack tout, the other a groom who'd been dismissed for reasons he refused to specify. When provender lacked and tempers grew short in the Peninsula, he'd set the men to building earthworks or digging latrines, whether they were needed or not. That wasn't an option here.

And then there were the children, solemn-eyed as children should never be. They needed amusement.

He glanced down as Timmy tugged on his sleeve.

"Yes?" he said, attempting a smile he was afraid might not quite reach his eyes.

"Please, Uncle Arthur—Mr. Fitz didn't take nothing from us. We have five shillings and a sixpence. D'you think Aunt

Sally would take half? You already paid our shot, so we won't need near so much."

"The sixpence is mine," Alice threw in. "I got it in our Twelfth Night cake. It's for luck. Aunt Sally can have it."

He truly smiled then, ruffling the boy's hair and hugging Alice's warm body tight.

"I'll see to Aunt Sally, lad," he said, gazing into Miss Bowen's suspiciously bright eyes over the top of the moppet's curls. "I'll see to us all somehow. But thank you, Alice. Thank you both. You're infinitely generous—offering to frank Aunt Sally."

"Yes, thank you," Miss Bowen agreed, a catch in her voice, "but you must keep your sixpence as it's for luck. Is it a shiny new one?"

Alice nodded.

"There's nothing quite so wonderful as a shiny new sixpence from a Twelfth Night cake, is there? I remember when I discovered my first. I thought all of heaven had opened up to me."

And then he had it. Of course! A revel. What did it matter that Twelfth Night was long past, Shrove Tuesday creeping up on them on scurrying mice feet? They would pretend, all of them, if only for the children's sakes, and do their souls and spirits a deal of good in the process. And somehow in all the hilarity and confusion he would corner Miss Bowen and convince her the most reasonable solution to her problems would be to wed him. He already had a fair notion of how he'd manage it if all else failed.

"Would you do me a favor?" he said, looking from Alice to Timmy. "Would you go build me a card house over by the windows?"

"You want to say something you don't want us to hear," Alice returned wisely, slipping from his lap. "That's all right. Mama and Papa often ask us to build card houses, Uncle Arthur."

It didn't take much once he'd made his proposal and

stated his case. Timmy's and Alice's offers had been heard by all. And, for a miracle, faces that had been surly moments before were taking on life again. Even Mr. Burridge approved the notion, and Archer suspected Mr. Burridge rarely approved anything.

He summoned the innkeeper and his wife and explained his notion. It might even, Archer suggested with an idea as to how to manage a true feast—for he and Charlie'd pulled the same trick in the Peninsula often enough—be a friendly act to invite the entire village. Yes, even the vicar and his wife. The whole was being done, he insisted, nodding significantly at where Alice and Timmy were dutifully constructing their card house, for the sake of the poor mites delayed on their way to their aunt's deathbed. Each family could bring what contributions they wished. And foolish gifts—they must have some of those. Nothing of value, merely mementos of a bad situation made better.

And that was all it took. The innkeeper's wife scurried to the kitchen in the throes of culinary desperation. Peg was sent to find boxes of favors stored in the attics. The innkeeper was pulling on his boots preparatory to making the rounds of the village to issue invitations. The rest scattered to devise costumes and masks.

"You'd've become a general if you hadn't sold out," Charlie murmured in Archer's ear. "Masterfully done."

"I thought so," Archer agreed, rising from the table.

Moments later he was in the kitchen, slipping his signet ring from his finger as he explained what he wanted. Mrs. Short's eyes lit up, for all she said, "See to it you're honest. She's that fine of a young lady, work for her keep though she must."

The day that had begun in such an untoward manner passed in frenzied preparations. The travelers constructed masks with Mrs. Montague's nimble-fingered assistance, and devised costumes from the merest scraps of nothing. They decorated the taproom, hanging paper garlands fashioned by the children under Sarah and Archer's supervision. They watched from the windows as Alice and Timmy rolled great balls of snow about the inn yard and then stacked them one on the other with Charles's assistance, creating a Lord and Lady of Misrule so all the village would know where to come when night fell.

Through it all wafted delightful smells from the kitchen thanks to the farmer Tom had earlier importuned—turkeys turning on spits, pork pies, rabbits stewing in wine, apple tarts and rich cakes, and puddings steaming in bubbling basins. As the sun began its downward slide toward night village wives formed a steady procession to the inn's rear door, delivering all manner of specialties to be kept warm on the hearth while their husbands and children arrived at the front with bundles containing mystery tokens to be distributed by the innkeeper.

Archer managed a few moments of privacy during the afternoon to contrive his gifts for Sarah: a crude frog carved from soap sporting a tiny tin crown, and a pair of miniature slippers fashioned from bits snipped from the fur carriage robe that had hung forgotten in the stables since their arrival. He hoped they would please even if they weren't squirrel. Better yet, he hoped they would ease his way.

When not closeted, he attempted to convey his message in every manner he knew, inventing not a few new ones. Miss Sally Bowen, he discovered as the hours passed, had the most delightful manner of flushing when put out of countenance.

As for Sarah Timmons, she had soared into an unexplored realm from which she would have admitted, if hard pressed, she had no desire to ever return. The *coup de foudre* did not exist, so that could not be from what she suffered, but it must be something rather akin to it. Love at fourth or fifth or tenth sight in any case. Best of all, Arthur Hunt believed her penniless given Mr. Fitzmorris's light fingers. At last the perfect suitor—one who wanted her for herself, not her father's mills and fortune.

How shocked he would be when he learned the truth, she thought, smiling as she donned the mistletoe wreath intended to transform her into a Druid priestess after she and Mrs. Montague had assisted Timmy in belting one of the ostler's smocks about his waist, tied a black patch over his eye, and handed him his crude pirate's sword.

"Avast!" he shouted, waving the sword. "Fire all cannons! There's a rich ship off our port bow, me boys, ready for the taking, and fine wrenches."

Alice, already sporting the tattered lace bedhanging, paper wings, and crown that proclaimed her a fairy princess, waved her wand. "Abber-dabber," she giggled. "You're a toad, Timmy. What d'you know about wrenches?"

"I know Papa calls you his fine little wrench, and Mama his fine big one."

"Children, children," Sarah reproved absently, her heart not in it as she examined her reflection in the tarnished dressing table mirror of the inn's smaller bedchamber. "Shouldn't this sheet be pinned a trifle higher, Mrs. Montague?"

"How high d'you want it? All the way up, so even your pretty face won't show?"

"But so much of my, ah, front is exposed."

"Less than the most missish London debutante reveals over the breakfast cups, believe me. No, leave it as it is," Mrs. Montague snapped, struggling with the mass of copper-colored wool that signaled her to be Good Queen Bess. Ancient curtains draped over baskets they had strapped to her waist provided the illusion of a farthingale. A stomacher embroidered with string and a high paper ruff completed the illusion. "I don't want the effect spoiled. Gimcrackery such as I'm sporting's easy. Simple elegance never is. Ready to make your grand entrance?" she said, giving the wig a final pat, then holding out her hands to the children.

Their grand entrance must have overjoyed Mrs. Montague. Conversation ceased. Heads spun. It began as polite applause, Mr. Burridge—Moses, complete with tablets of the law—leading the way. Then it degenerated into whole-hearted cheers.

The rest had done their best. There were shepherdesses, nymphs, wise men, and Romans. There was an executioner with ax and "severed head"—in reality a cleverly carved gourd. There was a donkey with gray ears and tail. Mr. Short had become a jolly Bacchus. Peg, apron covered with paper flowers, was Spring. Even the vicar and his wife had donned masks, becoming golden sun and silver moon.

None compared with the queen, the pirate, the fairy, and the Druidess.

Sarah hunched her shoulders as the others swept across the taproom, little Timmy offering to shiver the timbers of all those present, Alice to transform them into anything they wished. And then a blue-faced stranger was bowing before her, a fur rug flowing from his shoulders as he offered his arm.

"Our costumes go well together, don't you agree?" he said with a grin she recognized on the instant. "The Pict warrior and the Druid maiden. Of course, Mrs. Montague gave me a hint earlier so I could manage it."

"A giant moth appears to've made merry sport in your cape," Sarah said to turn the subject. His carriage robe had been crudely hacked along the edges, and was in dire need of a trip to a furrier for repair.

"An extremely giant one. How d'you like the new tone of my skin? Am I ridiculous enough for you?"

"Berry juice?" she managed.

"No, some sort of laundry thing beaten with egg white so it would adhere—Mrs. Short's special recipe. There's a layer or two of dried yolk beneath so it wouldn't sink in.

Not authentic, but at least it's stayed on so far even if my face feels like a starched neckcloth. I'll wash it off once you've told me what a fine, strapping fellow I am, and that you'll be pleased to guide my tribe in all the traditional observances."

"Oh, heavens," Sarah laughed, "you're positively stunning, Mr. Hunt. Now, do go make yourself comfortable. No one should suffer a crackling face for a bit of fun."

"The one who's a stunner is yourself, my dear Miss Bowen," he said, his smile causing a shower of pale flakes as he ran a single elegant finger down her blushing cheek. Beneath his crumbling paint lingered a decided tinge of blue. "And now, if you'll excuse me?"

She nodded, and he was gone.

"When are you going to put it to the touch?"

Archer plunged his head in the basin and came up spluttering like a grampus, water streaming down his bare chest. Charles was still there.

"When I'm ready," he said, grabbing a towel and scrubbing his face, then turned to his old companion. Behind them the kitchen bustled with activity. "Better?"

"Not really. Where it's gone your face is red. The rest's still blue, except for a few touches where it's actually purple."

"Blast!"

"So, when are you going to ask her?" Charles pressed, leaning against the wall, legs and arms crossed, rope tail draped over his shoulder, the devil in his eyes a fine match for the straw horns on his head and the pitchfork propped beside him. "You are, aren't you? I haven't misread your intentions?"

"No, you haven't misread 'em. See here, what business is it of yours anyway? You're becoming as bad as my blasted godfather."

"None of my business," Charles said hastily. "Just curious, is all. The roads'll be passable soon. Y'don't want to be caught napping and lose all."

From the taproom came the sound of a rasping fiddle. There was music, there was laughter, there was dance—except for Archer. There was food—a veritable feast covering the bar and the big table, which had been moved against the wall—except for him. And he was hungry. Had there ever been such a nodcock?

"Hand me the soap and that brush when I surface, would you?" he said just before he plunged his head back in the basin.

Archer lathered. He scrubbed. He rinsed and toweled and began again.

It took a bit of doing. By the time it was, Archer knew he wouldn't be able to shave for days, but only the faintest hint of blue lingered except for an unfortunate streak beneath each eye where the skin was too tender for vigorous scrubbing, and another down the center of his nose where the egg yolk had apparently not performed its task. He would have to do, he decided with a sigh, examining his reflection in a gleaming pot. It had seemed such a splendid notion at the time. As with so many of his splendid notions, while it had achieved his object—taking little Miss Bowen so off her guard that she'd forgotten to be shy at her appearance—it had also had a few unpleasant consequences.

"Himself'll be giving out the tokens in a minute or two, Mr. Hunt," came a caution behind him, the voice choking back laughter, "and then I'll be serving the Twelfth Night cake. You'd best stir yourself."

"My thanks for the warning, Mrs. Short." Archer gave his nose a final rub and chucked the towel on the pile beside the sink. "Charlie, hand me my shirt, would you?"

He made quick work of dressing. Then, carriage robe flowing from his shoulders, he gave his coat pocket a pat.

The license was where it was supposed to be, and the lump that was one miniature fur slipper.

Was it terror he felt? Uncertainty as to the outcome?

Logic said there could be no doubt—not given all he had to offer penniless, intrepid, delightful little Miss Bowen of the glowing sapphire eyes and golden curls. The trouble was, she didn't know that. To her he was a stranger, chance-met during a winter storm. He might be almost anyone or anything. Disabusing her would require explanations he wasn't willing to offer just yet. Given the streak of contrariness he'd witnessed in her, she might actually insist it was his duty to present himself to Sarah Timmons and be rejected before she'd consider his suit. That he would never risk, so she'd have to take him as he was, a doting stranger complete with blue streak down the center of his nose, and nothing to offer but his love and a currently shallow purse.

Shoulders squared, head high—and with the same icy hand gripping his vitals that seized them during the last charge at Waterloo just before he was hit—Archer followed Mrs. Short back into the taproom. Behind him ambled Charles, an enigmatic smile quirking his mouth.

Villagers and guests perched on benches and stools rimming the room, waiting for Bacchus to distribute the contents of his great sack before the cutting of the cake. Archer spotted Miss Bowen immediately, surrounded by a phalanx of country swains. From the looks of it, the village maidens were feeling their defection sorely. Time to set that to rights, and insist on his own prior claims to the lady's winsome smiles.

He helped himself to two cups of Charles's punch and strode directly to her, cutting across the floor.

"Thank you for seeing to Miss Bowen for me," he murmured, handing her one.

His nod of dismissal held a touch of an officer's arrogance combined with the rueful self-deprecation of a gentleman who knew himself and his world very well, and found both a trifle overblown on occasion. On the far side of the taproom, Charles had joined the swashbuckling pirate and diminutive fairy princess.

"Enjoying yourself, my dear?" he said, as Miss Bowen's bucolic *cicisbei* drifted away. "Certainly no Druid maiden ever did greater justice to white sheets and mistletoe wreath, for you give them luster rather than the reverse."

She blushed and stammered incoherently. Good. If he could keep her a bit off balance, things should go just as he desired. Besides, Sally Bowen mired in confusion was even more delightful than Sally Bowen with all her wits about her. Had no one ever flirted with her? If not, he'd spend the rest of his life flirting with his wife and telling her how lovely she was, and tutoring her in the proper responses.

And then Mr. Short in his guise of Bacchus called out her name—the last, just as he'd been instructed, for Archer wanted the special slice of cake to arrive before she'd recovered her equanimity.

She swallowed her punch in one enormous gulp, eyes like a hunted hare's, and handed Archer the empty cup. Then, cheeks aflame, head high, steps barely faltering, she floated across the taproom to receive his tokens. If only she'd understand them! And, please heaven and every god and godlet that ever existed or ever would, let Bacchus have saved out the right one, and not some Yahoo's attempt at cleverness.

Archer watched, heart in mouth. She was making a stalwart attempt to exchange banter with the innkeeper, and not doing too badly at it either. Ever quick, his little Sally Bowen. Perhaps she'd concluded they were all merely overgrown children, and so not to be feared? If she had, there was a certain truth to her opinion.

Archer heaved a sigh of relief at the reassuring wink Mr. Short sent him. And yes, it was the proper parcel—small, clumsily wrapped in one of the scraps he'd hacked from the carriage robe so it could be mistaken for nothing else, and tied with string.

As soon as she reached her stool she toyed with the lumpy thing, glancing at him uncertainly.

"Open it," he said. "The knots aren't difficult, but if they give you trouble I'll be glad to cut them for you."

"As you did the carriage robe?"

"As I did the carriage robe."

"What a criminal waste," she scolded.

"I'll buy us another."

That set her to blushing again. He took the package, pulled out his penknife, and sliced through the string, then placed it in her lap. The crude wrapping fell away. There, in all their splendor, lay the soap frog and a single fur slipper. His hand perhaps shaking slightly, he pulled the other from his pocket and set it beside its mate.

"I believe you misplaced this one," he said.

Were those tears he saw in her questioning eyes?

And then Peg was handing her a plate holding what he prayed was the right slice of Twelfth Night cake. She juggled plate and gifts. He retrieved the frog and slippers and slid them in his pocket beside the special license for luck.

"Careful," he murmured as she took her first bite. "One never knows what these things contain, and I shouldn't like you to chip a tooth or choke."

She began crumbling the cake then. Yes, it was the right piece, and she was trembling like a raw recruit just after his first battle. He had her on her feet, guiding her into the corridor where he'd first accosted her what felt like a lifetime ago, before she knew what he was about.

There was no doing the thing gracefully—not unaccustomed to honeyed words as he was, and not with the sounds of revelry streaming from the taproom and women brushing past them carrying more food to the tables.

"I find," he managed to say, gripping her shoulders and forcing her to meet his eyes, "this poor frog is in need of precisely the person you are to make his sorry life complete. Not a simulacrum. Not a pale imitation. You yourself."

"But—"

"Hush. Let me have my say before I forget half the words. I promise you we shan't starve, and I promise you shan't be bored, and I promise to behave like a proper gentleman every other Sunday, and I promise you no rotter shall ever importune you again, and I promise never to destroy another carriage robe. I also," he gulped, drowning in her eyes, "swear to love you with every fiber of my being for the rest of my life. Miss Sally Bowen, will you give over bear-leading the infantry and take me in hand instead? I have more need of you than they do."

And then Archer Huntleigh-Bowes succeeded in doing what he'd failed to do two nights before, and succeeded very well and thoroughly indeed.

"But you know nothing of me," she whispered when he lifted his head.

"And you know nothing of me. There'll be surprises in plenty for us both, I don't doubt. I'd wager my life on their being pleasant ones. Well, I am, aren't I?"

"Yes, you are." Her eyes were serious then, so serious the look in them almost frightened him. "And even the best may harbor drawbacks of one sort or another."

"Sally, will you marry me?"

"You have no notion who my people are, or what my history may be."

"Will you marry me tonight, here and now, and the devil take the hindmost?"

"You could discover I'm the most disreputable of lightskirts."

"And you that I'm a wastrel who's gambled away every sou. Perhaps I'm a highwayman. Perhaps I'm a murderer with a price on my head. I've a special license in my pocket, and a great desire to hand it to our Sun-vicar for instant use."

"How does that happen?"

"The license? A joke of a sort on another's part, though he'll soon learn the joke's on him. It's real enough, if that's what troubles you. Will you marry me, my darling Miss Bowen?"

"But what of your family?"

"I have none—not really, beyond an interfering old marplot who'll adore you the instant he sees you. Will you marry me?"

Her tremulous smile, her slight nod, were all he'd been waiting for.

"You will never regret this, that I swear, sweet Sally," he whispered huskily, gathering her against him. "We'll explore heaven together for the rest of our lives."

Dear God—was it she who trembled so, or was it his own arms that shook so violently he could barely hold her to him?

Archer managed it all with an efficiency that amazed even him. A private word with the vicar—and proof of his actual identity—laid to rest that gentleman's doubts as to the propriety of the proceedings. If Archer had had to explain rather more than he'd intended, including relating the tale of his godfather's holding a gun to his head while clutching purse strings that weren't truly his to clutch, and his dread of encountering Miss Sarah Timmons of Brevett-on-Chipple, so be it. Charles'd sworn to his *bona fides,* and even had a few private words of his own with the vicar. After that, instead of repressive frowns the vicar was all smiles, promising to slur his name a bit during the ceremony, though he did take Sally aside to assure himself she was entering into this lifelong compact of her own free will.

A veil and a wreath of silk flowers were procured from an attic trunk to replace the mistletoe, little Alice given a basket of paper scraps to strew in lieu of rose petals, and

Timmy his signet ring to bear on a pillow, the village fiddler struck up something that might have been Handel's *Hallelujah* chorus were a few notes added or a few omitted, and suddenly Sally was coming toward him on the beaming innkeeper's arm.

There were words. A lot of them. He managed the responses well enough. Charles handed him the ring. Then it was done. The fiddler was scraping away. People were cheering. He was turning his wife, lifting her veil, meeting her bemused eyes with a tender smile in his own, bending to give her the first kiss of their married lives.

He ignored the sudden pounding on the inn door, and Charles slipping away to see what the trouble might be. And then, just as his lips were about to meet his bride's, some sixth sense made him glance across the taproom.

"Oh, Lord—this tears it!" Charles was saying, pulling the door wider. "Why couldn't you've delayed just a day longer, sir? Heaven help us, for we'll need it."

Rubbing his hands in the cold, stamping his feet, bundled to the ears and above, was Sir Evrard, a stranger at his side. Behind them light streaming from the taproom caught on a sleigh containing two ladies peering anxiously toward the inn.

"Good Lord, sir—what the devil're *you* doing here?" Archer roared.

"Papa?" Sally gasped at Archer's side.

And then she was shrinking against him.

" 'Papa?' " he demanded, turning on her, hands on his hips, scowling.

"Yes, 'Papa.' Heaven knows who that other man is, though you appear to."

"My godfather, for my sins. Sir Evrard Huntleigh-Bowes."

What followed wasn't pretty. It definitely wasn't to the credit of any of the principals, nor did it display their understanding to advantage. The beginning provided as fine a farce as the village revelers had ever witnessed. In due course, Charles measured his length on the floor, blood streaming from his assaulted nose courtesy of Archer. Timmy—intent on defending Aunt Sally, or Miss Bowen, or Miss Timmons, or Mrs. Hunt or Huntleigh-Bowes, or whoever she might be now—attacked the bride's irate father with his sword, catching that worthy gentleman smartly across the shins more than once before he was pulled away. Alice climbed on a stool and beat Sir Evrard about the shoulders with her wand, sobbing and proclaiming him a toad for turning her first wedding ever into a war in which almost everyone was shouting at everyone else. The diplomat's wife proclaimed the child had the right of it, and Georgiana Timmons so far forgot herself as to burst into laughter at the spectacle they were making of themselves.

It was, to put it mildly, a shambles.

Then the innkeeper's wife offered the family parlor as a private spot in which all might be sorted out, and the vicar's wife pleaded that more level heads might prevail. A hush fell over the combatants. Charles scrambled to his feet, laughter in his eyes despite the rag containing snow he held against his nose.

"I really don't understand where the problem lies," he said in the sudden silence.

Three gentlemen and one young lady opened their mouths. He raised his hand.

"Yes, Archie, I knew who *your wife* was the morning after she arrived. Her card case spilled. No, I didn't tell you. Would you ever've bothered to get to know Miss Bowen, ah, Timmons, if I had?"

"You know the answer to that one, damn you!"

"Archie—ladies present."

"I don't give a da—I don't care *who's* present. I will not be manipulated by *anyone*. That includes you, you two-faced, conniving, unprincipled—how much did my godfather pay you to pull this off?"

"Archer, moderate your tone," Lady Huntleigh-Bowes threw in sweetly. "No one paid anyone anything."

"As for you, young lady," John Timmons growled, "you will gather your things and march yourself to Sir Evrard's sled on the instant."

"You have the temerity to order my wife around?" Archer snapped.

"Your wife, is she? Not what you were saying a moment ago. Said you'd been entrapped and you'd procure an annulment if it was the last thing you did. Well, she was my daughter before she was your wife, and it's high time she made her departure from this den of, of—"

"There are only honest people here, sir," the vicar protested. "I'll vouch for every one. And *I* was aware of the identities of both bride and groom, as both told me their stories in private. That *they* weren't matters not in the least."

"You'll even vouch for that blue-faced miscreant over there?" John Timmons sputtered in disbelief, pointing at Archer.

"Yes, sir—even him."

"Who held a gun to your head when you asked Miss Timmons to wed you, Archie?" Charles Moreland demanded, clearly out of patience with them all.

"No one," Archer admitted.

"Did anyone need to?"

"Hardly," he said with a wry grin. "My heart was in my mouth for fear she'd refuse."

"Who forced you to wed Archie?" Charles said, turning on Sarah.

She shrugged.

"You fools," he continued with the labored patience of one dealing with fractious children, "so you've begun oddly, and your pride's been dented a bit. Where's the inconvenience in that? Probably done you both a world of good. Archie's learned a prank can turn on one—though he's a most fortunate devil in this case, rather than to be pitied. And you?" He laughed. "You appear to've learned that you can dress in sheets if you wish, Sarah—and I insist on giving you your name, as you're the wife of my oldest and dearest friend—and still be a lady. And you've found a husband who wanted you for yourself alone. Best of all, you'll never be able to pull caps without remembering tonight. Disagreements should be short, and end sweetly.

"As for the two of you," he continued, turning on fulminating father and incensed godfather, "this is precisely the end you desired, isn't it? Forgive me for being a blunt military man, but you're a pair of blithering idiots! Who cares if they believed they were disobeying your wishes? The war's won, unless you insist on losing the battle."

The company held its collective breath.

"They're all gotten up like mummers," Sir Evrard muttered, then winced at the swift kick to his shins delivered by his wife.

"When my daughter weds, it won't be to a fellow with a blue face," John Timmons snarled, "and she'll certainly not be gowned in sheets!"

"Interesting." Georgiana's voice was silk scraping on velvet. "Is it the type of fabric one wears that makes a wedding valid, or the sort of stuff one's made of inside? And what do you intend to do about my cousin? He's broken no law that I know of."

"I'll find one, don't you worry! And see him in hell before I let him lay a finger on Sarah."

Charles strode across the taproom, fire in his eyes, and stopped directly in front of bride and groom.

"Are you going to cede *them* the field?" he demanded. "Especially when you both went to considerable effort to gain it for yourselves? For feather-brained, irrational, easily manipulated dunces, you two win all prizes! What do they matter, blast it? What do your names matter? What does anyone or anything matter but yourselves? If the games, *all of them,* rebounded on every single player, does it really *matter?* There wasn't a one of us innocent in this beyond Mrs. Timmons and Lady Huntleigh-Bowes, when all's said and done."

"On *everyone?*" Archer spluttered.

"Yes, everyone."

Archer met Charles's eyes, a question in his own. Charles nodded.

"Charlie, I'd like to confer privately," Archer said in the silence. "Don't worry—I won't try to draw your cork again, old fellow."

And then they were in the corridor leading to the kitchen.

"You love her too," Archer said the moment they were out of earshot.

"Top over tail, but she never saw me, not even that first night. Not much I could do except ease your way."

"I could step aside, give you a chance."

"There are some lengths to which friendship may go, and some to which it mustn't. She planted you as much of a facer as she did me, though it took you a bit longer to realize you'd been felled. And it was a glorious rig, you know—perhaps the most glorious I've ever run. But if you ever cause her a moment's misery—"

Archer nodded. "She's like that girl after Waterloo. If there're two, maybe there's another somewhere."

"Maybe, though I sincerely doubt it. Now, go make your peace. You'll forgive me if I don't watch. Here's the recipe for my punch. Consider it your wedding present."

Slowly, ever so slowly, Archer extended his hand. Charles gripped it.

"Go to her," he said. "Make all right. For me there's always the Lottie Leighton sort until someone better comes along."

And so Archer did.

* * *

It took only a few words concerning surprises, and the fact that they'd both had a few and would doubtless be in for some more during the course of their lives. Sarah Timmons, who'd had a moment to consider while he was gone, was forced to agree. Sir Evrard and her father halfheartedly admitted that perhaps young Moreland had had it right, and all was well that ended well. The revelers cheered. The fiddler struck up a shaky waltz. Bride and groom took the floor, at first smiling tentatively, then bursting into good-natured laughter at the trick they'd played on themselves.

In the corridor Charles clenched his jaws and strode unseeing through the kitchen and into the dark night, nursing his sore nose. There he stood alone in the snow and the cold, the sounds of revelry echoing in his ears as he stared at the sliver of moon and cursed the fate that had made him invisible. When he joined the revelers after a bit, lifting his tankard high in salute to the newlyweds, there was a tightness to his smile and a wistfulness to his gaze that caused the fairy princess to slip her hand in his and refuse to leave his side for the rest of the evening.

As soon as the roads were clear, Archer and Sarah Huntleigh-Bowes departed on an extended wedding journey that included a stay in Kent to visit Miss Althea Saunders, which delighted Sarah's former governess every bit as much as John Timmons had predicted. In later years an odd bibelot protected by a glass dome graced their drawing room mantel: a frog carved of soap perching on what appeared to be a pair of miniature slippers clumsily wrought of fur.

Sir Evrard and his wife continued to Brevett-on-Chipple, where they made an extended visit. Sir Evrard had a right to a bit of a holiday after all that effort, and so he informed anyone who would listen. If Whitehall disagreed, let Whitehall look to itself. It was very few days before the bumbling matchmakers were proclaiming they had succeeded in bringing Archer and Sarah together against all odds, a conclusion from which nothing either of their ladies said could sway them.

Timmy and Alice arrived to find their aunt miraculously recovering. No one believed the tale of their adventures—pirates, and thieves, and runaway lovers—until their mother came upon the notice of the marriage of Miss Sarah Timmons and Mr. Archer Huntleigh-Bowes in the London journals. Then even she wondered.

"Mrs. Tizzet" vanished, of course. That was, as William Fitzmorris told his rib with a chuckle, his stock-in-trade. Sometime later, when the sentimental thief's store of pounds and shillings shrank to troublesome levels, a robust schoolmistress who declared herself to be Miss Sally Bowen boarded a stage bound for Bath accompanied by her long-suffering abigail, there to take the waters and, perhaps, lighten a few purses.

And Charles Moreland? Contrary to the hopes of his closest friend, he never did find a young lady who equaled either Sarah Timmons or the intrepid physician's daughter they'd encountered briefly after Waterloo. He did, however, one day literally run down one who far exceeded either in beauty, intelligence, and grace—at least in his eyes. Best of all, she saw no one but him.

LOOK FOR THESE REGENCY ROMANCES

WATCH FOR THESE ZEBRA REGENCIES

LADY STEPHANIE   (0-8217-5341-X, $4.50)
by Jeanne Savery
Lady Stephanie Morris has only one true love: the family estate she
has managed ever since her mother died. But then Lord Anthony Rider
arrives on her estate, claiming he has plans for both the land and the
woman. Stephanie soon realizes she's fallen in love with a man whose
sensual caresses will plunge her into a world of peril and intrigue . . . a
man as dangerous as he is irresistible.

BRIGHTON BEAUTY   (0-8217-5340-1, $4.50)
by Marilyn Clay
Chelsea Grant, pretty and poor, naively takes school friend Alayna
Marchmont's place and spends a month in the country. The devastating
man had sailed from Honduras to claim his promised bride, Miss
Marchmont. An affair of the heart may lead to disaster . . . unless a
resourceful Brighton beauty finds a way to stop a masquerade and
keep a lord's love.

LORD DIABLO'S DEMISE   (0-8217-5338-X, $4.50)
by Meg-Lynn Roberts
The sinfully handsome Lord Harry Glendower was a gambler and the
black sheep of his family. About to be forced into a marriage of convenience, the devilish fellow engineered his own demise, never having
dreamed that faking his death would lead him to the heavenly refuge
of spirited heiress Gwyn Morgan, the daughter of a physician.

A PERILOUS ATTRACTION   (0-8217-5339-8, $4.50)
by Dawn Aldridge Poore
Alissa Morgan is stunned when a frantic passenger thrusts her baby
into Alissa's arms and flees, having heard rumors that a notorious
highwayman posed a threat to their coach. Handsome stranger Hugh
Sebastian secretly possesses the treasured necklace the highwayman
seeks and volunteers to pose as Alissa's husband to save her reputation.
With a lost baby and missing necklace in their care, the couple embarks
on a journey into peril—and passion.

*Available wherever paperbacks are sold, or order direct from the
Publisher. Send cover price plus 50¢ per copy for mailing and
handling to Penguin USA, P.O. Box 999, c/o Dept. 17109,
Bergenfield, NJ 07621. Residents of New York and Tennessee must
include sales tax. DO NOT SEND CASH.*

ROMANCE FROM ROSANNE BITTNER

CARESS   (0-8217-3791-0, $5.99)

FULL CIRCLE   (0-8217-4711-8, $5.99)

SHAMELESS   (0-8217-4056-3, $5.99)

SIOUX SPLENDOR   (0-8217-5157-3, $4.99)

UNFORGETTABLE   (0-8217-4423-2, $5.50)

TEXAS EMBRACE   (0-8217-5625-7, $5.99)

UNTIL TOMORROW   (0-8217-5064-X, $5.99)

ROMANCE FROM HANNAH HOWELL

MY VALIANT KNIGHT   (0-8217-5186-7, $5.50)

ONLY FOR YOU   (0-8217-4993-5, $4.99)

UNCONQUERED   (0-8217-5417-3, $5.99)

WILD ROSES   (0-8217-5677-X, $5.99)